Flight to Ohio

Edited by Kelly Luce
Cover Photographs courtesy Shutterstock
Cover Design Wabi Sabi Design Studio

Flight to Ohio

FROM SLAVERY TO PASSING TO FREEDOM

MARY ANDERSON PARKS

DEDICATED WITH LOVE TO MY MOTHER

Lucy Maude Jones Anderson
May 4, 1903 - June 30, 1980

HER PICTURE AS A YOUNG WOMAN IS ON THE COVER.

ACKNOWLEDGEMENTS

With gratitude to my husband, daughter, sons-in-law, grandchildren, daughter Rachel's spirit, Publisher, Kermit E. Heartsong of Tayen Lane Publishing; Editor, Kelly Luce; Michael Urbano and Mark Kohr, invaluable technical support on video; Erwin A. Thompson (deceased in 2015 at age 99), a great help on farming questions; Steve Murray and Tiina Nunnally; Paula Morrison; U.C. Berkeley Writers' Workshop; Novel-writing group: Susan Austin, Betsy Hess-Behrens, Diane De Pisa, Margaret Judge, Mary Tolman Kent, Joan Mastronarde, Susan Miho Nunes, Shiho Nunes, Kaye Sharon, Phyllis Smith; Readers of manuscript: Lois and Michael Anthony, Elena Balashova, Ruth Bardakci, Penny Brogden, Beth Cochran, Michael Griffin, Lois Segal, Sarah Parks Urbano; All my relations, The Great Spirit.

CHAPTER ONE
1836

It be dark as inside an ear the night we leave. I guess we lucky the moon and stars wants to hide too. When the clouds lift, we gonna be out in the open. It cold like happen sometimes to a Virginia June. Mama has on her sweater, both dresses and who know what stuffed down in her big pockets. She wearing her shoes, but mine too fulla holes and I got on marsa's old ones. I ain't used to em and they be painin me fore we run a mile.

"Wait!" I call out to Mama, though it a damn fool thing to slow down when we not even off the plantation. "I run better barefoot."

"Put em in your knapsack, Tom," Mama says when I yank the shoes off, bout to sling em in the ditch. "You'll need shoes later and them be good ones."

We set ourselves to a harder run. I reach back to be sure Big Jim's map ain't fallen outta marsa's hip pocket. Besides his shoes, Mama stole me a pair of pants. Grabbed marsa's pants right off the clothesline along with his brown plaid shirt.

"When he find us gone missin, he ain't gonna study on no clothes," she said.

Marse Tom and I are bout of a size. I got his straight, narrow nose, same brown hair only mine darker and curly. His eyes are blue, mine green-brown. It drive the missus crazy how alike we look.

We got eight or ten hours till they know we gone. In the morning, cook Jessie gonna tell marsa we down with fever. But ole marse will come right in the cabin and look for hisself to see if we playing at being sick. First, he'll have breakfast.

I hope Jessie don't get beat for lying. She a house slave, probably never been beat. I'll miss Jessie. When I told her I could read words, she got me a book called "Pamela." "The missus won't nebba notice," Jessie said. "And effen she do I'll git it an put it somewheres she'll think she laid it herself."

White folks do be strange critters. Between the odd way they talk and carry on, and a mess of words I never heerd of, "Pamela" were hard going, but interesting to see how things turn out for that young servant girl. She had her troubles she went on and on about in them letters she wrote.

Ain't nobody owned her though, like they do us. Pamela, she white.

Big Jim holding onto the map, that's a true miracle. He got beat so bad after they dragged him back he can't see now out his right eye. I never knew marsa to beat any of us across the face before that. The dogs were first to go at Big Jim. That's how he got his limp.

Sharp yelps send my feet flying. Mama speeds up beside me. We're passing Atkinson's. It's their dogs we roused up. If I thought our own was already on our tail, it would sap the strength plumb outta me. I seen what them dogs can do. Yet here we are, Mama and me, making a run for it. I glance over and see she's pacing herself, breathing the way she does in the field.

A whiff of far-off skunk, then a frog bellowing not ten feet away. We running so fast we make our own breeze. I like the power of that. I've been aching to run since the last beating marse Tom gave me. I couldn't get up from that one, just lay there, my nose in the mud. After marsa went off, Mama turned my head to one side so I'd go on breathing, though I'd as soon not have. But once I started healing, I was glad to be still kicking around.

One thing a body can say for marse Tom, he does his own dirty work. He's his own overseer. Says it saves a heap of time and trouble. Money too, I reckon. I hope I didn't get that temper of his, but sometimes I feel it boiling away down under. And it's his own stubbornness I got, though Mama can be a mule if she take the notion. I never thought I'd get her to go with me, and I weren't gonna run without her. We'd a kept on out in those tobacky fields till we dropped dead if marsa hadn't gone and sold Janey and her kids. After that, Mama said there wasn't nothin to stay for.

I saw Mama's face when she watched her three granchillun and Janey ride off in the back of that trader's wagon, the baby sucking at Janey's breast and little Willie Joe staring at us, his eyes begging not to let them be taken away. Janey's eyes were blind black stones. Mama had to turn away. I wondered if my face looked like Mama's, bout to break in pieces. Ole marse had doubt showing in his eyes. Was it dawning on him he'd maybe messed up his own life too?

Marse Tom been coming to Mama's bed since before I was born, twenty-one years ago and never stopped, only slowed down some. Two years after me came Janey, and when ole marse saw Janey's color, way darker than Mama, he found out who the man was and traded him off the next month. Marsa's the kind of white man with reddish pale skin the sun likes to torture. He knew that weren't no baby of his.

Funny how much can flash through your mind like it's all right with you even when you running for your life.

Mama stays just a touch behind me, silent like she my shadow, knowing not to waste breath talking. We gonna stay near the road and skirt the towns, over to Kentucky and north to the Ohio River. Once we cross that river, it be freedom land! But Big Jim warned: "Git tuh Canada effen yuh kin, case that law rise up that low marsa to bring yuh back."

Mama's breathing harder, so I slow down a tad. Legs pumping, heart pounding, Mama and me putting miles between us and ole marse, I start to feel good, like we gonna make it. I reckon that's because Mama's alongside me and I never known her to do nothing foolish.

Big Jim was old when he tried to run, older than Mama. Mama thinks maybe she's thirty-eight. She's a tall woman and don't carry extra pounds. Both of us got feet caked hard from fieldwork. In summer the dirt gets tough and pointy like sharp rocks. The shoes they give us don't never fit. Our feet blister up, get rubbed raw. Unless the ground so hot we be dancin round or so cold our toes freeze up, we better off without shoes. Right now it's grateful I am for those long days working barefoot. Ole marse could never make a run like what lie ahead of us. He's nothing without a horse. Our power be in our bodies. Don't that make us better than him? I chuckle to myself.

High in the sky, the moon sails out from behind a cloud, helps us see our way, then runs back in. Out and in, like it up to something. An owl hoots, not far off. Are they wise old birds like folks say? Can it see us out in this black night? We fall into a smoother, slower run, always keeping near the road, passing through fields and woods, more fields. We skirt the town Big Jim's map show to be the first we come to. I know that map by heart from so much studying of it, Big Jim and me lying on the hard dirt behind the cabins, the map spread out in front of us. It shows the way clear up to Canada. Long ago when I was small, he took me outside, showed me how to find the North Star and tell directions. "That star shine on freedom," he told me.

We won't go north right away, not till we're in Kentucky. We'll go west so when we come to the big hills we'll be in the low part.

When we get past the first town, a feeling of being free comes on me real strong. Mama can tell. She reads my mind without even looking in my face.

"Settle down," she says, between deep steady breaths. "We got a long piece to go and who knows what's ahead? It sure ain't us what knows." She doesn't break stride. The moon is faint now. I smell skunk again.

My right leg starts giving me fits. Mama looks over, sees the way I'm favoring it. She points to an old shed about a quarter mile away, behind a barn. "Head for that. I got my salve to put on your leg, but you need sleep to heal." She knows my right leg ain't been the same since I got beat so bad. All I did was stand up to marsa and say Janey's boy was too sick to go out in the fields.

"No nigger slave's gonna tell me what to do," he yelled. He started on me with his whip and the more he beat on me the crazier mad he got. I'm your own son was the thought leap-frogging through my mind. There be eighteen slaves here and we all know I'm the only son you got. I don't know which of us was madder.

The shed looks like it ain't been used in a long time, but when we come up to the door, hanging by one hinge, I follow Mama's gaze to a wad of chewing tobacco on the ground.

"Ain't been here long enough to dry all the way up. We best keep goin till we find another place." She looks up at the first pink lines of dawn streaking the sky.

"I can't go on without no rest. I'll mess my leg up real bad if I keep running on it."

The farms we passed have been far between. Is it worse to risk daylight out in the open or someone finding us in this shed? I see worry in Mama's eyes. She stoops to go through the small doorway. I follow. A rusty shovel, hoe and rake lean into one corner of the sagging rotten walls. Two moth-eaten blankets cover a thick layer of straw packed down on the ground. A stack of old books stands next to a half-empty whiskey bottle and a kerosene lamp. I start to back out.

"No!" Mama says. "See that dusty window? I'll keep watch. I kin see somebody comin a fair piece away."

"That don't make sense, Mama. They'll see us too, when we run outta here."

"Leave it to me." She says it that way, means I'd best ask no questions, pressing her lips tight together.

My leg's paining me something fierce, and I lay myself down on the blankets. The deep gash on the back of my right calf healed, but under the scar it still hurts. Mama kneels down, rolls up my pant leg to rub in the salve she brings outta her pocket. She takes holda my leg and works it over good and strong, then hands me the whiskey bottle.

"Here, drink." That shocks me. Mama always say whiskey the devil's brew. I take a long pull from the bottle. It burns right down my throat into my stomach. I close my eyes.

It is night when I wake up. I musta slept the whole day. My body feels rested. The salve and whiskey did their job. I reach over in the darkness, but Mama's not there. Straining my eyes to make out objects in the bit of light the moon sends through cracks, I see Mama standing near the door.

"We need to git started," she says.

It's not till I'm on my feet that I see the man, a medium-size white man in overalls and blue work shirt, fresh blood drying in his yellow hair. He's lying on his face just inside the door.

"What . . . ?" I stare at Mama.

"Jes step over him."

"You did this?"

"Course I did it. I stood watch, holdin onto that shovel, and when he busted in here I hit him over the head with it. Hard."

I never known Mama to hurt no one. Ever. I stand over the man's body and ask.

"Is he dead?"

"He breathin real weak-like." Her voice catches, and I reach out to hold her trembling arm.

"Can't git it to stop shakin," she says.

I am awed by what she done so I could sleep and get back strength. So we wouldn't be caught.

"He might be a man lives alone. He missin two buttons." She don't seem quite right in her mind. I tighten my grip on her arm.

"We got to get ourselves far from here, Mama."

"I know that."

So we start out again, with no more words. We don't eat any of the food Mama brought till many miles later when we come to a creek. The moon is far above us. We drink creek water from Mama's tin cup and eat pemmican and shelled walnuts. Mama sees me watching her, finishes chewing, stands up and rubs her palms on both sides of her back. I stand up too.

"It don't bear talkin on. It somethin I'll have to live with. Let it make you run harder." I know by the way she speaks it's all she'll ever say about the man we left in the shed. She lays her hands on my shoulders and gazes in my eyes for the longest time. I feel her love pour into me. I'm so connected to her it's like I never left her womb.

CHAPTER TWO

We run together the rest of the night like one runner. Toward dawn, we bed down next to a creek, covering ourselfs with brush and branches.

Each day the weather grows warmer, the air kinder, and we find wooded places to sleep where we pray nobody will see us if they come hunting, for us or some other poor critter. Thick bushes by a creek are best, Mama says. We can split up if we have to, me across the water, her running off the other direction. So far we been lucky. I check the map against road signs when we see one. We right on track. The closer we get to Kentucky, the luckier I feel. Streams and small rivers, Mama and me been able to wade. We had some hard rains, got soaked through by a thunderstorm one afternoon. I shivered and shook so bad we laid low that night and the next. Made ourselfs a leanto. Did my leg good to rest.

Mama know what herbs and roots to use when we feeling puny. I been catching possum, coons, rabbits. I'm getting good at throwing stones to make the kill. Mama dresses them and I have a tinder-box, flint and steel in my knapsack to light a fire. I use dry wood so the fire won't smoke. Feeling lucky ain't making me careless.

I think a lot about Janey. I wonder is she still in Virginia. We'll be on somebody's land and I think, maybe this is the plantation Janey's on now. Is she sorry how she done things? She was crazy in love with her husband, Willie Joe. They jumped the broomstick and we had us a shindig to beat everything. Marse Tom was off on a trip. We made the most of those times. Since he did his own overseeing, he'd leave the missus in charge when he had to be away. She'd be up there in her room tipplin the bottle, didn't give us much grief.

Janey wouldn't never let ole marsa sleep with her. He been trying since she was thirteen and turned so lovely. But Janey hates marsa with a fire gives her a power way more'n a normal human. She could always see right into him, see the meanness. There's something wild about Janey. Puts me in mind of a bobcat. She bit marsa, places we could see and places we couldn't that she boasted about. He finally quit trying but any fool could tell by the way he eyed her how much he wanted her. After she and Willie Joe had chillun, Janey got even fiercer when marsa looked at her that way. She'd stare right back, taunting him, eyes flashing. Marsa never did beat her. Maybe couldn't bring hisself to, kept thinking he'd wear her down some other way. Mama worried he'd sell Willie Joe, but none of us thought to worry about what he did do, selling Janey and Mama's only granchillun. That way he could hurt all of us.

I couldn't bear looking at Willie Joe's face the day Janey and his kids went off on that wagon. I saw his shape, his strong tall body slumped over like it'd never be straight again. And it never has. His tears came flowing out. Me, I was too filled with hate to have any tears.

Janey's eyes, as she sat there in the back of the wagon, went blank. I'd seen it in other slave women, but I never thought Janey's eyes could go empty like that. Little Willie Joe had a face on him said he knew he was being taken away from us forever and didn't know why. He looked at Janey, then his father, then Mama and me, out of his big owl eyes. His sister, two years old, hugged onto Janey, buried her face in Janey's skirts. And Janey stared out from that wagon like a blind woman, the baby latched onto her breast.

Willie Joe don't talk to nobody since.

Those pictures never leave my mind. Now though, I also think about that white man Mama maybe killed, bout how he liked to sit out there, get away from people, read books, drink whiskey. Maybe I can do that someday. I'm not to let nobody know I can read. Mama said a slave can be killed for knowing how. I feel real bad if we had to kill somebody to get away to freedom. I'm pretty sure that man was gonna die.

He couldn't have been that bad if he likes to read books, could he? It seems a peaceful thing to do. Why'd he have to hide away from folks to read? I guess there be lots I don't know, not ever being off the plantation. I wonder where we gonna end up, Mama and me. Leastways we'll be together, like always. Both of us can do bout any kinda work. I try to imagine working and getting paid for it, then buying things with the money, like marse Tom when he sells his tobacky.

A house! That's what I gonna buy. A little house for Mama. We can live in it peaceful the rest of our lives. I smile wide when that idea comes. It our fifteenth day out, me on my back in the sun, Mama asleep in the shade of a low-hanging willow. I roll out here into the open, happy to laze like a cat in the warm sun and not have to toil in no tobacky fields.

That crackling! What is it? It's coming from real near. I want to roll back to where Mama lies hidden, but only my eyes move. I hope it's an animal sound, but it's more like a man's feet stepping on underbrush. Out hunting, could be.

And we ain't in the North yet. Why did I roll out into the open, letting myself feel a freedom I don't have? My body goes rigid.

And then I see him. A big white man, maybe over six feet, though it's hard to tell with me lying on the ground. He sees me, stops in mid-stride, startled. I wait for him to point his rifle at me, but he's still holding it by his side.

"You all right?" he asks.

I can't understand why he don't aim the gun at me.

"These here ain't my woods," he says, "but my neighbor, he lets me hunt em.

Usually I don't run into nobody out here. Guess I caught you restin?"

He talks friendly, almost like we two white men coming across each other in the woods. I get up slow, brushing twigs and leaves off marse Tom's pants.

"Yessir, I was restin," I manage to say. I take a few steps away from the tree.

"You walkin this way apiece?"

"Yessir, I am."

He looks about fifty, with a broad wrinkled face and smile lines round his blue eyes. Don't he know a nigger slave when he sees one? All I know is I have to get him away from Mama and not raise up suspicions in him.

"Where's your gun at?" he asks.

"I'm not huntin, just passin through." How far will I have to walk with him? How long can I keep up this pretending? Won't he figure out I'm a runaway? I'm skeered to say much. Whatever reason he thinks it'd be okay for a slave to be out here with a gun! Now that beats everything! Do he maybe think I'm a free black?

"Nice day, ain't it?" he says.

"Yessir, sure is." My mouth's gone dry.

From how low the sun be, I figure it getting on in the afternoon. I hope he's heading home, out of these woods. We come to a clearing and he says, "Well, I turn off here." He points to the left. "My place is over that way. Sure you know your way, wherever it is you're going?" Curiosity is plain in his eyes. He stands still, watching me.

"Yessir, I do." I force my lips to smile, and hope he doesn't see the trembling I feel pass over my face. I wait for him to head off in the direction he pointed. Not till then do I start walking. After a few steps, I look back and he be stopped, staring at me. I raise my hand and wave, and then so does he.

I have to keep going the way him and me was going. He might turn back again. I ain't breathed normal all that time I was with him and hardly can now.

I keep walking but I don't go far. I need to get back to Mama. I turn and run toward where I left her, making myself slow down when I come to the clearing. I glance all around. No sign of him. Maybe he went off to get more men. Maybe he was afraid I'd grab his gun cause I'm younger and stronger, so he just pretended to be friendly.

I run to the tree, push through branches, frantic cause I don't see Mama. I shove through thick leafy branches hanging down near the ground and there she stands, crouching over next to the trunk. I grab hold of her hand.

"Mama, we got to get going. Even though it be daylight. Did you hear that man come by?"

She nods, like she too skeered to say words.

"He didn't seem to know I was a runaway, but we can't be sure. Anyways, he may get suspicious and come back, bring somebody with him."

"You mean he didn't hurt you none? He jes went away?" Mama sounds disbelieving.

"He treated me real friendly, Mama." I shake my head, not understanding it.

"Treated you real friendly?" Mama stares at me, an odd look in her eyes.

I tell her what the man said and what I said back.

"You always was a good talker," Mama says slowly, "even as a chile. Member how you could talk jes like the massa and make us fall down laughin?"

"I still can. It comes natural. All the reading I done help too. I listen how people talk, then I do it the same way."

Mama's thinking deep. "Mebbe that'll come in handy." She stares at me like she's seeing me for the first time. I feel strange, her looking at me like that.

"Come on, Mama. Us not safe here." I pull her by the arm.

CHAPTER THREE

This be the biggest woods we seen yet. It twilight time when we reach the edge. We sink ourselfs down at the roots of a big tree, waiting for darkness to hide us.

Then we run all night till the sky look the way it do when it about to lighten. I be all heated up from the long hard run. Panting, sweating, I tell Mama to wait in the field we in, then I go looking for a road sign. When I come up on one, I can't believe my eyes. I check the map to be sure. Racing back to Mama, I yell, "We comin to Maysville, Kentucky in twenty miles! We almost to the Ohio River!"

"God almighty!" Mama cries out.

A skinny man in raggedy shirt and pants appears outta nowhere. "Y'all betta quiet down effen ya wants to git to Ohia." He grins. "Foller me. Name's Herman." He leads us to his cabin and we pass the day there sleeping, after telling our story to him, his wife, son and three daughters. All of em have to go to the field when the horn sounds. That night, they come back when it too dark to work. Herman looks tired as an old plow horse.

His wife goes off for a bit while the daughters put together a cold meal the eight of us share. I hope we ain't eating up what's meant to last till their peck of corn on Saturday. Maybe they get more in Kentucky. When it dark as pitch, Herman goes with us a distance to help us get past the dogs and not be seen from the house. Then he stops, hands me the bag he been carrying.

"Got room in your sack? It be food my wife went an got from the kitchen. All of em know you here. We all wants to help."

Mama moves forward, takes hold of his shoulders, her eyes full of tears. "Please thank em for us, an pray we be in Ohia when we eats it."

He gives us a long sad look. "I hopes ya make it. I'd run effen I had no fambly."

After we leave him, I keep hearing those words, "I hopes ya make it," and it gets me nervous, reminds me that coming this far not being caught don't mean we gonna make it all the way. We not out of the South. These slaves have it better than us in Virginia, they have their family still together, but that don't make em any less slaves.

"Let's run," I urge.

"Nope. We too near the road. We don't hear as good when we runnin."

She right. We don't. It's real late when a wagon comes up on us. When we hear it we have the time it take a pig's squeal to dive into the cornstalks. I peek and see four white men on the wagon with guns. Pattyrollers. Passing so close they'd hear if we sneezed. Big Jim warned me bout em. They catch runaways, get money when they take em back. Give em a good beating first.

I hold my breath, but feel like I'll for sure sneeze with corn dust tickling inside my nose. The wagon rumbles on by. We keep silent. We don't move. What if it turn around and come back?

At last, without a word, Mama gets up, trembling a little, and we go on, not talking, careful not to trip on ruts or step in holes. It takes a while to calm down after them pattyrollers pass so close, but soon our feet be eating up the miles. It quiet, the moon out, the night air crisp and cool. There ain't as many dogs in Kentucky. More often than dogs barking, we hear the soft neighing of horses and smell their powerful odor. I can't help doing a little leap in the air. Mama been using her salve on me every day and I feel real good.

The scent in the air changes.

"Mama," I whisper. "I smell the river. I'm sure I do."

She takes hold of my hand, squeezes it so tight it hurts.

CHAPTER FOUR

All a sudden there it is. The Ohio River. Flowing between us and freedom. Dark, fast-moving. I never seen nothin like it. Bout a quarter mile wide. Can I get us across? This part worries me. Big Jim said go along the river till we find a boat with oars, and showed me the way a man move his arms and shoulders when he do what's called rowing. How did he learn such stuff?

"You ever seen a big river?" I asked him. "Mebbe I did," was all he'd say. Like it was his secret.

"That's Ohia on the other side," Mama breathes. "We best start lookin."

We set off in the direction the water's moving. I feel more and more uneasy, watching how fast it goes. It one powerful river.

"We both strong," Mama says, reading my thought. "We git us a boat and we gonna cross that river, one way or nother."

We go a long distance, stumbling in the dark on tree roots, before we come on a little boat tied to a tree. At first I don't see no oars, but Mama point to where they be, one on each side of the boat, held there somehow.

I untie the knot and push the boat into the water, holding onto its rope.

"I'll git in first." Mama steps in and the little boat wobbles but Mama keeps her balance and sets herself down on the bench in the middle.

"Here I come!" I step in the near end like she done. The doggone thing tips way up while I still got only one leg in.

"Wait!" Mama says. "I'll move back. Throw me your knapsack."

She catches it, eases herself backward, and I try again. This time the boat wobbles and I wobble but I end up setting in the middle of it.

"Be careful with them oars," Mama warns. "Don't let em slip outta the holders they be in. Lessen they end up in the river."

I grab hold of the oars like Big Jim showed me, only all we had was two sticks. Pretty soon I get the hang of rowing except we moving down river faster than across it.

"That don't matter," Mama says. "Don't matter what part of Ohia we land in so long as we gits there."

She right, like always. So I keep rowing strong as I can. It's not dawn yet and hard to make out the other shore. I stand up to see better. The boat tips like crazy. Before I know it, I'm out in the cold, freezing water, desperate, looking for where the boat got to. We come so close, I be thinking, but like a fool I had to go and stand up. I thrash around, trying to row with my arms to keep my head above water.

I hear Mama call, "Over here, Tom!"

I see the boat now, see her laying flat on her stomach, reaching out for me to take hold of her arm. I move the way I seen a dog swim, toward where she is. I reach to grab onto the boat but it trying its best to get away. Mama stretches out long so I can grasp her hand and then pulls me till I can hook my arm over the side of the boat.

"Haul yourself in real easy," she says, "or we'll both be out there."

I do like she say and at last get back in my place, breathing hard, grateful as a stuck mule pulled outta mud. We still got a chance. Dripping, shivering, I throw all my power into rowing. The current sweeps us along and I fight it till my arms feel like they gonna drop right off my body, but I scare up enough strength for one last big push that gets us through to the other side. We scramble out in knee-deep water, grabbing handfuls of tall thick grass so as not to be swept away. Both of us be sopping wet by the time we set our feet on land.

The sky turns lighter by the minute. Soon the sun will warm us. I take deep breaths as we stand watching the river surge by, carrying the boat with it.

"Thank you," I murmur to the boat and its owner who won't ever know where it went or how much it meant to us. I'm also thanking the world and its maker, though I ain't had much truck with all that till now. I throw back my shoulders and gulp in freedom.

"Ain't this the best feelin in the world?" Mama says. A slow, beautiful smile lights up her face. I feel I been waiting all my life to see that smile. I just didn't know it.

I leap up in the air, waving my arms, kicking my feet out. "We in the North, we free! We made it! Look at us, Mama, here we be!"

Mama keeps on smiling. I run and pick her up, swing her round and round till us both fall on the ground laughing with tears in our eyes.

"We been so lucky, Mama."

"God been with us, son."

Wasn't God with Big Jim, I think to myself, but I don't ask out loud. Maybe there really is a god. Maybe he finally showed up.

We sit close together on the grassy riverbank, shivering, and Mama lays her arm on mine. "Son, it'll be hard in the North too. It ain't easy nowhere bein colored. But we have each other." Her eyes light up as though a fire warms them from inside. "Nobody kin sell us away from each other." She grips my hand and I feel her strength enter into me. "You hear? We don't belong to nobody no more. Cept ourselfs! You kin have a wife and chillun and we'll all be a family together and nobody up here in the North kin change that. You hear?"

"I hear, Mama." I like thinking how my family will be my own now. How nothing can change that.

Mama grips both my hands, her glowing eyes look deep into mine. "That's the main thing, son. Remember. Here we kin be a real family. That's a chance we never had."

It almost too much, the feelings I'm having and everything Mama's saying.

Her big smile comes back, spreads over her face. "Now let's have us a picnic. Look in that bag Herman done give us and see what in it."

What's in it is wet but it's mostly the wrapping cloths got wet. We sure can still eat the food.

"Fried chicken, Mama! Us ain't had fried chicken since last Fourth o'July!"

"They eats good in Kentucky." Mama opens a damp packet of cornbread sliced and buttered, spread with honey, put together like sandwiches. "Here a jar of green beans been cooked with ham!" She looks thoughtful. "They musta stole stuff from the big house. Or the cook and house slaves went hungry so us could have it." She looks up at the sky and I know she's praying. Seem like Mama's getting religion long with freedom. We dig in and that soggy food taste so fine we can't help ourselfs letting out a whoop and a holler. We finish every bite, and then climb up the riverbank to the road.

"Here we are free and had ourselfs a fine picnic!" I shout.

A buggy come along just then, and a hard-faced white man stares out at us. He looks like he gonna stop, but then goes on and Mama and me feel good about him going on and leaving us alone, and us whoop some more. We trudge along that beautiful free Ohio road the whole long day and evening, and sleep the night in a soybean field, the ground hard and stubbly, unyielding. But Ohio will yield to us. I know it will.

"We oughta have some money," I tell Mama in the morning. "How bout we look for work in the third town we come to. Three's a lucky number!"

Mama looks me in the eye. "Son, we best try to git to Canada. We can't stop long, you hear? No way atall kin marsa git us once we in Canada. Big Jim said so."

"Course, Mama. You be right. That what we gotta do. When we earn some money." My feet keep jumping round. It's all so new. We never been free till now, Mama and me, not one minute. I try to shake off the stab of worry that came from her to me just now. Was it the hard-faced man in the buggy worried her? He the first Ohio person we seen.

MARY ANDERSON PARKS

CHAPTER FIVE

We tramp along the road a good spell till we come to a town. Feels funny walking right out in the open, not hiding ourselfs. We do a lot of looking and wondering. About three miles later, we come on another little town. Leaving it behind, we glance at each other.

"Where all the colored folks be? Seem like we a rare sight. Everybody be starin."

"I know, Mama." It ain't long before we come to the third town. The sign say its name: Blanchester.

Blanchester got nice houses, most made of logs with little gardens out to the side. Mama says we should each go on our own to find work, so she take off one way and me the other. When I see a man unloading crates of potatoes off his buggy, I ask real polite, "Can I be of help with that, sir?" He's a short, brown-haired man with a big belly, his eyes small in his broad face.

"Sure son, you can give me a hand. Arnett's the name."

I think how no white man ever called me son before. Or told me his name. We carry the potatoes into his grocery store and he say the fellow used to work for him's gone, and do I have time to help him make home deliveries.

"Yessir," I tell him. "Work's what I'm lookin for."

We load up the buggy with all the orders. That's what he calls them, orders. Each box got a name writ on it. Mr. Arnett takes off his bib apron and goes with me for the first delivery. He shows me how to take the groceries, set the box on the back porch and knock real loud two times on the back door. The second one he lets me do by myself, while he stays in the buggy. Then he drives us back to the store, saying I can do the rest on my own.

"What's your name, son?"

"My name's Tom, sir."

"You have an honest face, Tom. And you catch on quick. I think I can trust you to do it right." He draws a map, writes people's names on it to show me which houses to go to. Then I drive around matching up street names on the map with street signs on the roads, and names on the orders with names on the map, cocky as a rooster that I learned reading from Mama, and here in Ohio I don't need to hide it.

When I drive back after the last delivery, Mr. Arnett meets me with a smile. "Son, how'd you like a regular job?"

"Thank you, sir." I remember what Mama said this morning when we went our different ways. "Don't say 'Massa.' Don't never say Massa to no white man ever agin."

"Well, consider yourself hired. You'll need to be here at eight in the morning. How's that sound?"

"Fine, sir. Jes fine." What do he mean, a regular job?

"I've got one more delivery for you. It's the last house up the road." He hands over a box of groceries and points the way. "Have a glass of apple cider before you go." I put down the box, take the glass he hands me and drink it down in thirsty gulps. I never had cider before but I take to it right off. He goes inside with my empty glass and I be wishing he might offer me more when I see Mama sitting on a big rock across the road.

I walk over and tell her what Mr. Arnett said about a job. "How you doin, Mama? You found work yet?"

"No, and I don't understand it." Mama looks tired, even kind of old. "I can't git these women here to talk to me. They jes turns up their noses and goes bout their business." She pulls her sweater tight around her, hot though it be, and hunches over.

"Don't worry, Mama. I'll be able to take care of the both of us. It's time you had a rest anyhow. Just wait here for me, all right? I got one more delivery."

I see Mr. Arnett watching us from the doorway of his store.

"I gotta run. Don't want him thinkin I lazy and foolin around."

I pack the box in the buggy, gee up the horse and make the delivery quick as I can. When I get back, Mama's dozing off on that rock where I left her. I feel bad she had to sit on an ole hard rock, tired like she be.

Mr. Arnett says, "Well Tom, I'll see you in the mornin. You got a place to stay?"

"O yessir, yessir. I sure do."

Mr. Arnett looks across the road with squinty eyes, something dangerous glinting in them. "I saw you talkin to that nigger gal," he says, frowning. "Hope she knows she better be outta town by sundown. We don't allow coloreds in this town after the sun goes down. We ain't gonna have no trouble here like happened in Cincinnati in April. "

I guess it's good I've learned not to show what I be thinking. I guess all those years learning how to do that are worth something. Because I don't let anything on my face tell Mr. Arnett that my mama he be talking about. No, I don't let any of that show in my eyes or my mouth. I keep my face just like it's supposed to look, but all the while I be thinking don't he know I'm a nigger too? And what do he mean, coloreds have to be outta this town by sundown? Ain't Mama and me in the North? Ain't us free?

I just say, "Evenin, Mr. Arnett," and I walk off fast.

And Mama follows behind me like I know she will.

I walk right to the other side of town, to the sign that say "Leaving Blanchester." Mama don't catch up to me till then, causa the speed I going.

"What be wrong?" She looks up at me, her eyes full of worry.

"This ain't the right town for us, Mama." I want to keep walking, I don't want her to ask why it's not the right town. But Mama's not like that.

"What did that man say to you?" She grips my arm, pulls on my sleeve till I have to stop and look at her.

"Tell me!"

"He say coloreds can't stay here after sundown." I mumble, half hoping she won't hear.

She drops her arm to her side, stares at me that way she has so I have to look back and can't look away. "But he wants you to come back in the mornin, don't he?" I nod. "An he think you stayin in town." Her eyes probe into mine. It ain't till I see it in Mama's eyes that I know it for what it is. And then she puts words to it. The words come out as if she don't want to say them.

"You passed."

Her lids drop down, half cover her eyes. She stands there like she's waiting to see what I gonna do. I sway on my feet. A wave of nausea passes through me.

"Come on, Mama. We'll find a place to sleep the night."

She follows me then, but she don't walk beside me like we been doing all our long journey. She trails me by a few steps. And I don't say nothing. I feel ashamed of why. It's because I hear a buggy coming behind us, and if she's walking in back of me, they'll think she's my servant. Maybe they won't be bothered by that.

What kind of people have we run all this way to be with?

* * *

I lie awake wondering, worrying. I feel like a big broad beam hit me across the forehead, stunned me to the ground where I be lying here next to Mama in some farmer's shed. We're taking a chance we hadn't even reckoned on. Is everybody going to see me as white or just Mr. Arnett? But there was that man in the woods. And who will people think Mama is? I see her saying, "You passed," with all those feelings in her face I couldn't read. She was waiting, Mama was, to see what I'd say to her. Lord almighty! Could she be thinking . . .? I try to make my mind turn off. The thought goes by as I stare into the dark that I can't call her Mama no more. Not so anybody can hear. I drop deep down into sadness.

In the morning, I wake before Mama and for a few moments I wonder where we are, then remember sneaking into this shed last night. I lie thinking about how she taught me letters when I was small, then words, tracing them in the dirt behind our shack with a stick. "Letters be good to know," she told me, wrinkling her forehead. "They make words when they be put together right. It be words folks write down to tell their stories and ideas."

"How'd you learn letters?" I asked, but she'd never tell.

"Don't you never let nobody know you kin read." Her eyes glinted with fear I would. "There's some whites who'd kill you for it." I wondered how come then she was teaching me to read. She must have thought it awful important.

Before I know it, I'm thinking bout Mr. Arnett, how he'll be expecting me soon. I could still make it on time if I ran all the way. I see through the cracks it's past first light but not long past. He ain't paid me yet. I could tell him I need my first two days' wages because I'm new to town and low on money. Then I could hightail it back here to Mama before dark. But no, someone might find her here. Who knows what could happen to her all alone? And there's no way on earth she'd go back to that town. Proud and stubborn as she is. I guess we should jes keep heading north. Maybe Ohio gets better the farther north you go.

Waiting for her to wake up, I watch her eyelids flicker like she might be dreaming. Her skin is a warm milky brown. "I got white in me, too," she told me once. I lay my arm next to hers. I'm tan color but no more than some white men get from the sun. My arm touches Mama's and her eyes fly open. I see her remember where she is, take in the look on my face. Her glance goes to my arm next to hers.

"You got my eyes, that's all," she says. "And even them's mostly green, so they really not like mine except the shape and the way they be set in your head. Your mouth's more like marse Tom's, your nose too." Her glance travels over my face. "My forehead, you got that." She frowns. "And my jaw. If somebody look close, they'll know we kin."

"No, Mama! Nobody looks that close at . . ."

"Coloreds," she finishes when I hesitate. "But they would if they had doubts about you and you was with me."

"Mama, it only Mr. Arnett who somehow didn't know I was colored. Maybe his eyes are bad—"

Mama's sad smile cuts me off. Who I aiming to convince? I remember those ladies I took groceries to yesterday, how they treated me so good. One gave me a glass of water and another poured cold tea for me and both of them rinsed my dirty glass under their kitchen pump and set it alongside her other glasses to dry. They stood and visited with me while I drank. And I thought that was the way white folks act with coloreds in the North, friendly and polite-like.

Mama sits up and straightens her shoulders. "You got a decision to make, Tom. You got a job offer and you kin still be on time the way you knows how to run."

I can't make myself look at her. "If you think you'll be all right, I'll go work one more day, then ask for my pay." I push my feet into marse Tom's shoes. They seem to fit better today.

It don't feel right going off without Mama, but it's just one day. Anyways, I don't have time to think on it. I got to use all my wits getting outta this shed and not being seen.

Once on the road, I give myself over to running.

MARY ANDERSON PARKS

Chapter Six
Nellie

It were ole marsa made me name him Tom. I hated the name, but since my boy been wearin it all this time I've come to live with it. He think I kin read his mind, my Tom do. Well, he wrong about that. How kin I read his mind when he don't know hisself what he gonna do?

I crawl behind the pipes they got stored here, carryin along the burlap sack I been usin for a pillow. I gonna stay flat, so if somebody look in I kin hope they won't notice me. It's dark in here and feels peaceful, like nobody's disturbed it for a time. I reckon I'll be safe here till Tom comes back.

I won't think about what I'll do if he don't.

I wanted more chillun. Janey's father and me both did. Mebbe he been able to have some. Most likely. He were such a gentle man. Any woman would be glad of a strong kind man like Jake. After ole marsa sold him, I couldn't stop thinkin about his gentleness. My body ached from missin him. He could git powerful mad if he was pushed too far, but it weren't his nature. Maybe all that changed after he was sold away.

The one I know stayed mad, deep down dangerous mad, was ole marse Tom. I didn't let him come near me after he sold Jake. I guess he thought I'd git over it, and when I didn't, the madness come risin up in him and he decided I hadn't been punished enough.

One night he came to my cabin where I lay aginst one wall, my two chillun ginst the wall across. I always had my own cabin. That way when he came to me he'd have the place to hisself. Jake knew better than to try to sleep in there with me. I'd always go next door to him. Even though there were five others sleepin in there with him. If we heerd marsa come lookin for me, I could run over to my cabin and pretend I'd been out back doin my business. Jake and I never let ourselfs fall asleep together. We weren't gonna take that chance.

The night marsa got his fill of how I hadn't let him in since he sold Jake, I could smell alcohol before he even powered the door open and sent flyin the planks I had propped aginst it. One plank jes missed the baby. Could of crushed her pore little body flat. Tensed up like a new-strung fiddle, I turned to the wall, but he jerked me around to face him.

"Still thinkin about that black buck?"

He was holdin somethin in his hand. I don't know why I did, but I reached out toward it. I guess I was worried what it was, my chillun bein so close by.

"Oh, you want this, do you? I thought you might." His face twisted ugly as sin, and I wriggled on my back away from him. It was an ear of corn in its husk. I could see that now. What harm could he do any of us with an ear of corn? That what he give us as our food every week, a half bushel of corn ears, we had to grind them ourselfs to make meal for hoe cakes. I member havin that thought right before he plunged it inside me. It were a big husk and he pushed it deep in as he could git and stabbed it into me over an over till I thought I gonna die. My thighs clench together now, feelin the pain.

When I came to, it were still dark and I felt blood on me like it was my time of the month only it weren't. I tried to git up so's I could go clean myself before light came and the chillun saw, but it hurt too bad when I moved. I pulled my nightdress down over me best I could.

Tom was sleepin and I didn't know what he might of seen or heerd. I let him sleep and when he woke up at daylight, I told him to carry Janey to cook Jessie and ask her to git somebody to take care of Janey because I wouldn't be able to. It weren't more'n ten minutes till Jessie was there beside me, liftin the torn nightdress to look at me. She made Tom stay outside.

I watched her glance off to the side and saw her jaw muscles tighten. I turned my head to see what she be lookin at. The bloodied cornhusk lay there next to me.

"God almighty, what that devil do to you?"

I started shuddering, and she covered me with all the blankets we had. She and Suphronia the kitchen girl took turns carin for me. They'd bring me Janey to nurse. Janey was five months and Tom two and a half years. After a month, I had to go back to work in the field, carryin Janey on my back.

I thought there'd be one good side of marse Tom messin me up like that. I figured he wouldn't ever come near me agin.

I was wrong.

It were a few years before I understood I wouldn't never be able to have more chillun.

What got me through that time was havin Tom and Janey near me, then later Janey's chillun.

Now all I have is Tom.

CHAPTER SEVEN

"There you are, right on time!" Mr. Arnett's voice booms out as he ties on a clean apron. "Good thing too. Wednesday's always a busy day."

He's right about that. I do nine deliveries in the morning, all the time thinking I gonna wait till the end of the day to ask for my first two days' pay. He'll see the need, won't he, and give me it? I hate asking. I keep going over in my mind different ways to say it. It's hard to believe a white man's really gonna give me money for doing work. It ain't even hard work.

When I come in at noon, Mr. Arnett brings out ham sandwiches and points for me to sit down on one of the two chairs he put there in the dim coolness at the back of the store. He pours a cup of coffee, hands it to me and asks do I use cream or sugar. I about choke on my sandwich getting out the words, "I like it plain, thank you sir." I can't get used to being treated so polite.

Do it ever taste good, that coffee and ham. I ain't never had a fine thick slice of ham all to myself. We lucky to get a hunk of fat on Sundays.

Come afternoon, I stop the buggy at a house where a lady looks up from her gardening and smiles at me.

"You must be the new young man Bob Arnett hired." She stands up, takes off her gardening gloves, comes right over to me with her hand outstretched. "I'm Mabel Yeoman," she introduces herself, and for the first time in my life I hold a white woman's hand. She's sweet-smelling like the lilacs she's tending. Tall for a woman, like Mama, and on the thin side. She has her gray hair braided and pinned up round the top of her head.

"And what's your name?"

"Tom, ma'am. My name's Tom."

"Just Tom? That's all?" Her smile is so kind I know she don't mean no harm, but I don't have a last name to tell her. Nobody ain't never asked me for a last name. Marsa's name is all I can think to say.

"Tom Jones," I blurt out and then feel like a fool. What if marse Tom comes here looking for us? She'll know right away it be me he after. She'll be letting it out to Mr. Arnett that my name's Tom Jones. All I told him was Tom, and he seemed satisfied. Pretty soon the whole town's gonna hear it. Course marse Tom might never come to this town. Our luck might keep on. But I feel stupid.

"Tom Jones, I was widowed last year and I happen to have a room to rent. Would you be interested?" She's still smiling that kind way. I guess she just a real good woman.

"No, ma'am," I say. "I have a place to stay."

"Oh, well that's too bad. For me, I mean. I could use someone handy around the house, and you seem like a nice, hard-working fellow."

"Thank you, ma'am."

I ain't used to lying and I worry that somehow she can tell I don't really have no place to stay.

"I better get your groceries, ma'am."

"Yes, well I hope I'll be seeing a lot of you, Tom Jones. The last fellow Bob Arnett had working for him took to drink and wasn't any good at all."

I wish she wouldn't keep calling me Tom Jones. I'd hoped she'd forget the last name.

I ask should I carry her box of groceries to the back door and she says no, she'll take it in herself.

"Save you a few minutes that way," she smiles.

After I gee up the horse and drive off, I can't stop myself thinking about that room of hers she want to rent. Imagine having a whole room to myself! Then right away I feel bad cause of course any room I have I'll be sharing it with Mama, except Mama's not welcome in this town. Yet it seems I am. That thought I can't get used to. Don't want to, neither. I back away from it like a horse skeered of something up ahead.

At the end of the day when I ask, Mr. Arnett gives me two days' pay without any questions. He says he's counting on me to be back tomorrow morning.

I walk away with money in my pocket for the first time, my head filling up with troublesome thoughts. Will somebody else take Mabel Yeoman's room right away if I don't?

MARY ANDERSON PARKS

CHAPTER EIGHT
Nellie

My legs gittin awful stiff. I been sittin a long time with my back aginst the wall watchin it git dark outside. Now there's no more light atall comin in through the cracks. This been a long day, all by my lonesome. For a spell I could hear a man gruntin an grumblin and I lay still as a stone, hopin nothin would bring him to open the door to where I am. Once I felt a sneeze come over me, hardly had time to stuff my face in the burlap sack and muffle the sound. It got quieter; the mumblin stopped as if the man lifted his head to listen. Then came clankin noises and I could tell he gone back to what he was doin. I heerd his wife when she come out to feed the chickens. Heerd her callin, talkin nonsense to them while they ate the corn she musta been shellin out. I felt all queer, with her so nearby doin that. What would they do if they found me here? I made up a story in my head I could tell them, but it didn't make no sense even to me when I thought about it. If I told them I couldn't find no work, don't mean it okay to be lyin out in their shed. What could they do to me? Could ole marsa come and claim me even here? The slaves told so many different stories. And how would any of them really know? There's one thing I know for sure. Big Jim was still in Virginia when marsa and the dogs caught up with him.

I breathe easier, reach deep in my pocket to touch the bar of pemmican I got left, two hard rocks of biscuits, a bit of parched corn. Tom left water for me but I didn't drink much. Tom's always needed lots of water.

I hear crickets singin, no people sounds. They must be in the house for the night. Crickets sound like they right here in the shed with me. Mebbe they is.

All day long my mind been turnin to Tom, but I don't know where to go with the thoughts I be havin. He always jes been my son, way lighter than Janey, but that to be spected. Never in my life would it have come to mind anybody would take him for white. I heerd tell of passing. We all have, but the stories were of folk far away like they was in another world. There was one about a woman who passed and years later her husband found out. Somebody jealous told on her. The pore thing jumped in the well and drownded. Worse stories, too, about what happened to them when they was caught out in their lie. I s'pose there must of been some didn't come to a bad end, but them we never heerd of.

My mind jes won't go past the place where it thinks about Tom bein treated like a white man and how that would make him feel. It hits a wall and drops back. I be tired from bumpin into that wall over and over. Tired in my bones, though it my mind doin the bumpin.

I thought today about what makes marse Tom sech a bitter man. I seen him gittin poorer over the years, the place runnin itself down. He done wore out that land plantin tobacky season after season. Soil needs a rest from it. He should of planted more corn, wheat or rye between times. But no, he thinkin about the money he gonna git takin his tobacky to market. Not about what us and the animals gonna eat.

Come soon, Tom. We kin sleep and tomorrow we kin move on to a better place. Mebbe you gonna have money to buy food. How I'll love walkin on the road agin! Never in my life I had to stay hidden, cramped up in one place this long. It sure don't feel like freedom yet.

MARY ANDERSON PARKS

Chapter Nine

Walking to the edge of town, I pass a house I delivered groceries to this morning. The lady calls out hello from where she's sitting on her porch swing.

"Evenin ma'am." My stride gets freer as I walk on. I'm already known here by a few folks. Odd thoughts rear up and peer at me, like they daring me to do what I oughtn't. I can't help thinking what a pretty town Blanchester is, with all these nice shade trees and porch swings, like Mabel Yeoman has, and how pleasant her house would be to live in. The thought slides in next, slick as you please, how this might be a good place for a slave trying to pass, because no other coloreds live here. Most coloreds would see me for what I am. I've seen other slaves light as me, when they come to the plantation with their masters, and I'm pretty sure I'd know they had colored in them even if they was off someplace by theirself, if they had yellow in their skin color, or mouth a bit too full, nose too wide. Now I think on it, I'm pretty sure marse Tom or the missus would know, too.

But if a man was all dressed up in a suit, like I seen some here in this town? Would anybody, slave or slave owner, know?

I tan real nice, no yellow. Mama say my nose and mouth like marse Tom's. Most folk think he's a good-looking man.

Folk that don't know how mean he is. I take a deep breath and rest my mind from thinking.

There ain't no more houses. I left town not even knowing I was leaving it, so full my mind was. The warm evening air comforts my skin and when a breeze comes up, I breathe deeper and slow my steps, letting myself enjoy being alone here on this road. There be trees along both sides and I love watching the leaves flutter in the breeze. A wagon rattles by. The farmer driving it lift his hat to me. I do the same. I'm glad Mama made me wear the hat. She had it folded up in her pocket all the time we was running.

When I come to the shed where I left Mama, I keep on walking, wondering where my feet be taking me. It's too early is what I tell myself, too risky till darkness comes. It feel so good walking on the open road. Like anything's possible. Lightning bugs are coming out, their little bits of light jumping first here, then there. I do a hop, skip and dance right in the middle of the road, thinking how far these legs of mine have taken me. I think of Mama rubbing her special ointment on the leg that sometimes troubles me. She knows to do that soon enough it don't git too bad. She always knows when I'm achin and need rest. My god, she even knocked a white man senseless, maybe dead, so I'd git the rest I needed to go on running.

I turn and head back slowly toward Mama. It's dark now, crickets singing powerful loud, like they have something important they want to say. I try to hear, in case it be for me.

Chapter Ten
Nellie

Mebbe I doze off. Next thing I know, I hear the shed door close quiet like it don't want nobody to hear it.

"Mama? You awake?"

"I be sittin here in this corner."

"I can't make you out."

"Well, here I be. Big as life."

Don't know why I feel techy all a sudden.

"Yeah, I see you now."

Tom comes to sit beside me. He hands me somethin round. "Here's a apple I saved for you from lunch. Mr. Arnett gave it to me, and a ham sandwich."

"It's good he fed you. Here are biscuits and some water." I drop the apple in my pocket. Ham, huh? Guess dry biscuits don't taste like much after ham.

"Mama, he don't work me hard at all. And he paid me for the two days right away when I asked. Gave me a half dollar!"

Has he forgotten what that man said about me havin to be outta town by sundown? I guess I had too much time to think today. Mebbe that ain't good for a body.

"Such a day I had, Mama!"

"That right?" Tom be chewin fast, like he do when he excited to tell me somethin. What is it, I wonder, worried but knowin I won't have to wait long. Tom never been able to keep nothin from me.

"You won't believe this, Mama, but a lady I brought groceries to wanted to rent me a room in her house!" He laughs a laugh I ain't never heerd from him.

"Well, what did I tell you? They think you white, son."

I keep my voice calm. "Yes, you were right about that, Mama. It the strangest thing, ain't it?"

"Yes, it is. Which road you goin down with that? What you gonna do bout them all thinkin you a white man?"

"Do?" He finishes his biscuit and stretches out next to me. "We have to act like you're my servant, I guess. Will you mind that too much, Mama?"

I suck in my breath. "No, but I hardly see how we kin make a life like that."

"Can't we just start out that way and see what happens?"

"I s'pose. So we'll be on our way tomorrow and try to git to a town where coloreds ain't run out by sundown?"

"There's jes one thing, Mama."

"And what that be?"

"Mr. Arnett's spectin me back an I don't want to start out our new life on a lie."

"What you be thinkin, Tom?" He sure don't be thinkin bout the biggest lie of all we be startin out on. I almost want to laugh, the way his mind work.

"I don't know. Ain't there somethin I kin tell him so I kin leave honorable like?"

I think on that, bout Tom wantin to be honorable. Not truthful, but honorable.

"You kin go in tomorrow mornin and tell him you got word in the night your mother's very sick and needs you to come right home. Then rush off before he kin ask any question."

"That's good, Mama! I knew you'd think of somethin. Where shall I say my mama live?"

"Say Cincinnati. That's a big city here in Ohia."

"That's what I'll do, Mama. He mentioned the place himself." Tom pauses, frownin. What he holdin back? He holdin back more'n he sayin. That's not like my Tom.

"I jes don't want to leave feelin Blanchester's a place I kin never come back to. Not after folks here been so good to me."

I guess he's too young to know how those words cut into me. He rolls away on his side and soon I hear from his breathin he's asleep. I feel like I can't do nothin bout all this. It jes gonna go on happenin. Nothin ever gonna be right agin. Not that it ever was. Was there ever a time things seemed right, or it felt like they could be? I think when I learned to read may have been the best time of my life. And the worst. I had jes lost my mama. She died birthin my sister, born dead when I was six years old. Mistress felt sorry for me. She brought me in the house to sleep in her room and do for her. It warn't marse Tom's wife. I hadn't been sold yet to marse Tom. It was a few years later he'd have his go at me. The mistress I lived with back then was Mistress Elaine, a golden-haired girl married to a man three times her age. They had one chile, Lydia, a girl of seven, and mistress was learnin her to read. My job was bringin things to Mistress Elaine when she needed them and fannin her when she was hot. I slept on a mat in the corner where I could hear when she called out in the night and wanted water or her headache medicine. It was the only time I ever slept inside a regular house. It lasted two years, till Mistress Elaine took sick with pleurisy. In those two years, I heerd all Lydia's lessons her mama learned her, and learned them right along with her. Mistress Elaine knew it. She'd hold the book so's I could see it almost as good as Lydia. She could tell how much I loved the learnin. If ole massa popped his head in, she'd send me on an errand so he wouldn't see how I was hangin on every word.

When Mistress Elaine got too weak to git outta bed, they sent Lydia to her grandparents. Lydia knowed her mother would be comin to join her there, but I spect she knowed too her mother was gonna end up the same place my mama and baby sister went. When Lydia said her goodbye to me we looked in each other's eyes, each of us holdin the other's two hands, and us neither one wanted to let go.

She said, "I'm sorry, Nellie, about your mother, and I wish I didn't have to leave you." She'd never mentioned my mother before. I weren't able to speak a word. Did she know the empty space it filled in me when the three of us read stories together, Mistress Elaine and her takin turns readin, me followin along? I wished there was somethin I could give Lydia that would do that for her. But I didn't have nothin to give.

After Lydia left, I offered to Mistress Elaine I could read to her to comfort her while she lay there in bed. She took my hand and said no, massa might come in and hear and then he'd beat me. I'd never been beat yet, and I told her mebbe that wouldn't be so bad. I'd take the chance. She jes squeezed my hand with her little bitta strength and tried to make a smile.

I roll over, put my arm round Tom's shoulder. I spect to drop right off to sleep but it don't happen. Instead I start to wonderin what do he mean, I'll be his servant? We won't get to sleep in the same place. Mebbe not even eat together. I bury my hand in his thick wavy hair and he stir a bit, then sigh, peaceful-like. Is this the last time I'll git to touch him? It be so long since I cried, at first I don't know I doin it. My face scrunches up, sounds come outta me same time as tears. At last I sleep too; next thing I know I hear a rooster crow and see a sliver of light between two loose boards. My hand's still in Tom's hair. His hair's growed down to his shoulders, like most men here. An it not that much curlier than some. I draw my hand out slow, lettin my fingers move down his cheek, around his chin and up the other side. Tom be smooth-skinned. He ain't never had no beard.

"Mama," he sigh. "It be mornin?"

"Fraid so. An doan call me mama. I'se yuh suhvant."I feel him smile under my palm.

"Aw, Mama. You don't have to talk like that."

"Ah sho nuff do. Ah needs tuh practiss."

"Ain't you had enough practice on the plantation?" He sits up and I raise up too. I watch him remember what he told me he was gonna do this mornin.

"You be all right here a little longer, Mama?"

"I got to git outta here, Tom. I'll wait up the road apiece. First clump of trees I find, I'll set an wait."

He frowns. "I may be a while."

"I'll wait," I say, not lookin at him. Is he thinkin bout that room for rent?

"When I see you come by, I'll git up an follow."

"You'll come along an walk a few steps behind? That how it gonna be?"

He's got his head bowed down and I kin tell how bad he feel bout the way it goin to be.

"It all right. I kin take care of you jes as good bein your servant as bein your mama." I give him a push to git him goin.

He goes out, cautious, slow. The door shuts. I sit quiet awhile, listenin for signs of trouble, an prayin.

"Is you there, God? Is you watchin over us?"

I guess he is cause it ain't long before Tom's back from town, finds me waitin under a big ole tree and soon we out on that dusty road, Tom as a white man, me a free colored servant, trottin along behind him fine as you please.

"When's I gonna git my first wages?" I call out.

Tom turns, sees my wide grin.

"Soon's I get a job!"

He start steppin more light.

Chapter Eleven

Mid-afternoon we reach a town called Milford, bigger than the others. We seen no coloreds living in any of the towns we passed through. Are all the towns like Blanchester? Yet we know slaves made it to Ohio. Free coloreds, too. Maybe most of them went to big cities?

So when we get to this place, Milford, we're glad to see colored folks. Least I think Mama's glad. I been looking back at her real often, because of how serious her face has turned. She's been doing some heavy thinking. Now she looks downright mournful. It don't take long to notice the coloreds live in the rundown part of town.

I slow my steps and let Mama catch up. It comes to me I have a choice to make. Live there with Mama, and be dirt poor all your life, a voice in my head butts in. Mama knows me awful well. She sees in my face what I be thinking. She says in a low voice, "Tom, you want to go find a room to rent like that lady in Blanchester offered?"

I look in her tired eyes and no words come out.

"Promise them you'll pay at the end of a week. Say you new in town but findin work's never been a problem. That be true enough."

She gives me a long look, probably seeing in my face I'm imagining a job, a room to myself, a new kind of freedom.

"I'll git me work too," she says, turning away. "You'll know where to find me."

She walks off without another word into that part of town I know few white people ever walk into. I could follow her. I could catch up easy and say, 'No, Mama, we'll always stay together, no matter what.' She ain't walking as fast as usual, and I wonder is it because of how tired she is or is she waiting for me to make my choice. And I really don't believe I've made it yet. She is the length of two barnyards away when I take a step toward her. Or maybe it is only in my mind I take that step.

CHAPTER TWELVE
Nellie

Every step I take away from Tom, my mind's sayin please, please give up this foolishness, please jes come with me an be my boy. Why you wanna be one of them? Then I tell myself I bein selfish. Course he thinks his life gonna be a whole mess better, what with findin out he kin pass as a white man. I see it in his eyes and the way he lift his head up kinda cocky. It won't be me, his own mama, standin in his way if that's what he thinks best. But it feels like the whole world's outta kilter.

I don't know what I was spectin Tom to do when I said that to him about rentin a room from a white lady. I been hidin my heart best I could, like when he took to the idea of me bein his servant like a baby to the breast, and now him lettin me walk away, not tryin to stop me or comin with me. Is it a mistake, hidin my heart? Should I let him see the pain he causin me?

I been a slave too long. I jes take what comes and try not to let it knock me down. All my tryin go into that. There's nothin left over. But oh it hurts.

I'm hot, sweaty and tired from walkin through towns where folks look at me so unfriendly. Then when we come to this place that finally has coloreds, and we see they all live off to themselfs in ole shacks, well all I knows is the North ain't what I hoped.

I kin hardly believe I done walked off from Tom.

Chapter Thirteen

After a bit, I get into the part of town where the stores are. A man in a gentleman's hat crosses the road over to my side. He's probably in his late fifties, wearing nice trousers and a good pressed shirt.

"Hullo, young fellow! You're new in town, ain't you? My name's Fullerton. Dan Fullerton. Can I buy you a drink?"

I'm thinking how unbelievable this is. He takes my arm and carries me along with him. I can almost taste cold apple cider like I had the other day.

Neither me or Mama turned to look back. Or did she?

Is this how important stuff in life happens? I slide into being a white man by accident? Or do I want to think like that so I don't have to face I'm breaking Mama's heart?

It ends with Dan Fullerton offering me a job as his assistant, but not till he asks me lots of questions and tells me about his business. He calls it 'real estate.' He explains that means he buys land, or helps somebody else to, sometimes land, sometimes a whole farm, other times a house in town, and then he sells it for more than he paid. Not right away. He waits till it's worth more. He says prices keep going up. You can't lose. And it's not apple cider but whiskey he buys me a drink of.

"That all sounds real good," I say.

"Tom, you catch on quick. How are you at reading and writing?"

"Well, I read some. I reckon I could learn to write."

"I'm not so good at it myself. Never got past fourth grade. That ain't held me back none when it comes to making money. I've been feeling the need of help. Most young fellows are busy on the farms. Looks like you came along at the right time for me and for you too. You can ease into learning the business. You have a good honest look about you. I think I'll take a chance on you. I can't pay much but when times get better I'll give you a raise."

I told him that was fine. So I started driving him around in his buggy drawn by two handsome black mares and we'd check out property. Or anyways he did. I watched how he did it, listened carefully to all he said. Back at his little office, he'd set me to copying what he call documents. All I had to do was make the letters, spaces and dots come out looking like what I was copying from. If I didn't know what a word meant, I'd ask him, and that way I learnt.

Dan Fullerton spent a lot of his time with his feet up on his desk, smoking cigars. He says smoking cigars helps him think and thinking is a big part of real estate. He don't mind at all when I interrupt to ask something. He says, "The more you learn, Tom, the more you'll be worth to me." He says that a couple times a day.

So I set myself to reading everything I can lay hold of. A book on Mr. Fullerton's bookshelf explains how folks supposed to talk. It's from back in his schooldays. Got his name on the inside cover in squiggly little boy handwriting. I study that book every chance I get. Mr. Fullerton has two shelves of books. I wish he had more. I figure out writing from what I read.

He lets me sleep on a cot in a room behind the office. He lives upstairs. I hope Mama found a place to stay right quick. I keep busy so I won't think about her so much. Milford's not that big a town, but I haven't seen her yet. The place Mr. Fullerton and me eat meals never has a colored person in or near it. The first time he said, "Let's go get ourselves something to eat," we walked across the street to the saloon, where it turns out they serve food as well as liquor, and I noticed not only weren't there no coloreds, there weren't no women neither.

I was already known at the saloon because that's where Mr. Fullerton and me had our first drink together. He introduced me as Tom Jones who walked up from Virginia. He found that out by asking me questions before he hired me. I told him the same name I used in Blanchester, so if somebody from there comes around, they won't catch me in a lie.

Dan Fullerton had a way of asking that made it easy for me: "Where you from, Tom?"

"Virginia, sir."

"Came up here by yourself, did you, Tom?"

"Yessir."

"Reckon you're a young fellow who wants to move up in the world, that right?"

"I hope so, sir."

"Yes, I can see that. You've got that fire in your eye like I had when I was a young man just starting out. And you're a strong healthy fine-looking fellow with an inquiring mind. You carry yourself well, too. You afraid of hard work, Tom?"

"No sir, I surely ain't."

"Well, you might just be my man."

"I hope so, sir."

"I knew straightaway you're a hard worker from how tanned you are by the sun. You're a farm boy, am I right, Tom?"

"Yessir."

"Farm boys are good workers. It don't matter what they're working at, it don't have to be farm work at all. They just keep at whatever job they're given till it's done."

"Yessir."

I liked Dan Fullerton well enough. But after I'd worked for him a month, and in that time he made two big sales, he said not to expect my raise yet. He said new workers who don't have experience have to prove themselves and that takes six months. Then we'll see about the raise.

Part of me's thinking I can go back to Mama when I get the raise. I'm already saving most of what I get paid, in a sock under my pillow. All I bought is a few clothes. Weather's so hot I don't need no coat or jacket. But I sweat and then I need a change of underwear and shirt, even trousers. I bought those things and washed the clothes I've been wearing all this time.

I left my slave clothes behind when we ran. Marse Tom's trousers and plaid shirt held up pretty well, his shoes too. I washed in creeks when I could, so I didn't look too bad when we got to Ohio.

Yes, I can go back to Mama and then . . . I get confused. How can I keep my job or any good job if folks know I'm colored? I've heard the men talk in the saloon.

"There seem to be more of those damn niggers all the time," a man named Butch said the other day.

"So long as they stay out of my way, they don't bother me none," Dan Fullerton put in. I about choked on my stew meat.

"Well, that goes without sayin, Dan. I mean, they sure as hell better stay out of our way." He squinted his eyes and looked around at the other men. "Know what I mean, dontcha?"

"Yep, sometimes niggers need to be taught a lesson. Like folks did up in Cincinnati." The meanness in the eyes of the man who said that sent fear through me. He was sitting in a dark corner. Was it my imagination he stared straight at me?

It was a relief when Dan Fullerton stood up. "Time for us to get back on the job, Tom."

A few days later, he told me he had to stay in the office to close a deal, but he had another client insisting on seeing a certain piece of land.

"Can you drive him over to Goshen, Tom?"

"I sure can, sir."

"The land is a couple miles beyond Goshen. Mr. Steele will show you the way. He's been there before." Then he muttered, "Don't know why he has to see it again this very day. But he's a hard customer, Mr. Steele is. You'll learn something today, Tom. Mr. Steele wants to see the land after these thundershowers we've been having, wants to make sure it perks. If there's a lot of standing water, he'll back out on me."

I'm thinking how I'll be alone with a man I never met. I gotta remember to talk the way they do when I'm with these white folks.

CHAPTER FOURTEEN

It's not long till Mr. Steele knocks on the door. A tall, thin man wearing high boots, a black rain slicker and rain hat. Right off I don't like the look of him.

"This your new assistant, Dan?"

"Yes, this here's Tom Jones. Tom, meet Mr. Steele."

"How do you do, sir."

"We're in for a wet ride. The rain started up again." His small smile never reaches his eyes. His mouth has hard lines on each side that settle quickly back in place after the smile comes and goes.

I hurry into my room for the yellow slicker I bought last week. When I get back, Mr. Steele's saying, "Thanks for the use of your team and buggy, Dan. My mare's not up to it today. I had to walk over."

"What's wrong with your mare?"

"Guess I rode her too hard."

"Well, that'll do it."

"She's getting old. Keep an eye out for me for a strong young horse, will you?"

"Even a strong young horse won't last if it's ridden too hard. You've been through a lot of horses, Sam."

"Well, that's my business, ain't it?"

"Sure is, Sam, sure is."

Mr. Fullerton claps me and Mr. Steele on the back.

"You two better get on your way if you're to be home before dark."

I'm surprised he spoke up about the horse. But one thing certain sure about Mr. Fullerton is he takes the best care in the world of those two mares of his. So off we go in a rainstorm, me and Sam Steele, who of course I'm supposed to call Mr. Steele because he's older than me by a good twenty years.

"Go slow where the mud's bad, Tom," Mr. Fullerton calls. I turn and wave to him where he stands in the doorway, looking worried.

"I will, sir."

We are almost out of town when it happens. I see a woman carrying two big white sacks. She starts across the road up ahead of us. She's hurrying so she won't get some white family's laundry soaking wet. I'm thinking she'll be across by the time we get there but I slow down anyway, because that stretch of road is real muddy.

"You were going slow enough," Mr. Steele snaps. "No need to slow down more."

Just then the woman slips, falls to her knees in the mud, along with her white bags.

I yank hard on the reins, call out "Whoa!" to the horses. The woman looks up at the sound of my voice.

It is Mama.

The expression on her face pierces right through me. I move to jump down and help her. But Sam Steele grabs my arm, shouting, "Get out of our way, you goddamn nigger!" He seizes the reins and the whip and whips the horses over and over. "Giddyup, you damn beasts!" Mama scrambles up from the mud and is able to get herself and one bag out of the path of the buggy, her gaze fixed on Sam Steele.

He keeps on yelling. "You damn fool nigger, why did you cross in front of us? Can't you see we're in a hurry?" He throws me the reins. "They're the slowest, laziest people on earth. Now let's make some time."

I don't speak a word that whole trip and back. He talks, and I nod.

I drop him off at the fine house he says is where he lives and drive on to Mr. Fullerton's, shaking, dazed. I towel the horses dry, lay blankets over them, pitch them hay to eat.

I go in and tell Mr. Fullerton, "I'm going to bed. Took a chill, don't feel so good."

"No, you don't look good at all. A solid night's sleep will fix you up, Tom, and a big breakfast in the morning. Take an extra blanket or two from your closet."

I don't sleep for a long time. I lie in bed under three blankets, seeing Mama's face and those muddy bags. I begin to understand I won't ever live with Mama again. I don't have words for how that feels. I'm not proud of myself.

In the morning my head hurts bad, upside, downside, across, all the way through. Mr. Fullerton looks in on me.

"I'll skip breakfast," I tell him. "I'll be ready to work when you get back."

After the front door bangs shut, I go out to the pump in the backyard, pump it hard, douse my head under it for a long time, then dry my head with a towel, gently, so as not to kick up the ache. I feel a warm day starting, that special scent and softness in the air that turns brutal later on out in the fields under the sun. I lift my face to the sky, breathe in and out, deep and slow.

And still I see Mama's hurt, questioning eyes in front of me.

I brew up strong hot coffee, drink two cups. The rain let up some after we drove off and left Mama there in the road. She hadn't been injured, far as I could tell. She would have made it to wherever she was going. How strange not to know where she lives. She don't know where I am neither.

Later, copying out a Bill of Sale and Transfer of Title, I tell myself how glad she'll be I'm learning all these new words. Won't she? How I want to believe that! I'll work my hardest, learn all I can about real estate, be as good a man as I can. A voice inside mocks me. "A good white man?"

When I have more money, I'll find a way to help Mama without anybody knowing.

CHAPTER FIFTEEN
Nellie

I watch Tom and the devil-faced white man drive off and I stand there till I know Tom's not gonna turn around to come back, not gonna jump off that buggy and come to me. Even after he saw with his own eyes and heard with his own ears how that man treated me.

So I make my way across that muddy road and pick up my bag the buggy passed over. The wheels thank the Lord didn't run over it. I head back to my place I found to stay, with a lady who lets me use her bucket, well water and soap to wash white folks' dirty clothes. I try to push out of my mind what just happened and think about her instead.

She gave me a room and food to eat. Says she was lonely before I came along. She was born free, this lady and her husband too, but he up and died a year ago March. Died of pneumonia. Her name's Mary Walker and she thinks she's almost sixty though she's not sure. She was born in a town called Richmond, in Virginia, and her mama had eleven children. After she married her man, they made up their minds to come up here to Ohia where their babies could have an education. In Virginia they wouldn't be allowed. She thought maybe in Ohia they could. Turned out it isn't so. But the Lord never blessed them with children. She told me with eyes as sad as any mama on the auction block. I could see freedom don't always mean you're happy. I knew marse Tom and the missus weren't happy, but I thought us colored folks would know how to do a better job of it. We wouldn't be living with our foot on somebody else's neck. How can you be happy doin that? I see God has lots more to learn me. I think about all this, walking the mile back to Miz Walker's little house.

It's helped me all these weeks to think about stuff that don't bring Tom to mind. Trouble is, most all that comes to mind brings Tom trailin right behind. What helps most is having work to do. And I like going to church with Miz Walker. Marse Tom didn't let us. He was always afraid we gonna get ideas in our head.

When I finally get there, Miz Walker takes one look at me, puts on her coverall apron and lifts the muddy bags from my arms.

"Oh Lord, Miz Jones. You jes get cleaned up and dried off. I'll start in washing these bags and the clothes that need washing again. Some fool musta splattered you with his buggy?"

I feel too discouraged to answer. I got four ladies I wash for. This one wanted hers by evening. I was on my way over to give it to her. Using the clotheslines I got strung up in my bedroom, no way can I have things dry and ready till morning. She'll jes have to wait.

I take off my muddy shoes that Miz Walker gave to me, an old pair of hers. Rubbing my face and hair with a towel, I slump down on a chair at the kitchen table.

"It not as bad as it could of been." Miz Walker offers up, trying to comfort me. "Looks like only these few things at the bottom got to be done again. I can do them in the blink of an eye. You jes rest."

"Thank you, Miz Walker. You more than kind."

"You'd do the same for me. I know that. And look how you help me, keepin me company, havin supper all cooked and ready most days when I get home from my job!" She's a maid for a white family six days a week, so I guess it's true I'm a help to her. "You always have the place swept up neat as a pin."

I think for a minute before saying what's on my mind, crowding out all the rest. I think how to say it.

"Miz Walker?"

"Hmm?" She's busy scrubbing.

"If someone was to come askin for me, you know, like if another slave from the plantation was to make it up here like I did, all alone, tryin to find help gettin started, do you think they'd have trouble locating me?"

She turns with her hands held up, dripping water, her eyes round with surprise.

"Why no, Miz Jones. All they'd have to do is come here to colored town and ask for Nellie. Nellie Jones. Every living soul here knows you be stayin with me. Except if the one askin be a white man, then they'd all say, 'No suh, ah nevah heerd of no Nellie, not in dese parts.'"

She smiles at me before going back to scrubbing. "So don't you worry none, Miz Jones."

I think about what she said, and can't keep my glance from going to the door, can't keep from hoping.

Tom would say he's looking for Nellie, his mama. Wouldn't he? He'd even know to say how long ago I came here.

Miz Walker goes off to bed before I do. I sit in the dark till my head slumps over and I know how stupid I am. There's nobody up and about at this hour, nobody Tom could ask.

Maybe tomorrow.

I'd best get some sleep.

What I can't no way believe is that he'll want to keep staying around folks who act like that man whipping those beautiful horses.

Chapter Sixteen

I'm used to getting advice from Mama. Since we went separate ways, I have to think for myself. I worry, am I making wrong decisions? It seems like some decisions make themselves. I get carried along like a boat by the river current. Like when Mr. Steele made me keep driving the buggy that day I saw Mama. The days pass quick cause I have work to do, new stuff to learn. Even months hurry by. Business picks up and Mr. Fullerton depends on me more and more. I know that gotta be a good thing for me and my future. Imagine me having a future!

"You sure do learn fast, Tom," Mr. Fullerton tells me one day. "You've got a way with people and a head for business. Folks trust you. You're nice and polite."

I'm thinking, of course I'm polite. I was a slave. We get flogged for looking the wrong way at a white person. We learn to act like they want us to.

What I say is, "Guess I don't know how to act any other way."

That makes him laugh for some reason. Then he gets serious again.

"It's more than that, Tom. It's like you read folks' faces and know what they're thinking, how high they'll bid."

It seems like a good time to speak up about an idea I been kicking around in my head.

"Know what I'm thinking, Mr. Fullerton? I'm thinking we could branch out into livestock. Trading livestock would give us no end of business. Folks buy land, settle into farming, and for years to come they got to keep up their livestock. Even if a farmer's got just one mule, or let's say two old nags. Sooner or later one's gonna give out on him and he'll be lookin for another."

Mr. Fullerton's eyes turn thoughtful. He's really taking it in, this stuff I've been thinking on for quite a time.

Sitting on the chair cross from me, he slaps his knee. "Dang it, Tom, you've got something there. Livestock!"

He hooks his thumbs in his red suspenders. He's put on weight, Mr. Fullerton has, with all the good meals him and me eat. He don't move around much, eats like a farmer, but don't work it off like them. He acts more and more like one, from dealing with them so much. But he's not a farmer. My thoughts keep running along their own track.

"I put the cart before the horse!" I burst out. "Before a man trades livestock, he got to have some! And before that he got to have a farm!" I let out an excited laugh. "I've got to get me some land, Mr. Fullerton."

He rests his chin in his hand, like when he's considering an offer. "Yes. Land. I reckon that is why I never got into trading livestock. I never had a farm, always lived in town." He seems to drift off into a daydream. He does that lately. He's way up in his fifties, or even sixty, and showing his age more.

I get up, pour him a cup of coffee, set it near him on the desk. He nods, stroking his chin.

"Let's have oatmeal cookies, too, Tom. Help us think better."

"Fine with me, sir." I set cookies on a plate and pour myself half a cup more coffee.

"You know, I had a wife, Tom. A fine good woman. She used to help me out here in the office. But we never had children. That was a great sadness to Ruth. To me too." He gives me a long look I can't read. "Turned out she had weak lungs. It ran in her family." He munches on a cookie. I reach over and take one for myself. "Anyway."

I think he's not going to go on but he does. "So I've got no heirs. What I'm thinking is, I know of a big piece of good farmland we could get for a low price right now, things being down the way they are. If you felt up to farming it. You come from a farm family down in Virginia. Grew up on a farm, right?"

"Yessir, I've got experience making stuff grow."

"And I know something about horses," he says. "Cattle, I suppose we could learn that, don't you think? Hogs too, maybe?"

He's saying 'we!' I wonder can he hear my heart thumping? It sounds awful loud. I stop chewing the cookie I stuffed in my mouth.

"You could do up a title document with us as joint owners, right of survivorship."

I swallow hard. "Mr. Fullerton, are you sure? Do you think we could handle it?"

"I think you could handle it, Tom. Young and strong as you are. We'll tackle it a little at a time, of course. Maybe start with some chickens, a few milk cows." He grins. "You'll need to find you a wife, Tom. A good healthy farm girl."

"Mr. Fullerton!" I'm choking on the cookie and all the emotions swelling up in me. Mama won't get to be part of it.

Will she? Is there any way she could? Would our servant idea work?

This isn't the dream I had for Mama and me. This is something else coming from nowhere.

"Tom, where are you? You off in a daydream? About taking a wife, I'll wager."

I look up in surprise. That was the farthest thing from my mind.

"You know, you're the new fella in town. I see them give you the eye, don't think I don't. Some widow ladies came after me when Ruth died. I know that look."

CHAPTER SEVENTEEN

Seeing Mama that day carved pictures in my mind. She's strong, and she's got a job doing laundry. That's a good thing. Means she's earning money. She must walk into our part of town, picking up dirty clothes, carrying them back clean. What will I say if we meet again? But mostly I stay right around here. If I'm out, I'm going at a good clip in the buggy.

I am so alone these days. I've never been so much alone, never used to be alone at all. And I've never been so free. I love that part. As long as they think I'm white, I can lie abed in the early morning, or in the evening like I'm doing now, and just stare at the ceiling, those cracks up there, or out the window at the leaves blowing in the breeze. Nobody cares. I can drink beer or whiskey, I can even get drunk, cuss and carry on, and nobody pays no nevah mind. Not that I really do those things. Maybe once. Twice. It didn't make me feel good to be drunk, wake up late and get looked at crossways by Mr. Fullerton, all disappointed in me. Wasn't worth it. I know there are rules even for white men. And I want to be among the best of them. I really do. I might say something stupid if I'm drunk. I need to be careful. What would they do to me if they find out who I am? I don't like thinking about that.

Some part of me thinks about Mama all the time. I miss her eyes, how she beams at me, proud and loving. When my leg bothers me, I wish she was here to rub her special salve on it. I bought some salve but it don't do no good. Nothing's the same without Mama. Especially me. Who am I anyway?

I go stare in the little mirror on the wall and I feel ashamed. On the plantation, they all knew who I was. So I knew. But out here in this white world, I'm making up who I am every minute of every day, and I'm all by myself doing it and sometimes I wonder why I'm doing it.

I see young women glance at me that way that means they'd be pleased if I came over and said, "Good morning, how are you today?" I see other young men say such things and I know where it leads. I even know it'll happen to me one day, and I got my eye on the one I'll say it to.

But it worries me to think of how it'll end up with her my wife, and me working hard to provide for her, and . . . here my mind balks like a horse you can't get to go the way you want. I know we'll have children and I can't make myself think about how they might turn out. I know I'm more than half white because Mama has a good bit in her, so there's a chance the black wouldn't show. Would I tell my wife before or wait and see if it happens? What could she do about it except hate me? Hate's bad. I sure didn't cut myself off from the person I love most in the world so I could end up being hated. See, here I am thinking about it when I said I couldn't. Can't help thinking about it is more the truth.

Oh hell, I'll go to the saloon and drink enough to forget but not so much I won't get up in time for work. I can do that, can't I? Stop when I want to?

I'm learning to hold my liquor. Even that time they talked about nationalities, I did all right. Most of them have German in them, so I said I do too. English and Welsh, I added, because once I heard marse Tom say that's what he was. And a little French, I threw in, because I think French are darker than those other folks. Seemed to me one fellow, Hank, looked at me funny, like he was weighing what I said or how I said it, and how it matched up with how I look. He's the one I noticed before, staring at me with a mean face.

"You're a real mutt, ain't you?" he drawled. "Probably got Irish too, the way you put away the liquor."

"Probably," I agreed. I was feeling pretty good by then. He's got his eye on that same gal I do. Her name's Sarah Long and I picked her for her dark hair and eyes. People won't expect her to have yellow-haired children with blue eyes. I like her, how soft she looks and she's nice to her brothers and sisters. She's the oldest of six. Her family rides into town Saturdays from their farm. I see her at church too, when all eight of them crowd together in one pew. Sometimes she looks sideways at me and then blushes pink when her eyes meet mine. She don't look at Hank that way.

Chapter Eighteen

Dan Fullerton is good as his word. The next day he asks me to drive him out to the place he has in mind. He gets the horses ready by himself, hitches them to the buggy. He's moving slower lately.

"It's near the settlement they call New Columbia, that has the Presbyterian church, a schoolhouse and the steam flour and grist mill," he tells me. "I've been keeping pretty quiet about it. The old geezer's finally ready to sell and I'm the one he trusts. I've known Ned Riley for years. He's been living alone out there in a two-story eight-room farmhouse. Keeps it neat and clean even though he's been all on his lonesome for years. Family died off or moved away. He and his wife had three girls who all married young. His wife died long ago and I know how lonely that can be. I visit him when I'm out that way, make sure he's all right. Well, here we are, Tom. Turn in at the lane."

I stare at the big house in awe. Are Mr. Fullerton and I really gonna live in it? I have tons of questions but no time to ask now. Ned Riley opens his front door, comes out on his porch to greet us. He's bent over with age, but still a tall, strong-looking man.

"Hullo, Dan." His blue eyes light up with pleasure at seeing his old friend. "Is this here the fellow you been tellin me about, the smart one?"

"Yep, this is the Tom Jones I been braggin on. One and the same!"

Ned Riley grasps my hand. He has the best grip I ever felt. He pumps my arm up and down.

"Come in, come in. Just come through the parlor and into the kitchen. I've got strong coffee hot and ready." He pours from a pot on the stove for all three of us and we take seats around his oilcloth-covered kitchen table.

"How you been?" Dan Fullerton asks.

"Pretty good, pretty good. Yourself?"

"Other than those chest pains I told you about, I'm all right."

I glance sharply at Mr. Fullerton. He nods. "That's right, Tom. Haven't mentioned it but I've had some pain in my chest. Sometimes even when I'm not doing anything but set in my chair."

"Have you seen the doctor, sir?" It feels odd to be talking about this in front of somebody I just met, but Mr. Fullerton's the one brought it up, and my question just pops out.

"Yeah, I've been to see him. He told me to take it easy and not eat so much pie."

Ned Riley grins. "Well, I won't offer you none then."

"Don't tell me you bake pies nowadays!"

"Nope, but my daughter brings me a pie now and then."

"She the one you fixin to live with?"

"That's right. Kathleen. My oldest. Lives over to Batavia. Has two sons at home farming. She's been after me for years to come stay with her. Her husband too. He's a good quiet fellow. Irish. His family came over from the old country about the time I brought mine. Among the first."

"What made you finally decide to take them up on it?"

Ned Riley takes a slow sip of his coffee, wipes his mouth with a big plaid handkerchief. "Two things. You saying you have this young man working for you, both of you interested in this here farm, getting it going again, and him ready to take a wife and you wanting him to get a good start in life. That's one. Then there's me realizing I'm not up to keeping even the vegetable garden going by myself. I can help out my daughter, but I'm too old to do all the work there is on this place. I like to see it ship shape, you know?"

"I know you do, Ned."

"Dan, you'll be getting a fine solid farm. That spring under the milk house, it's never run dry, not in all these years. And it's just a few steps from the back door."

"I see," Mr. Fullerton says, but it's plain to me from his expression he don't know the importance of a reliable spring close to the big house. Cook Jessie hates the distance she has to walk to the milk house to do the straining and churning, then carrying in the pails.

I lean forward. "That'll be wonderful. The farm I lived on in Virginia had a spring that ran dry part of every year. Then the milk would go sour."

A broad smile takes over Ned Riley's face. "This boy knows his farming, Dan. You two are lucky to have met up." He shifts his weight in his chair. "Let's wrap up the deal. You got the papers you want me to sign?" He glances over at the stove. "Chopping wood to keep that cook stove going takes more out of me these days than I got in me." He heaves a sigh. "Nope. I can't go through another winter here."

I'm thinking the place looks like heaven. All Mama and I ever imagined was a little tiny house with a patch to grow a few vegetables. It don't feel right at all for this to be happening without her. My right hand reaches out from my side, wanting to hold hers, imagining that possible.

"We can have the papers ready by tomorrow," Mr. Fullerton says. "I didn't want to rush you, Ned. This farm has been your whole life, I know that. You think on it tonight, see how you feel in the morning. I'll come out with the papers, make sure you're ready to take this step."

"Hell, Dan. I just had my eightieth birthday." He gets to his feet and pours the rest of the coffee into our mugs. "I reckon I'm sure as a man can be."

Chapter Nineteen

I wait until spring when buds appear on the lilac bushes. This Sunday morning is when I'll ask Sarah Long can I come calling in the afternoon. I wanted to see how Dan and me made it through winter at the Riley place and if a woman could be comfortable living here. We got snowed in a good part of winter and I did a lot of reading in Mr. Fullerton's books. He's got a big one called *The Complete Works of Shakespeare*. I especially liked a play about this dark prince name of Othello. That do be one sad tale.

We ate well. Did our cooking on the wood stove and in the fireplace in the kitchen, and our baking in the Dutch oven Ned Riley built into the bricks. I did most of the cooking because Mr. Fullerton's rheumatism laid him up quite a bit. In early fall, I fixed up the small room off the kitchen for him to sleep. With the door open, he gets enough heat from the kitchen to sleep through till I kindle the fire up again in the morning. I laid a featherbed underneath him and a featherbed comforter on top. Being hardier, I took the front bedroom upstairs, with windows looking out to pastureland we own across the road. I've got featherbeds for me too, and I love them. Right off I bought them and long underwear. How pleasing Mama would find all this. I feel a squeeze around my heart when I think about her, and I think about her every day. I mull over the servant idea but we probably couldn't keep up pretending and when folks see us together they're likely to notice the ways we look alike.

Our woods out back keep us in firewood. My bedroom has a small fireplace I plan to use a lot if Sarah says she'll be my wife.

Hank Dexter is still after her. Now that it's spring, folks can get out and about. I've driven the buggy by Sarah's house and seen him sitting on her family's big porch swing. Well actually her mother sits there with Sarah while Hank perches on a hard-back chair looking like a buzzard. Tuesday evenings is when he goes. I've seen him there twice. Her family's place is about two miles from ours. Theirs is closer to New Columbia so I go by coming and going. I always lift an arm and wave like folks around here do. The Dexter place is off to the other side of New Columbia. The Dexter boys, they're known for fighting. They back each other up, the three of them. It's a miracle Hank hasn't managed to pick a fight with me yet. It's not for lack of him trying. But it takes two to fight, and I know to go home when I see certain signals. One thing that helps hold me in is I'm tickled as a hen laying her egg to have a real home. I like to be here fixing things up, learning farming and most of all being the boss of myself. Don't want to lose all that by doing something stupid.

A woman can choose the man she fancies and I mean to put myself in the running. Hank Dexter's eyes are too close together. That's not a good sign. Neither is his low forehead. I reckon Sarah notices that sort of thing. The gleam in his eye puts me in mind of marse Tom. It's a look men with meanness in them can't all the way hide. It be lurking there behind their smile. Not that anybody ever saw marse Tom do much smiling.

I can hear what Mama would say. "You go in there boy and take your chances. You'll be doing that poor girl a favor. You worth a hundred Hank Dexters. She's probably longing for you to show how you feel about her. But how she gonna know lessen you tell her and how you gonna tell her lessen you pay her a visit?" I think that's pretty close to what Mama would say. I think every day how could I pay Mama herself a visit but the risk is too high. And now I'm out here on the farm with New Columbia the closest settlement, and it's a place no colored ever go. How could Mama and I have a talk?

We file out of church that Sunday, everybody there a white person, shaking hands with the minister as we go by, him grinning with happiness that we come at all when so many don't. Even Dan Fullerton don't go no more. But he has rheumatism for a reason. I linger around till Sarah and her parents come out, followed by her two sisters and three brothers. Her mother throws me a quick glance and I take off my hat and bow respectfully. She nods, a little surprised, and walks on with her husband. Then I fall into step next to Sarah.

"Please allow me to introduce myself. I'm Tom Jones."

Sarah blushes up into the roots of her hair and smiles kind of mischievous-like, the lights in her brown eyes dancing. "Yes, I know. You've moved into the old Riley place down the road from us."

"Yes, Miss. We are neighbors and I thought of coming by your place this afternoon to pay my respects to you and your parents." It's her I'm coming to see and I want her to know it. It's not her mother I aim to set next to on the porch swing.

My speech to Sarah is something I've been practicing in my upstairs bedroom, standing at the window, thinking how lucky I am to have something to offer such a fine young lady. Sarah looks like she stepped out of a picture frame, in a bonnet with pale green ribbons drifting down and a layered full-skirted dress she must have made herself out of green and white cloth with a spanking white collar and yoke. They don't sell nothing that nice around these parts.

She looks even cleaner and prettier close up. I feel in every muscle how close she is. When she spoke and I smelled the sweetness of her breath, my heartbeat speeded up. Yep, she's the best choice all right. And she's not a show-off, the kind can get a man in all sorts of trouble. She walks like a lady, not swishing her tail the way some do.

"Will you excuse me a moment?" Sarah's gloved hands flutter in the air until she clasps them firmly together. I'd like to think it's my nearness flustering her, maybe because I'm feeling that way myself.

"Sure nuff," I say, forgetting the fancy talk and manners I've been practicing.

"I need to ask Ma something," she explains. I hope I smell good to her the way she does to me. I scrubbed real hard this morning. I vow to wash good every day the rest of my life for this woman. Sure never did feel this way before.

She catches up with her mother and they go back and forth about whatever it is. Once her mother looks at me, gives me that up and down onceover. I'm real glad I have on the new gray britches, vest and jacket I bought last week. Her mother is a short woman with keen eyes and thin features. Not much flesh on her, maybe from running after six children. Finally she gives Sarah a brief nod.

Sarah hurries back to me. "Ma says to come and get introduced to her and Pa. Please?"

I follow close behind her till we're in a little circle, the parents, me and Sarah. Her brothers and sisters come to a sudden stop, almost running into us. They sure are a well-behaved bunch. I stifle an impulse to chuckle. Gosh, Tom. That'd be no way to impress this tall, serious man who stands so upright his chest puffs out, filling his black suit jacket. All the farm folks around here dress in their best for church. Often it looks worn and shiny like it's been their best for a lifetime. My clothes stand out, I realize, as new. I smile at the boys. The littlest girl runs to hold onto her mama's skirts. The other one looks to be about sixteen. She stands close to Sarah.

Sarah says, real proper-like, "Allow me to present our new neighbor, Tom Jones. Mr. Jones, these are my parents, Eldon and Naomi Long."

"Pleased to meet you." I bow slightly like I've seen folks do.

The mother gives me a small smile. At last!

"Pleased to meet you," Mr. Long says gruffly.

"We'd like you to join us for Sunday dinner." Mrs. Long speaks with an effort. It dawns on me she's shy. Likely doesn't get out much.

The invite takes me by surprise. "I-I'd be mighty pleased," I stammer. "But I didn't bring anything to contribute."

"We don't expect you to!" Mrs. Long responds with the first warmth I've seen in her.

"How's Dan doing?" Mr. Long asks abruptly.

"He's showing his age all a sudden," I say, glad for the chance to share my worry about him with someone who seems to care. "His heart's been acting up and he's got to take it easy. Now rheumatism troubles him too. It was bad this winter."

Mr. Long nods gravely. "Yep. Them things run in his family. They're not long-lived folks, the Fullertons. Don't know much about them. They've only been here a couple generations. Came over from Milford to church here in New Columbia because they liked our minister. Town folks. Never known them to farm before."

"I'll be doing the hard work, sir. He's not up to it. We'll need good farmhands to help plant. It's glad I'll be for any advice."

Mr. Long gazes at me levelly. "We'll see about all that."

Maybe I spoke out of turn. He must know I'm after his daughter. If he doesn't think he knows folks who've been here a couple generations, I better go slow.

Driving behind the Long's wagon on the dusty road, I sit straight and tall, prouder than anybody ought to be. Sarah got her mother softened up to invite me for Sunday dinner. I wonder if Hank Dexter's ever been invited? Reckon not since he hardly comes to church. Oh, I feel set up like all get out! Sarah likes me. Why else would she ask her ma to invite me? Then I get to worrying. What if my manners aren't good enough? Just be nice to all of them, I hear mama say. Be polite and respectful to the old folks and friendly with the kids.

And get up close to Sarah when you can, to send shivers up and down your spine, I add.

CHAPTER TWENTY

Once we're in their house, I have to sit with Mr. Long in the parlor while the women get dinner on the table. Everything looks so settled: lace curtains at the windows, lace cloths on the backs of chairs, little tables with doodads settin on them. Dan and me don't have no doodads. Books in the bookshelves look like they've been there over a hundred years. A gold-framed picture on the wall shows dogs going after a little fox they got cornered, men on horseback riding up fast. That's a real scary picture. I wouldn't want it hanging where I'd have to look at it. We don't have much except what Ned Riley sold us.

Mr. Long looks as uncomfortable as I feel. He clears his throat a couple times. "How did you and Dan Fullerton meet up?" he suddenly asks me.

I think fast. I'll tell part of it, the part I can without giving away Mama.

"He was about the first person I met after coming to Milford and he offered me a job in his real estate office."

Mr. Long thinks about that. "Did you have any experience?"

"No sir, I didn't. But Mr. Fullerton said I was a fast learner and a good worker."

He nods his head a few times. "Those are good qualities all right."

Then there is quite a long silence I'm afraid to break, afraid of where almost anything I say could lead.

He clears his throat again. "Where did you live before you came to Milford?"

Maybe I should never have agreed to come to Sunday dinner. All I'd bargained on was sitting on the porch with Sarah, her mother there too if she had to be.

"I come from Virginia, sir. Campbell County."

"Your family farmers?"

"Yessir."

"That'd be tobacco, would it?"

"Yessir."

He nods again. "That's real different from the farming we do here." Another silence. What is he thinking? I read the newspaper. Some think war might be coming and slavery the reason why. He would know they have slaves in Virginia. Is he wondering if my family had slaves? Is he for or against slavery? It's sure not gonna be me brings it up!

Sarah appears like an angel, coming in with her sweet smile. I hope her father don't hear my sigh of relief.

"Dinner's on the table," she says. "We do the cooking Saturday so there's not much to do but heat it up and set it out."

New worries attack me once we're all sitting around the dinner table. My hands start to sweat. I've never eaten a meal at a table like this, covered with a white cloth and cloth napkins at every place. They all bow their heads and I realize they're fixin to pray.

Mr. Long's at the head of the table, with Sarah on his left and me on his right. Her mother is at the other end. The three boys are lined up next to me and the sisters next to Sarah.

Mr. Long finds a lot to pray about. He asks the Lord's blessing on the crops we'll be putting in the earth, and good health for the farmers and farmhands who'll help with the planting. He asks a blessing on the farm animals, giving thanks they made it through the hard winter. Will he remember the chickens in the henhouse, I wonder? No, now he's giving thanks for the health of his children, his wife and himself, even me, calling me a fine young man who has come into their community with an honest purpose and the will to work. "In Jesus' name, amen," he finishes up, and everyone around the table adds "amen."

I open my eyes and take a good look at the food. Right quick they start passing around fried chicken and gravy, biscuits and butter, succotash, cooked carrots, applesauce, coleslaw, mashed potatoes, a bowl of pickles and a platter of sliced ham. Never have I seen such a feast. And this is just a family dinner! They use serving forks and spoons to get food onto their plates and I do like them. I take some of everything so if there's something here Sarah made I won't hurt her feelings. My plate gets piled so high I'm afraid I'll knock some off by accident.

I'm glad they all take eating so serious. Maybe I won't be asked any more questions about where I come from. It's what he cares about though. That's clear. And it troubles me.

Sarah and her sister, Carrie they call her, take away the plates and what's left of the food, leaving us our tea glasses and forks. Then they help Mrs. Long bring in chocolate cake, already cut in slices on plates.

"This is a mighty fine dinner. It's grateful I am to be invited," I say. Mrs. Long nods her head and looks down at her piece of cake.

Are they not supposed to talk?

Mr. Long finishes his glass of tea. Then he clears his throat. "Sarah, was it you made this fine chocolate cake?"

"Yes I did, Papa. Thank you." She gives me a quick smile.

When everyone is done and the table cleared, the children ask to be excused. They vanish upstairs. Maybe they'll get to change out of their Sunday clothes and play.

"Sarah," her mother says, "you can take Mr. Jones out on the porch and set for a spell." It takes me a moment to realize she means me. "Carrie will help me with the washing up." She turns to her husband. "The children will be down to have you listen to their Bible readings, Mr. Long." I can see more praying than playing goes on in this house.

He heads for the parlor, which I'm keenly aware has windows overlooking the front porch. I have to make the most of this. Who knows if I'll be invited again? Sarah sits in the porch swing and I settle myself at the other end of it, where I'm in a better position to look in her eyes. She sure is a pretty thing. She smiles like she wants to encourage me.

"I hope it wasn't hard on you meeting all my family at once like that."

I am surprised she'd bring it up. I hold her gaze and speak truth to her. "It was."

She looks down at her hands folded in her lap, then back up at me. "You don't need to be nervous with them. I'm quite sure Daddy likes you. He's not one to show his feelings but I know him."

I grin, relieved. I lay my arm across the top of the swing and move closer to her. And watch her blush. I don't touch her. I just let her think I might, maybe even wish I might. Now that I'm pretty sure I'll be invited back, I go slow so as not to frighten the parents, who may be keeping an eye on us.

"I have my own horse, you know," Sarah tells me. "Now I'm eighteen I'm allowed to ride into town on her."

"No, I didn't know you were all that grown up." I grin, wondering why she told me that.

"Not all that often," she adds. "Only twice so far. Her name's Cinnamon."

Then she tells me how useful it is to have a horse to ride out and check on the crops when they're in and how we'll be wanting rain once crops are in the ground.

She seems so young. But when we talk about farming, it's clear she knows all about it. Yes, she's the one I want for a wife.

"That's a real pretty dress," I tell her.

She blushes, like I knew she would. "Thank you. I made it from feed sacks but some of them have really nice colors and prints."

"You're a clever girl, Sarah. And about the nicest I ever met." She blushes a deeper pink. "I hope to visit again. Please thank your parents for me. I don't want to bother them when they're busy, and I need to get home." I stand up, bow slightly and shake hands with her. She gives me a big smile. I wonder, is this the right way for me to leave? Her hand is soft, her handshake very firm.

As I gee up the horse and start home, I still feel the thrill of Sarah's hand in mine. I held it extra long and I know we both of us liked it. I could see in her eyes she did. It felt a little like she already belonged to me. Will I really get to have a wife of my own that nobody can sell away? It's hard to believe.

CHAPTER TWENTY-ONE

My thoughts turn to Dan Fullerton and worries about his health. I took the one-horse buggy like I do often lately because he doesn't feel up to going with me on errands. Looks like the physical work will be up to me. I've been traveling around talking to merchants, traders, farmers, getting advice, learning all I can about managing a farm.

How grateful I am to have so much to offer Sarah. We have three milk cows now, four horses, two mules, thirty chickens and a rooster. No hogs or cattle yet. We hired a young boy from a farm a few miles down the road. He walks over to our place five days a week to help me. Mr. Fullerton has a good amount of money saved up. Even after paying for the farm, he told me there's enough to get it up and running. "Just give me all the receipts," he said, "and I'll make sure we stay in the black." That means not to owe anybody anything, he explained when I asked. "We've got good money coming in from selling eggs and milk. Are you gonna teach that young boy, Jeremiah, how to make deliveries and free you up for more important jobs?"

I turn into our lane, suddenly full of anxiety about Mr. Fullerton. He will have worried why I was gone so long. I wonder if he had anything to eat. I left chicken soup out for him, and bread.

Entering the kitchen by the back door, I call out, "Mr. Fullerton?" No answer. I look in his room off the kitchen. No sign of him. My heart starts to pound as I enter the dining room.

He's on the floor by his favorite chair.

At first I think he's dead. He's sprawled out on the rug on his right side, his left arm flung open. When I move him slightly to turn his face upward, I see his chest go up and down very slow, and my own breath starts up again.

"Mr. Fullerton!" I slap him a few times lightly on each cheek.

"Wha—what? That you, Tom? I must've fallen asleep." He tries to rise up and can't.

"Just stay there," I warn him. I grab a small flat cushion and lift his head gently to slide it underneath.

"Ah, Tom." He shuts his eyes.

"Yes, that's right, Mr. Fullerton. Rest yourself."

His eyes open. "I was waiting for you to come home. I think I fell. Maybe went to sleep here. Funny thing to do, huh?"

"Yes sir. We'll get you up and in your chair but there's no hurry. You'll be fine now. I'm here to take care of you. I should never have gone to the Longs for dinner. I wish to God I hadn't."

"Tom, I want to ask you something."

"What is it, Mr. Fullerton?"

"I wish you'd call me Daniel. My mother called me Daniel."

"I'd be honored to do that, Mr. Fullerton."

"Well then do it!" More strength comes into his voice and he tries to smile but the right side of his face isn't working. His mouth pulls down a little on the right.

I don't let worry show in my face. Instead I smile, like he's trying to. "Daniel," I say. "Daniel, I'm going to lift you up."

His eyes look straight into mine, trusting me.

"Can you put your arms around my neck and hold on?" I'm on my knees next to him and I lean toward him. His left arm goes around my neck.

"Okay, we'll try it one-handed. Hold on tight as you can." I brace my hand on his armchair to keep my balance and get up on one knee, pulling him with me. He's a dead weight. I heave us both up to standing, using all my might.

"Okay now, just ease yourself back into your chair."

I feel awful grateful for the strength I have. I can carry him to bed when the time comes, I'm pretty sure. Or maybe he'll be able to walk by leaning all his weight on me. Sweat trickles down my back.

"How do you feel—Daniel?"

"Damn glad you're home! What were you doing at the Longs anyhow? After that pretty girl, are you?"

I smile a real smile now. This is good. Him talking like this. I draw in a long breath and sigh it out.

"You had anything to eat while I was gone?"

"Nope, don't think so. Don't remember having anything. But I'm kind of foggy."

"How does chicken soup sound? It's all ready to be warmed up. I left it on the stove case you got hungry."

"Sounds real good."

"I'll get the fire going then."

MARY ANDERSON PARKS

CHAPTER TWENTY-TWO

The next few days I rely on Jeremiah for everything so I can take care of Daniel. His face stays drawn down on the right side. Worse, he don't have the use of his right hand and can walk only by leaning hard on me. He keeps telling me, "I'll be okay, Tom. Leave me be here in my chair."

Instead I tell him what a miracle Jeremiah is. "He's just a kid but he's got so good at all the chores, gives me time to set here with you and play euchre." Daniel loves that game and now that he's taught me, I do too. Jeremiah feeds the chickens, gathers eggs, milks the cows, cares for the horses, then goes out in the buggy and makes the egg and milk deliveries.

What I'd do without that boy I don't know. He's fifteen, one of ten children. I'm sure the family's in need of the money he brings in and the eggs and milk I give him, packing him up with all he can carry walking. I'm thinking of letting him ride Paint back and forth but haven't told him yet. Raised his salary because of the extra work he has to do. Probably raise it more at harvest. Sure don't want to lose him. A tall solid quiet fellow, hardly talks. Got a wonderful deep voice when he does. Dark blond hair, strong jaw, blue eyes with the longest lashes I ever seen, a real gentle look in his eyes. He mumbles and he's hard to understand. My guess is somebody's been cruel to him. That's why he don't speak up. Gets along better with animals than with people. He knows Daniel's a kind man and it's clear he feels real bad about what's happened to him.

I've been thinking how to help Daniel. This morning I woke up with an idea. Mama would know what to do. She used to go to the woods to gather herbs, and cook Jessie made special teas the way Mama taught her. I walk toward the barn where Jeremiah's doing the milking. Can I trust him with this? He looks up at me when I come in. Belle swishes her tail, cranes her head around so she can see me.

"She don't want to miss anything," Jeremiah grins.

"Nope, she sure don't. Jeremiah, I've been thinking on what you and me could do to make Mr. Fullerton better."

He nods.

"I want to ask your help with something."

"I'll do anything might help Mr. Fullerton." His eyes are astonishing, how much feeling they show. Brings to mind a young puppy.

"Well, this is what I'm thinking. I heard tell there's a woman in colored town name of Nellie, who knows a lot of secrets about herbs and roots and such."

The rhythm of his milking changes, the squirts come slower into the pail. Belle jerks her head back to check on us. The smell of manure hits my nostrils, suddenly suffocating. Jeremiah's gaze is on me, something different now in his eyes.

"A colored woman," he states. He seems to be thinking it over. I suppose he wonders how I know about her.

I take a breath and push on. "You could ask around, say why you want to find her." Nervous, I scuff my shoe in the hay. "Do we have extra eggs we can spare?"

"Eggs?" he repeats. I remember when I first met Jeremiah I thought he was simple-minded, going on how he talked.

But he isn't. He's real darn smart. Just keeps his thoughts to himself.

"You can give some to anybody who helps, save the rest for this woman Nellie."

"I won't take none home, then we'll have extra. What do I say when I find her?"

"Tell her who you work for, tell her my name. Then explain who Mr. Fullerton is and what happened to him, how his hand don't work right and his face pulled down to one side, and his legs weakened. Ask her what tea or ointment she has could help him. Say you'll come back if she needs time to make it. And tell her you have money to pay."

My hands start to trembling and I shove them in my pockets. It brings Mama so close talking about her like this.

"Do you want me to go now?"

"No. The deliveries need to be done first."

The sun is already low in the sky when Jeremiah sets forth with the eggs and bag of money. To pass the time I suggest to Daniel I could read to him.

"How high did you go, Tom, in school?"

"Not so high as you'd even notice." I grin, hoping to steer him off with a joke. "I don't think most farmers believe all that much in schooling."

"They're probably too busy to think about it! Let's play cards. We can get to the reading some other day."

"Sure. We can go through the books you've got, see what looks interesting." I walk over to the sideboard, bring back the cards, shuffle and deal.

"Jeremiah gone home early?"

"No. I—sent him on an errand."

Daniel studies my face thoughtfully, then looks at his cards. I'm grateful when no more questions come.

"I better pay attention," he mutters. "You know, Tom, I think it's good for the mind to play cards. No matter what Preacher Burns says about it being a sin."

That was my guess too. It's one reason I started it up, case his mind was affected some way by whatever caused him to pass out like he did. Holding and managing the cards is good for his hands, too. He mainly uses his left but sometimes the right has to help. We had the doctor out and all he could tell us was he'd seen a lot of similar cases and Dan was better off than most. "Try to move around as much as you're able and keep working that right hand even if it hurts," was his advice. "We ain't got no medicine for it."

After four deals, Daniel says, "Tom, you better light the lamp. Can't see the cards."

I don't want to admit to myself how dark it is fast becoming. The shadows in the room make me uneasy. I get up and light the coal oil lamp. Now the outside seems even darker. Maybe I'll get Daniel settled and asleep before Jeremiah comes back. I'm filled with fears for Jeremiah, myself, Mama. I should have let him go earlier. What was I thinking?

"Shall we call it a day?" I ask.

"Tom, I'm a big trouble to you, ain't I?"

"No, you sure as heck ain't. We're lucky we got us a good farmhand and can enjoy ourselfs playing cards. And it'll be good for my reading if I read out loud. Let's try that Shakespeare fellow again. We'll start tomorrow."

"Okay, Tom. Help me to bed."

He says it like he knows I'm anxious to get him out of the way. I don't tell him about the tea and salve I hope is coming, because I'm more and more afraid something's gone wrong. Old fears get stirred up along with fears about what's happening tonight. Maybe nothing. Maybe nothing's wrong.

Maybe Mama had him wait while she brewed up tea, or—well, I don't know, do I, what might or might not be happening?

After I get Daniel in his bed, I carry the lamp back to the dining room and sit waiting, straining my ears for the sound of the buggy. All I hear is a hoot owl. It brings back the night we ran off, Mama and me, and I shiver.

We need to get a dog. Maybe two. We're all alone out here. Daniel has a rifle. I look over at the locked cabinet where he keeps it. A lot of good that'd do! I never held any kind of gun. Wouldn't even know how to load it.

And then I hear the buggy wheels and dash through the kitchen and out the door, careful not to let it bang.

Jeremiah lifts his hand in greeting and steps down, favoring one leg, I notice. He hands me a bag.

"She gave me two kinds of tea and two jars of ointment. One's for his hand and the big one, she told me this twice, is for his legs and anybody else who has soreness in the leg."

"Looks like that might be you."

He gives a little laugh that don't come out right. I forgot to bring a lantern, so I can't see his face.

"Come on inside."

"No, I better get home."

"I'm giving you Paint to ride from now on. I laid the saddle out. So come on in."

"From now on?"

"That's right. I thought it over, Jeremiah. It makes good sense. You can get in more time working instead of taking so long walking here and back."

"I surely don't know how to thank you. Paint will come in useful tomorrow.

There's one thing I have to do, though she said it don't matter."

"What's that?"

"I couldn't pay her today. Even the eggs got broken."My eyes have grown more used to the dark. I step closer to him.

"You have a black eye!"

"So does he," he mumbles. "Maybe he's got two."

"Who? What happened?"

"You know those Dexter brothers?"

"I sure do."

"I ran into all three. They gave me a bad time, acted like it was teasing, grabbed away the money bag, even the eggs I'd packed up. I jumped out of the buggy with my fists up. 'He wants to fight!' Hank yelled and threw a punch. I knocked him out."

"On your first punch?"

"Had to. Three against one ain't fair. Another came at me and gave me this black eye. I knocked him out too. After the third one got him and Hank back on their feet, I still had my fists up. They rode off on their horses."

"How'd you learn to fight like that?"

"I was small as a young'un. Used to go to the barn and wrestle with our cows. Of course they knew me, knew we were just playing. I got strong doing that. And I grew a lot after I was thirteen."

"Jeremiah, come in the house. I need to look at you in the light. Quiet though. Mr. Fullerton's asleep."

In the dining room, I hold the lamp up to him. "Your eye's swelling bad."

"She gave me something for that. I've got it in my pocket."

"Well use it."

He brings out a small jar.

"Where in hell were you when all this happened?"

"The Dexter boys were out front of a shack everybody around Milford's heard of. A half-wit colored gal lives there alone and men take advantage. All they have to give her is a nickel. Or even candy."

My god! This is the man who's courting Sarah. Jeremiah must see the shock on my face.

"I've never gone there, Mr. Jones."

"I'm sure you haven't, Jeremiah."

"I think the three of them had just come out of her place. They were liquored up."

"Did they ask what you were doing in colored town?"

"Hank did."

"What did you say?"

"I told him, 'That's not your business, is it?'"

"And?"

"I heard you work for Tom Jones, that right?" he asked me.

"This was before the fight?"

"He weren't in no shape to ask anything afterward." Jeremiah looks so pleased with himself that I can't help grinning. "It was when they grabbed the money bag."

"And afterward you went to Nellie's."

"Yes. I asked a man where Miss Nellie the healing lady lives. He told me she lives with a Miz Walker and pointed me the way. He thought I needed her help, from my face."

"You think folks know how good a healer she is?"

"Well, you knew about her." He frowns, puzzled, but I risk another question. Can't help myself.

"Do you think any of the Dexter boys know what house you went to?"

"No, Mr. Jones." He smiles. "They hightailed it out of there quicker than jack rabbits. I'll get started home now. On Paint."

I don't rest easy after he's gone. He's a boy thinks on things, Jeremiah is.

There's so much I want to ask him, but I reckon I can't. How is she? Did she ask anything about me? I'm thinking, could I go there myself some day?

Who in hell would have thought he'd run into Hank Dexter?

Rubbing Mama's salve into my leg makes it tingle. The leg feels stronger and better right away. Mama's salve will fix Daniel up, I'm sure of it. I search through the cloth bag she used to put things in. Is there a note? No, she's protecting me, Mama is. I feel her spirit in the air around me. Will I be able to sleep? Any chance of that? I crawl into bed, sink into its comfort. So long as the Dexter boys don't know why Jeremiah was there and don't know where Mama's living, I reckon we're safe. But seeing Jeremiah in colored town, knowing he works for me and most likely was on an errand for me, that'll plant a suspicion in Hank Dexter's mind, even if he don't know yet it's there.

I burrow down under the covers, caught in the memory of Sarah's brown eyes, her soft mouth. I imagine what it will feel like when our lips touch. Yeah, she's gonna be my girl. The thought of her spending even a minute with Hank Dexter is unbearable.

I've got to move quicker. I'll be in church Sunday and every Sunday after. I toss around in the bed with a restless need to move on.

Will I always feel I'm running for my life?

CHAPTER TWENTY-THREE
Nellie

That boy Jeremiah comes by here again today, bringing the money like he said he would. This time he's on horseback. He sure is one sweet white boy. Big and strong, with eyes gentle as a lamb. Now how'd he get himself punched in the eye?

I can't get much out of him about the fight. But I keep trying.

"Somebody gang up on you?"

"Only two or three." He mumbles so I can hardly hear. I'm sure they'd be white but I ask anyway.

"Did you know who they was?"

"The Dexter brothers." He says it so low I have to ask twice. But then he speaks up, a warning flashing in his eyes. "Stay out of their path, ma'am."

"I will try to do that. Thanks for the name so I'll know what path to stay out of." I wink, and he gives up a shy grin.

"Did they know whose errand you was on?"

"I didn't tell them. But they already knew I work for Tom Jones, ma'am. Folks know Mr. Fullerton can't work since his spell. Mr. Jones takes care of him and everything else."

"Is Mr. Jones a good man to work for?" I worry should I be asking these questions but he's such a respectful boy I can't resist. He the only link I've had so far to my Tom. I don't want to let go of him.

"Yes'm, Mr. Jones is a very fine man to work for. He lent me this horse, Paint, to ride to work and back home."

So Tom owns a riding horse. And chickens. Jeremiah brought us eggs again. This time they didn't get broke.

Suddenly Miz Walker bursts in from the hallway, taking a step back when she sees the white man. "Oh Miz Jones. I didn't realize you—"

"It's all right, Miz Walker. This be the young man was here yesterday. His eye is more swelled up but it be gettin better all the same."

"Well, Miz Jones can fix you up if anybody can. I'll jes be going now. I was on my way out. Will you be all right, Miz Jones?" She shoots a sideways glance at Jeremiah.

"I be fine," I say, hoping she don't call me Miz Jones again. Will it seem odd to this boy I have the same name as Tom? I did notice him lift his head when she called out my name. Seemed to me those blue eyes got wider. Now is he studying my face in a new way? Or examining the wall in back of me? I turn to see what he's finding interesting.

"Do you be lookin at that drawing on the wall?"

"Yes, ma'am. It's real pretty. Looks like the Milford creek."

I smile. "That's what it is!"

"Was it you that drew it?"

"Yes it was. I have some free moments now and then, and that's what I like best to do is draw." I add, almost to myself, "Jes found that out since I been livin here."

"I like to draw too," he mumbles. "But my pa—"

I don't understand the rest of what he says. "Beg pardon?"

"He tears them up." I barely hear the words.

He shuffles his feet like he wishes he hadn't said so much and wants to get away now.

Not so fast, I'm thinking.

"Wait here! Now don't run off." I shake my pointer finger at him. "I got something for you." I hurry to my room and bring back my box of drawing pencils.

"I took out half for me," I explain. "These are for you." Seeing how that shocks him, I add, "I counted that money you gave me and it's way, way more than enough to pay for what you took home yesterday. Tell your boss you folks got credit with me!"

"Ma'am, if my pa found these on me, he'd whup me good." His eyes show his fear of his father. I think fast.

"Would your boss let you keep them at his place?"

"I reckon so." I watch the fear go out of Jeremiah's eyes and he lets me put the box in his hand. "I could keep them in the barn maybe. Thank you, ma'am. This is the best thing anybody could give me."

He looks distressed. I lay my hand on his arm. "Are you from a big family?"

"There are only ten of us kids now," he says. "The twins died two winters ago."

The poor sad boy, I ache to wrap him up in a big hug, but I guess I can't. "Well you tell your boss I gave you these for drawing and he needs to give you time to do it in, because you can't at home."

"Yes'm."

Does he wonder at me giving orders to his boss?

I glance at Miz Walker's old clock. "You best be on your way. Here's more salve, two jars. You'll be needing more before long if you using it proper. Now get on with you. Don't forget to rub the salve into your own leg. That's why I gave you two."

I might really latch on and hug him if he don't get out of this kitchen right quick. I sure don't want Zeke coming in and finding me hugging a white boy. Ezekiel Davison is a good man and I'm mighty glad he's come up in my life, but I know he wouldn't cotton to me being in another man's arms, no matter what color. He might not wait to hear the whole story.

Still, I risk one last question. "Jeremiah, where is the farm you work on? In case I'm ever out that way carrying my ointments and such, I could make a home delivery." He gives me a surprised look, but tells me what I want to know.

"This side of New Columbia. It's a big two-story white wood house with a green barn." He's probably wondering how I'd get out there. I'm wondering too. Could Zeke drive me out in his wagon to where Tom lives? Zeke's a traveling shoemaker. Could he travel out there?

I wave Jeremiah off on the horse called Paint, part of me riding right along in the saddle with him to where Tom is, in the big two-story house. How I long to look on his face. That would have to be enough, just to see him. But maybe he wouldn't like it, me showing up there.

I guess we never know how much loving we still got in us. I didn't tell Zeke, but I felt the old familiar stirring down below my belly when he caught hold of me and pressed me up against him. Zeke showed up at a time in my life when I thought that kind of thing was all finished. And I told him so. "Zeke," I said, "that kind of loving be all in the past for me." I think he knew better and he gonna be trying again soon. The old thing! What a handsome face he has on him. Even with the scar.

And here he is, striding in wild-eyed and yelling. "I heard a white man was in this house!"

"You heard right. He was respectful as could be, did his errand and left."

"Didn't hurt you none?"

"He jes a boy, Zeke, a farmhand. One of the men he works for had a spell, went unconscious and after that his right side don't work good. I sold them a root tea I made up for cases like that."

"Will it cure him?"

"It'll make him better. If he drinks it every day."

"So word's got out you're a medicine woman." He grins that charmer grin of his.

"Folks want the stuff I make. If they don't have money, they bring food to trade. And they know I'm no snake oil seller gonna be gone tomorrow."

"Same with my shoes. I make them to last so folks won't be back shaking them in my face."

It's because of shoes we met. I needed shoes real bad. Miz Walker told me go to Ezekiel Davison, the shoemaker. She said he learned his trade on a big Virginia plantation, made shoes for everybody miles around, then bought his freedom and came up here to Ohia. She didn't say how long ago. Well, Zeke's got to dropping by to check on how my shoes fitting me. Miz Walker won't stop funning me about that.

There's lots I want to ask this man. Before I go fallin for him if that's what gonna happen. But I don't want him knowing much about me. Miz Walker knows I escaped, but I keep the rest of my story to myself. I start talking about something else when it comes up.

"Set down a spell, Zeke." I pour us both a cup of the coffee I've been keeping warm.

"Tell me Zeke, was Davison your owner's name?"

"Nah. I took the name of the white shoemaker I learned from. Master kept him around enough months for him to make shoes for all master's big family, slaves too, and for me to learn how to do it. Then he run him off, knowin how much cheaper I'd be."

"He ran off a white man?" I stare at him.

Zeke's face hardens. "He were a Jew." Do I imagine a throbbing in the long scar across his chin? "A kind, patient Jew man."

"Did you see him get run off?"

Zeke's eyes narrow. "The master hit that old man. Pretended he'd been cheating him. Then shoved him real hard onto the dirt floor. I was thirteen. I grabbed Mr. Davison's work knife and went at master with it, but master was stronger, took hold of my wrist and made me slash my own face. Then we heard Mr. Davison's soft voice: 'Leave that child alone.' He was pointing a pistol at master.

"'Go back to the big house,' Mr. Davison told master. 'I'll be on my way soon enough. No need to drive me out by force. Or lies.'

"Master dropped the knife and backed out of the shoemaking hut and Mr. Davison brought out his medical box—now that's something I did know he had. He stopped the bleeding, cleaned and bandaged my wound, packed up his tools and his knife, then gave me a look would of froze a mountain lion in its tracks. 'Save up and buy your freedom,' he said. 'It will take years, but it can be done.'"

Zeke stares off into space. "I'd never known a slave could do that."

I sit next to him in silence, wait for him to go on.

"Course I was lucky because people came from outside the plantation and paid me to make shoes. Master took three-quarters and let me keep the rest. I was forty-six when I got enough saved up to buy my freedom. Master wouldn't let me go till I made everybody in his family one last pair of shoes."

MARY ANDERSON PARKS

Chapter Twenty-Four

This is the day I'm gonna ask her. I made my mind up yesterday.

I lie on my back, stretching out my arms and legs on the bed, wanting to forget the nightmare, but reliving it in spite of myself. It's a dream with a warning. The worst part was Mama, her eyes empty, staring straight through me like she didn't recognize me. And yet who but her knows who I am? I leap up, run to the mirror, check to make sure I'm here.

The ache in my leg brings back the escape, the long run together. Are we two different people now? Not the woman and boy we were? We were full of hope, fear too, but a cleaner, clearer fear than what I live with now. I reckon we knew we were in the right. That pure knowing is gone for me.

In the dream, Mama turned into Jancy, staring out from the wagon that took her and the kids away, and a slave up on the auction block was me, a dark-skinned me, terror in his eyes. He opens his mouth to cry out there's been a mistake, but no sound comes. Dragged away in chains, he twists his head back trying to see Janey or Mama.

A fearful need to hurry grabs me. I pour water from the pitcher and scrub up real good, then dress in my best clothes. I haven't felt safe since Jeremiah's run-in with the Dexters. They'll hold that against both of us. Don't make sense but they will. The way they'll see it, the fight was our fault and we got the best of them. They never gonna look at it they were the ones picked the fight with Jeremiah.

When I drop in at the Milford tavern time to time keeping up with gossip, Hank Dexter's usually there shooting off his mouth. That man don't care who he hurts saying crazy things. Tells tales on his own father, like how his pa owes somebody money and isn't gonna pay. Hank thinks that's funny. I need to save Sarah from him. And I need a wife. Bad. I need to be part of a family like the Longs. Then I'll feel safer.

So it's gonna be today I ask her.

I head downstairs, make breakfast for me and Daniel. After we eat, it's time for massaging the salve into his legs. I do a good job of it, then move on to his right arm.

"Feels good, Tom." He gives me the sad patient smile I'm growing used to. "Don't you get tired of doing this? I get better so slow."

"But you are getting better, that's the point! This and the walks we do twice a day, they're helping you heal."

"You're right. I'm just such a burden to you. I never felt that way in my life before. Funny how a man can worry about all the wrong things and then something like this strikes him and he realizes how lucky he was all along. He just never knew it. Kind of funny, don't you think, Tom?"

"Yeah." I smile, happy he can still look at me and grin the way he does. "But let there be no talk of being a burden. Where would I be without you, Daniel?" I choke up, saying that. In a way, it's hard to admit.

"You're doing a fine job of everything, son. Now Jeremiah's brother's working here too and they got the garden all planted—"

"Yeah, but now the garden's in and the soybeans too, Jeremiah says he don't need him no more, says keeping his brother on track's more trouble than it's worth. He's not too steady is how Jeremiah puts it."

"Do you agree?"

"I do. Jeremiah wouldn't say something like that without good reason. And I can see it myself."

"All right then. I tend to trust that boy's judgment, and certainly yours. Got time to read me a story from the Good Book before you go to church?"

"Sure do! Jeremiah's out there doin the morning chores. I heard the milk buckets clanking."

We've both gotten so we can hardly wait for these Bible stories I read to him. And it gives me something to talk to Sarah's father about. He do look at me odd though when I get all excited asking him questions, figuring he'll know the answers what with the Bible reading he's done all his life. Why does God play games with the devil do you think, Mr. Long? That makes me real mad, I told him. Poor Job. It don't seem fair, him being caught in the middle. Usually Mr. Long tells me to pray on it, God has his mysterious ways and will reveal things to me when I'm ready. Once he was silent so long I thought he forgot I was there. Then suddenly he said, "I don't understand it all myself." He had a lost look in his eyes. At that moment I felt almost close to the man.

"Daniel, I'm gonna find that story about Daniel in the lions' den. I told you Preacher Burns talked on it last Sunday? We're gonna love that one, I bet!"

"Tom, you better go, we can read when you get back. I'm tireder than I knew. Think I'll have me a nap. I see you left ham and bread. Hard boiled eggs."

"Applesauce, too."

"You'll be back after dinner will you, and your walk down the lane with Sarah?" He winks, and I feel my face grow hot, knowing what I'm gonna ask her.

Driving the buggy into town, I think about the trust they have in me, Daniel and Sarah's father. It's like they know I'm a good man and wouldn't hurt her for the world. She lets me have a kiss now at the end of the lane when we come to their pond, but I swear she's the one started it, looking at my mouth like she did and moving up closer. I get all stirred up kissing her but I make us stop even when she's clinging onto me. Then we turn around and head back to the house holding hands, and that too shoots tingles back and forth between us.

Mr. Long talks to me lots now about farming, like when to get the ground ready for corn. We worry together will the rains hold off. He says maybe I should have got mine in sooner, but too soon is risky because you might get a late frost. So a farmer never knows for sure.

Lately Mr. and Mrs. Long let me take Sarah in my buggy from church back to their place. We get a little private time that way. Her parents' trust means more to me than I even understand. I have to get her safely married to me quick as I can. Anger rages in me every time I think of where Hank Dexter was when Jeremiah ran across him in colored town.

Being part of Sarah's family will help me be this new person I'm becoming. "This white man," I say aloud, and then glance around, fearful, as if someone could hear. I hold the reins tighter.

That nightmare I keep having, I want it to stop. Sometimes I'm naked in front of a crowd of people. Their faces tighten with anger and I smell my own fear. With both hands, I try to cover my private parts. Always in this dream my skin is black. Their white faces leer at me. A woman bends over, picks up a stone, raises her arm to throw it. Who is she? I see the ground littered with stones.

I shake the reins, try to get back a sense of reality. The horses wonder why and trot faster.

Chapter Twenty-Five

After Sunday dinner is over and the table cleared, Mr. Long and I go in the parlor to have our weekly talk before his children come downstairs to read Bible passages.

"How far are you and Daniel in the book of Job?" he asks.

"More than halfway. We're at where his so-called friends and him argue about what's happened to him. They're full of words, those friends, but not much help." I shake my head.

"And what do you think of Job at this point?"

"I like that he defends himself. He sticks to his guns. He knows he's a good man and he argues back when they try to make him feel bad by saying he must have sinned or all the bad stuff wouldn't have happened to him."

I wonder, do he and Hank Dexter have talks like this? It's hard to picture. I like our talks. He told me a lot about how to get the ground ready for planting our first crop of soybeans. That was one helluva lot of work. Took days with me, Jeremiah and his brother, all three of us doing it together. We burned the prairie grass, then turned over the soil and worked it up proper. Jeremiah and I did the planting by ourselves. We used a little sled Mr. Long lent us. The runners make the marks for the rows. One man digs the holes, the other comes along with the seeds.

"What do you yourself think, Tom?"

I bring my mind right back to Job. "He didn't sin at all! He had some kind of faith that man did. My hat's off to him."

"We'll talk again when you've finished the whole book of Job. People have wondered and talked about that story for hundreds of years. Over a thousand."

I notice he said "that story" and didn't call it the Holy Word.

"There's more to it than I thought there'd be," I say. "It goes on and on. Daniel, I mean Mr. Fullerton and me, we puzzle over the way things are said. We figure back then certain words meant something different." I remember one of them and say it. "Like tabernacle."

My mind goes off with Sarah. I wring my hands and then make myself stop.

Mr. Long watches me as if waiting, as if he expects me to say something else. "Real nice day, sir."

"Yes. A real nice day."

When I don't say more, he adds, "Nice day for a walk, I suppose."

"Yessir." I stand up, relieved he brought up the walk idea himself. "I'll take my leave if I may, and go see if Sarah's done with the cleanup."

He gazes at me thoughtfully. "All right, Tom."

Sarah stands not far away, in the hallway tying on her sunbonnet. She looks at me with curiosity. Does she have any notion what I'm fixin to ask her?

"Let's go!" I take hold of her hand. We set off toward the lane. Halfway to the pond, she trips on a root and I catch her in my arms. Seems to me she don't want me to let her go. But I'm not ready. Not ready to hold her or kiss her or ask her what I plan to ask. Something holds me back. Have I thought this out enough?

I'd love to have five minutes with Mama, to see what she'd say. Have I waited long enough? Will Sarah say yes? It don't seem fair to be kissing her and then ask. She needs to say yes with a clear mind. I let out a loud sigh.

"What is it, Tom?"

Why is she blushing?

"Do you want to ask me something?"

"Yes. I do."

I stop dead in my tracks. And there are tracks in the dirt path, from all the people who walked this lane. Not just us. Lots of Longs, I guess. Not my own people.

Why can't I look in her eyes? Is it because of thinking about how nobody kin to me ever set foot on this land? It's a crazy thought. Of course they didn't! How could they?

"Tom!" She sounds almost impatient. That surprises me. "What are you thinking?" She peers at me from under her bonnet.

Why don't you take that damned thing off, I want to say.

"Don't it make you hot?" I blurt.

"What?" Her eyes widen.

"That bonnet." I scuff my toe in the dirt, the toe of my best shoes. And then I look into her clear brown eyes.

"Will you marry me, Sarah?"

"Oh Tom!" She smiles, but the smile changes into a slight frown of worry. "Papa gave you his blessing?"

"His blessing?" Is this Bible talk? What does she mean?

Her frown deepens. "You asked him, didn't you? Just now when you were talking with him?"

"Asked him what?"

"Oh Tom, you know! Don't make me say it all." She stares hard at me. "You do know, don't you?"

When I don't answer, she goes on. "You know you have to ask his blessing, don't you? For my hand in marriage?"

And then the darnedest thing happens. Tears come in my eyes. I have to turn away. But I think she already saw them. I'm so ashamed I didn't do it right. Ignorant slave! I bite my lower lip hard.

Sarah takes both my hands in hers. "Tom?" She tries to make me look at her, and finally I do. Her eyes have turned sad. I shake my head. I'd meant for this to be a happy time. I'd pictured it all so different.

She squeezes my hands, like I'm her child and she's comforting me.

"It's all right, Tom. You can ask him next Sunday." Thank God her smile comes back.

"Don't worry, I'll say yes!"

I love how she blushes.

I kiss her then, losing myself in the warmth of her face against mine, and move my mouth lower to kiss the hollow in her throat. She lets her head fall back.

This girl is mine, I think, confident again, so much confident that I murmur, "If Hank Dexter comes by Tuesday evening, send him packing, will you?"

The weight of her whole body falls back into my arms. "I will Tom, I will."

Chapter Twenty-Six

The Sunday after I get Mr. Long's blessing, I'm swaying back and forth on the porch swing with Sarah when she lays her hand in mine and asks, "Have you written to your people in Virginia?"

My stomach tightens. What does she mean? Why would I write to ~? The creaks of the porch swing, usually a comforting sound, grate into me.

"You speak of them so seldom. Never, really." She gazes at me, her brown eyes deep with concern. "Will they be able to come up here for the wedding?"

What can I tell her? I don't want to lie to Sarah. What absurdity though, not wanting to lie to her! That durn Shakespeare knew how to make comedy of people pretending to be who they're not. But those stories end up good, the whole thing a joke.

My people. Big Jim. Jessie. Janey, Willie Joe and their children. Marse Tom? I burst out with a bitter laugh.

"Tom! What on earth are you thinking? You should see your face!"

Sometimes with Sarah I let the mask slip. I allow myself that bit of restfulness. Probably a mistake. But she seems to me all gentleness and I fall into a feeling of safety. I wish I could share everything with her. Will I ever be able to?

Nothing is like I thought it would be. I wear my head out trying to think of a way to see Mama. Is she mad at me for what I done? What I'm doing? What I keep doing? I get deeper and deeper into it, don't I? I reckon I'll never be a truly free man, never have peace in my mind. It turns my stomach inside out imagining what these folks would do if they knew I'm colored.

"No, Sarah," I say slowly. "You know farmers can't get away. The cows have to be milked, the animals fed."

"But have you told them about us?"

"I'll write a line or two." That's true because I just this moment decided to write the news to Mama and have Jeremiah deliver it. We need more salve. I always have that excuse. And I need to get word to her how poorly Daniel's doing. Maybe she can come up with something to help. If only she could be with us, be his nurse.

Holding Sarah's hand, I study the contrast between her arm and mine, close together. I love how her skin is so white. Of course I wouldn't be this much darker if I hadn't been out my first twenty-one years in the fields, the killer sun beating down on me. Our children will come out somewhere between the two of us in color, our natural color when we were born. Isn't that how it works?

"Tom! See the bluebird in the lilac bush?" She lifts my hand with hers to point. "Isn't it cunning? Do you know what the bluebird symbolizes?"

I shake my head.

"Happiness! The bluebird of happiness, people say. Maybe it's a line from a poem, do you think?"

"Could be." It settles me down sitting next to her like this.

"Tom!"

"Yes?"

"Promise me something?"

"All right."

"Will you put up a porch swing on our own porch? Then when we're married we can go on doing this. Like we're still courting."

"But without your father inside watching us."She giggles. "Oh Tom, we'll be so happy."I squeeze her close to me, then let go. "Gotta get on home. Sorry. Daniel needs more help than he used to. I don't like to leave him alone long. Doctor says his heart's getting weaker."

Sarah leans forward in the swing to wave when I drive off in the buggy. Sometimes I wish I weren't bringing her to her new home with an old man in it she'll have to help take care of. It would be fun for the two of us to have the place all to ourselves. But that's an unworthy thought. I owe everything to Dan Fullerton, well, the house and farm and that's damn near everything. And she hasn't said one word of complaint. I doubt she ever will, no matter how hard it gets. She a fine woman, Sarah is. I think of Mama and how some women just give and give. Later, when I write the note to Mama, I want to tell her how Sarah is like her in good, important ways. I want to say they'd be friends, but it's a dream even to think they could ever have a chance to get to know each other.

Most of what I want to say I find I can't. Instead, I sit staring into my thoughts when I try to write the note. In the end, I write only that I'm getting married to Sarah Long, fold the paper small, seal it into an envelope with a few bills and give it to Jeremiah to take to Nellie for more salve, and tea to try and fire up Daniel's heart.

CHAPTER TWENTY-SEVEN
Sarah

After Tom runs off like a chased goose, I linger on the porch swing. It's still zigzagging from how he lurched off.

What is he hiding from me? He's keeping something locked in his head. I want to share my thoughts and feelings with him, and have him share back. Not be all closed off from each other like Mother and Daddy. But much of the time it's like Tom is somewhere else, in a place forbidden to me. Why do I feel I have no right to whatever it is he's keeping to himself? Doesn't he know I'd lie down in the road and let a buggy run over me if I thought it would save him?

No need to be so dramatic. There's nothing Tom needs saving from. It's just that I love him, is all. I always figured it'd be some local boy I ended up with, none of them very exciting. Tom's different, not being from around here. None of us know much about him, just how nice he is, and smart.

I want to be the one he tells everything to, the one he shares secrets with. And I do feel sure he's hiding something important. Dear God, don't let it be that he's changing his mind about marrying me! That would be the awfulest thing in the world. Yet if he is, I want him to say so. It would break my heart if he married me just because he thought he should keep his word.

Is there any other girl he likes better? I don't really think so. For one thing, he works all the time. Travels around this county and the next trading livestock. Always gets the better part of the deal, I notice. He's a great judge of horses, and trades them off soon enough I won't have to worry about getting too attached to them. Of course he would never dream of selling Mr. Fullerton's fine black mares. Or his own Midnight.

I like that Tom talks to me about his work. As if I'm his partner. He respects my opinions and says I have a good head for business. I know from the spark in his eye I'm his girl. There's nobody else. So what is he hiding? I'd bet the six gold pieces Daddy gave me for a marriage present that there's something he's holding back. Maybe it's the kind of thing you don't find out till after you're married. But what kind of thing would that be?

I know one he'll find out about me. I tie my hair up in rag strips on Saturday night so it'll be wavier for church. Will he laugh at me looking like a pickaninny? I stretch my arms way up, yawn, then lace my fingers behind my head and tip my head back. It feels so good to loll it around..

"Sarah!" There's Mother. "I need your help with supper."

Mother's been working with me hemming pillowcases and towels. "Can't have too many towels when the babies come," she said. "Little blankets, too." How much there is for me to learn! But Tom will be patient with me, I'm sure he will. And I know a lot already from being the oldest. I wonder if Tom's the oldest in his family. I'll have to ask him. He'll probably change the subject, like he always does. Is he ashamed of them, his family? He did say they're poor. That's nothing to be ashamed of if they're respectable. I should reassure him of that.

I stand up and leave the porch swing zigzagging again. Of course I wouldn't really bet my gold pieces. Daddy says betting is sinful.

MARY ANDERSON PARKS

CHAPTER TWENTY-EIGHT

A flock of blackbirds is going plumb crazy in the oak tree. Out my upstairs window, I watch them fly off in a panic down the road toward Jeremiah's place. I've ridden by his place, never been inside. It's a falling down house maybe once had paint on it but no more. Kids out front playing on bare dirt. Tomorrow they'll likely be slopping around in mud. Or later today. A helluva wedding day, rainclouds low and heavy overhead. We gonna be married in our one-room wooden church, its steeple sticking up into the most threatening sky I've seen all this June. Is it the mood I'm in makes me feel the sky's aiming its threats right at me? Sarah told me folks here come from all around when there's a wedding. After the service in church, the bride's family puts on a feast, ending up with snow white wedding cake. Snow white. That's what she said.

"Never chocolate?" I asked.

"That's my favorite."

"No, Tom!" She laughed, gave me a poke in the ribs. "It's a wedding cake!"

I shut up then, cause the way she said it I could tell she thought I'd been to a wedding before. Jumping over a broom's not what she means by a wedding. Though we knew how to throw ourselves a shindig. Sarah had more to say on the wedding cake.

"The cake should be white all the way through because it symbolizes purity." She blushed and I reckon I knew what she meant. Ignorant though I am, I know what a virgin is and she sure is one.

I wish I could get those words 'white all the way through' out of my head. Sets me to thinking how our children might turn out.

I was over to her house yesterday, wanting to set in the swing a spell and get her around to telling me more about what our wedding gonna be like. All I learned so far is her father will 'give me away' is how she put it. I gather I'll be up there in front standing next to her oldest brother, waiting for Mr. Long to do that whichever way he plans on doing it. I have the ring to put on her finger. It's a worn-thin gold band belonged to Sarah's mother's mother. Don't look likely to last through washing dishes and clothes, sheets and such for another lifetime. Maybe Sarah will keep it in a box or at least take it off and put it on the windowsill when she's doing dishes or laundry. I get to studying on these things to a point that's hardly natural, probably because I don't understand much of the whole marriage thing and I latch onto what I can see, like the ring.

When I went over there yesterday, all three women, Sarah, Carrie, Mrs. Long, were running around the kitchen up to their elbows in flour dust. It smelled delicious. They had bowls of berries and sliced apples settin on the table and were rolling out dough, shaping it into pans, spooning in fillings. Sarah gave me what she named a cinnamon roll to munch on and told me to get on home and out of the way. Lord, how pretty she looked, warm and flushed from pie making. And how good that baked dough tasted, filled with butter, cinnamon, sugar. Now that was something I could latch onto and know what to do with. Maybe that's why

Sarah gave it to me. She's a comforting sort of woman. But I could see there'd be no settin on the porch swing yesterday.

Daniel's clomping around downstairs. What's he up to? I wash myself carefully and dress in my Sunday clothes. It's hard to believe the day is finally here. Later I'll be bringing Sarah home with me to stay. That's the strangest of all. I hurry down the stairs to drink a cup of Mama's tea I been brewing up. Jeremiah told me what she said. "It's for Mr. Fullerton and also Mr. Jones since he's gittin hisself married. It's good for lots of things, this tea." Jeremiah kept a straight face but had mischief in his eyes.

I almost collide with Daniel, wearing his best suit and hat. I stare in surprise. He hasn't gone anywhere for months.

"How do I look?" He grins.

"Mighty fine. You look ready for something special, something don't happen every day."

"That's about it, ain't it! That's how I figured it too!" A furrow comes between his eyebrows. "Will I be too much of a nuisance if I go? You have a lot on your mind, with all those words you'll have to say. Must be worried your voice will shake or some such thing. I remember how I felt on my wedding day."

All those words I have to say? What's he talking about? I take hold of his arm. "Come on in the kitchen, Daniel, I'll kindle up the fire and we'll have our tea."

When we're settled, I blurt out, "Nobody told me about words I have to say."

He looks at me, his eyes sympathetic. "They didn't have no practice or nothin?"

"No. Was we supposed to?"

He considers. Sips his tea. Keeps eyeing me.

"You ever been to a wedding, Tom?"

"No sir. I have not."

"Well don't worry, Tom. You look awful worried to me. You got wedding jitters is what you have. Can't even eat or drink coffee? It's okay, we'll have a feast later. And here you are dressed so fine. Sarah's going to be proud as a bantam hen to be marrying such a fine-looking man. And a good man. Hard-working, kind. If anyone can vouch for that, I can. Yessir. Now let me tell you, here's what's going to happen. It's Preacher Burns has to do most all the talking. There'll be a part where he tells you what to say. See, this is how it goes. He says the words, a few at a time, mind you, not more than you can remember, and then you just repeat those words of his, understand?"

I nod. I'm holding my breath, so grateful I am to learn more about what a wedding is.

"Breathe, Tom. You have to breathe. Else you might pass out up there in front of everybody. I seen that happen once. The groom just fell over. Maybe had too much whiskey the night before. Don't you worry. Just drink your tea and breathe. Steady there, Tom. Guess I shouldn't have brought up about that fellow passing out. He was a weak sort anyhow, now I think on it."

Daniel takes a big swallow of tea, smacks his lips. "The preacher does the same with Sarah."

"Says words for her to repeat?"

"Yes, that's right. Just listen to the preacher and he'll make clear who's to talk when. You'll catch on. Every man's nervous at his wedding, Tom. I've even heard of men not showing up at all."

I choke on my tea at that.

"Women seem to take to this wedding stuff more than men do," he adds.

"Daniel, look at me please. I want you to know I'm tickled as a rabbit loose in the garden that you fixin to go to my wedding. I feel okay about it now, knowing you'll be there."

"I'll be up near to the front as I can get. I'll sit with Jeremiah."

"Jeremiah's coming?"

"You think he'd miss your hitchin up? Why, he's part of our family!"

Daniel's right. We're a family, I suppose. Daniel has no other family left. And Mama's a memory in my mind. How have I let this happen, the only solid links between her and me the healing salve and tea? It's all wrong! The family I pictured was colored, with Mama safe in a house of her own, a proud grandma.

"Ain't he?" Daniel's questioning voice, his pale face close across the table, startle me. It takes a moment to collect myself.

"It's just that he don't come to church hardly ever."

"No, maybe he don't. But believe me, he'll be there today." Daniel presses his right hand to his chest. "You gave me a turn there, Tom. Your face changed. Do you know that? You looked for a minute like someone I didn't know."

That's right, I think, you don't know me. I'm not at all sure I know myself. But I need to ease his worry, it's not good for him. "Just wedding jitters, Daniel, like you said. So much change in our lives all in one day."

I try to picture Sarah coming back with us later, going up to the bedroom with me. As if reading my mind, he winks.

"I'll make myself scarce, Tom. I'll likely be worn to a frazzle and go out like a lamp the minute my head hits the pillow."

My face feels hot. Am I blushing?

Daniel and I both turn toward the sounds coming from outside. Squeaky wheels. Could it be a visitor? I go to the kitchen door and fling it open. Daniel stumbles along behind me.

The most dilapidated buggy I ever laid eyes on comes to a noisy stop, piece by piece. Surely the horse pulling it is Paint, but who is the gentleman in black sitting very upright, holding the reins? Then I notice his sheepish half smile, the familiar long-lashed blue eyes.

"My God, it's Jeremiah!"

He jumps down. "I figured Mr. Fullerton could ride in with me, if he's not ashamed to be seen in this contraption." Paint tosses her head, looks in our direction and smiles. Yes, it most surely is a smile. "Mother got Pa to let me take it for the day. The old thing sits out in the barn all the time anyway. Nobody in our family hardly ever goes anyplace. I cleaned it up best I could but I guess you'd never know it."

After this surprisingly long apology, Jeremiah twirls the black hat he's holding and stares at the ground.

I swear, sometimes it's all I can do to keep from hugging him. Now that he's standing, I see his sleeves and pants are a few inches too short. He's wearing his socks high and since everything on him is black, that sort of works. His face shines even more than the old suit. Looks like he scrubbed his whole head several times over.

Daniel walks around the buggy, admiring it. "Haven't seen one of these in some time. It's a real antique you've got here, Jeremiah. I'll certainly be proud to ride in it with you."

Jeremiah's head jerks up, his eyes show relief.

Daniel glances at me. "You look a little shaky, boy." He has no way to know how him calling me that pierces right into me. I can tell he means it the same way as when he calls me son. It's affection he's feeling. But it rankles. I clench my fists before I know I'm doing it.

"Do you want a medicinal whiskey before we set off?"

I do. I want it so bad I have to force out the words, "No thanks, Daniel. Mr. Long would smell it on me. That'd trouble him. I know how he feels about a drinking man."

Daniel laughs. "He might call the whole thing off, eh? Refuse to give her away to you? Well, suit yourself. I'll go in and have me one. How about you, youngster?"

Jeremiah scuffs his shoe in the dirt, ducks his head. "Maybe not, Mr. Fullerton. Not today."

"I see," Daniel says. "Maybe some other day, right? I'll have to remember to offer you a drink some other day."

He smiles and limps away into the house. Where does he keep his bottle stashed? Probably best I don't know.

As Jeremiah walks to the barn, I hear him mumble, "It's no joke around my house when Pa starts drinking." He brings my buggy around and stations it in front of his own. I do not feel ready to go. I want to start walking backwards instead of toward it.

I guess I'd look funny walking backwards away from my own wedding. That makes me want to chuckle, but the chuckle sticks in my throat.

MARY ANDERSON PARKS

Chapter Twenty-Nine

I never felt as lonely in my life as I do driving into town. I envy Daniel and Jeremiah having each other for company. I want to be with them, or have one of them here with me. The groom's not supposed to be all alone, is he? On the plantation, we were never alone.

I want to turn around and go back. Back to the house. Or all the way back to Mama. My breath starts coming real fast. For a minute I can't see the road. What am I doing? It feels like I'm losing my mind. I shake my head, wanting to feel normal, like I belong in this world I chose. But it's too hard. I hate it. I won't do anything right. It'll be like my nightmares.

Lightning snakes across the field I'm passing. Automatically I count. I only get to two before the loud boom of thunder. One of Daniel's horses, wild-eyed, tries to turn her head back toward me. I call out, "Don't worry Dolly, Louisa, it'll be okay. Just keep goin." I gee them up. Can't get soaked. Have to beat the rain. A sopping wet bridegroom? I look back but they aren't in sight. What the devil are they doin? Daniel mustn't get wet or chilled. They better hurry up.

"Dammit, boy," I say aloud. "It ain't even raining yet. Calm down!" And a laugh comes. Out of nowhere, me laughing at myself. "You're free, boy! Don't you know that yet?" Yes, I can call myself boy. No harm in that. And Mama knows it's my wedding day. She's right here with me. In the lightning and the thunder, trying her best to tell me she's here and always will be.

The first drops fall as I drive up to where they are, Sarah's father and brothers lined up near the church door. When they see me coming, her brothers follow their father inside. I see relief on their faces. Well, they're right to worry. I wanted to go the other way.

Where's Sarah? And her mother and sisters?

I go in and her oldest brother takes me by the arm and guides me to the front of the church. Most seats are filled. Golly, am I that late? Or was it the threat of rain drove them in? There's Sarah's mother in the front pew, wearing a bright pink dress I've never seen. She must have made it special. And Carrie? What's she doing standing up in front? She's got on a real pretty dress too, a lighter shade of pink than her mother's. Mrs. Long catches my eye, gives me an encouraging smile. Does she sense how hard this is for me?

Alma Stiles is at the piano, like always, and now Betty Ruth Henderson gets up, stands next to the piano and begins "How Great Thou Art" in her strong soprano. She's a fine singer. It thrills me to my toes listening to her. After her song, I see Jeremiah and Daniel slip in, but they're too late to find seats up in front. There aren't any left. And I'll be damned if the Dexter boys don't come in and plop down in the very last row. Seeing them sends a chill up my spine.

Alma Stiles bangs out a stirring march tune with a strong beat, loud and slow, that makes everybody sit up and take notice. In fact now they're standing up, one after the other, turning to look at the back of the church. Lord if it's not Sarah, hanging on her father's arm. They start walking slow toward us, side by side, one small step at a time down the aisle. She is a vision if I ever seen one, an angel in a beautiful white dress with a white veil over her face. Carrying flowers. White ones. They finally get up to where we are, me and all three of her brothers. She hands her flowers to Carrie, then looks straight at me, smiling the sweetest smile I ever seen, a smile that makes the whole world fall into place. I'm not sure what all happens after that, the air thick and humid, charged with excitement, thunder close and loud, lightning flashing at the windows, but I'm not scared anymore. I hear Mama's voice, "Jes say the words after preacher tells them to you, Tom. You always been good with words. Say them nice and clear."

Portly little Preacher Burns waits while claps of thunder shake the room. Then, after I do my repeating and Sarah does hers, Preacher Burns still has more words to say, something about if any man knows a reason why we should not be joined together in holy matrimony, speak now or forever hold your peace. He pauses, like he's waiting. A commotion erupts in the back of the church. Horrified, I imagine marse Tom striding forward, claiming me as his slave. But no, it is Hank Dexter noisily stomping out, crashing the door shut behind him.

The preacher's mouth drops open. Then he recovers, goes on smoothly with his talking and ends up saying to me, "You may kiss the bride."

What? In front of her father? And all these people? I am struck dumb. But Sarah lifts her veil, steps up to me and kisses me on the mouth. I'm grateful it's a quick one. Then she takes my hand and starts out down the aisle and I realize I'm to go with her. It's over, thank the Lord. Sarah Long is my wife.

We're delayed some at the door with ladies crowding round, wishing us well.

Finally we step outside into the crisp freshness that follows a storm. Blue sky appears between dissolving clouds. Sarah squeezes my arm, does a little skip, gathering up the white skirt of her dress in her white-gloved hand.

"Let's run to the buggy, Tom! We should get home before guests arrive. See! My family's already in their wagon."

She's right. Mr. and Mrs. Long are settling into their places as the boys clamber into the back with their sisters, where blankets are spread out to protect their good clothes. They won't need the rain cover they've got back there.

I feel proud helping Sarah up to her own rightful place.

"This is Daniel Fullerton's buggy, isn't it," she comments as we start off behind her family.

I slow the horses to wave to Jeremiah. He is boosting Daniel up into his contraption.

"Is that your hired hand? All dressed up like that?"

Sarah's words startle me. I better set her straight right away. "I don't think of him as a hired hand, Sarah. Jeremiah's been with Daniel and me almost from the beginning. He's part of it all. He may be a fifteen-year-old kid but he knows more about farming than Daniel or me. He's at our place more than with his own family." Images fly through my mind: Jeremiah intent on his drawings, using the special pencils Mama gave him; staying all night to help me birth our first calf; keeping a setting hen's secret until she strutted into the barnyard trailed by seven yellow bits of fluff; fighting off all three Dexter boys that time in Milford, then glaring at Hank Dexter today when he crashed the church door behind him and walked out on our wedding. Thunder was deafening at that point and I don't think many people noticed Hank. I bet they'll all three show up at Long's. Those boys won't miss a feed.

Sarah keeps silent, thinking her own thoughts. Then, "I recognize these beautiful black mares of Mr. Fullerton. They're in splendid condition."

"Yes, when he was doing so poorly, I took up the full care of them. Trying to keep up to his high standards. All winter, he couldn't make it out of the house and he'd ask after them a couple times a day, how they were wintering, if they were off their feed, if their coats were glossy. I sure was glad I could give him good reports."

"What are their names?"

"Dolly and Louisa."

"Dolly and Louisa! I wonder where he came up with names like that!"

"Well, you can't imagine how special those horses are to him. He told me he named them after the wives of presidents James Madison and John Quincy Adams."

I feel proud to know these facts to tell her. But Sarah giggles.

"What's funny?"

"I almost got named after a president's wife too! My parents considered naming me Martha. But Daddy really liked the name Sarah, and he always has better arguments and wins out."

"I like the name Sarah too, because it's yours." I glance over and smile. Now I'm hoping she'll talk about something else. That's all I know about presidents or any other history stuff. I've picked up a lot about real estate, livestock, even the Bible and Shakespeare, but when it comes to most else I don't know more than a hog.

"I can't wait to start bringing my things over and settling in." I look at her in surprise. Her eyes are shining. She's taken the veil off and has it on her lap.

"Uh, what things are those? Oh! Your clothes?"

"Well of course there's all that. But also my hope chest and what's in it, and then several boxes of linens and towels Mother's giving me to start us off. Mother saved everything, our baby blankets and baby clothes." She blushes at her mention of babies, hurries on. "And Cinnamon. You can ride me over home tomorrow, then I can ride Cinnamon back to our place."

It thrills me she's already saying "our place" so naturally.

"And the things from Carrie's and my room that belong to me. Pictures, souvenirs, books. My little rocker."

Gosh. It sounds like maybe two full wagons of stuff. Well, Jeremiah can help me.

After a moment I notice Sarah is silent again. I slow Dolly and Louisa's pace, realizing I'm in no hurry at all to rejoin those folks we'll have to spend the best part of the day with. Some of them pass us on the road and that's fine with me. Sarah turns sideways on the seat toward me. Her face is smooth and relaxed, her brown eyes soft.

"Tom, I'm not scared. Because you're my friend. You wouldn't hurt me, no matter what Mother says about the wedding night."

So! Her thoughts too have been on the night ahead. All this chatter was a way not to talk about what's really on our minds.

I reach over and pick up her hand. We twine our fingers together, caressing in that way that sends shivers of excitement between us.

"I tried to go slow but we're here already." The huskiness of my voice and a sudden thickness in my throat surprise me.

Sarah heaves a sigh. "Yes dammit."

For her to curse about our time alone being cut short excites me a whole new way. "I've got some kind of woman on my hands," I say, grinning as I put my arm around her, the reins in my left hand.

Is that relief in her eyes? Was she afraid she'd gone too far, been unladylike? What all fears and worries has that mother of hers filled her head with? I don't think she succeeded. I think I'm blessed with a woman who follows her own good sense. How I hope I'm right. I feel danger ahead though, that Sarah will have to face. Now I'm the one with fears looming up like the thunderclouds forming above us.

"We set up the tables inside." Sarah gazes upward, breathing in air heavy now with the sultriness of more rain coming. "Minnie Holstein, she's a cousin of Mother's, came over to help and brought a table and extra chairs in their wagon. And our neighbors Pearl and Eric Schmid brought chairs, and food too of course. It'll be crowded, but we didn't want to take a chance on setting up outside and a downpour ruining everything."

I help her down from the buggy, wanting to kiss her but not doing it. In the house, everything is a swirl of activity. Minnie Holstein turns out to be a severe-looking woman with penetrating dark eyes, who gives me a quick strong handshake and tells Sarah she's not to do a lick of work on her wedding day. Minnie, Carrie and Mrs. Long scurry around with platters of food, the little sister helping. As guests arrive bringing more food, there is hardly room for it all. The men fill their plates and gather in groups. I notice a small table set apart for the white three-layer wedding cake Sarah has told me about.

"I'm going to run upstairs and change out of my dress," Sarah whispers in my ear.

"But this one's so pretty!"

"Thank you, Tom, but I need to put it safely away. That's what brides do." She smiles and hurries off, leaving me standing by myself. I see Daniel sitting among a group of men, clearly enjoying the talk and company. Jeremiah hands him a plate of food he's brought for him, then stands awkwardly by a wall. I walk over to join him.

"Jeremiah, you know you love fried chicken. Let's get ourselves some before it's all gobbled up."

"That's why turkeys gobble," he mumbles. "They know what their fate is so they get themselves used to it."

I laugh, and see his body relax. Maybe he'd been about to sneak out, go wait outside. I bet he wishes he was fishing in the pond. That's always where he'd rather be; he's told me many a time fishing is best in the rain. I wouldn't mind being there myself. It's a real humid day for us all to be stuffed in suits like we be. I can't wait for this to be over.

Sarah comes back, still in her pretty wedding dress. "Mother says I can't change until after you and I cut the cake." She makes a face I've come to know, widening her eyes and pursing her mouth, lifting her hands up in the air.

"Hi, Jeremiah. Be sure to have pie. That's what Mother and my sister Carrie and I made yesterday."

"Yes ma'am."

I'm relieved she's falling right into a friendly manner with Jeremiah. I guess it would break my heart if they didn't get along. I'm surprised to find myself thinking that. Do I love them both then? But something troubles me.

"Sarah, why would I be cutting the cake? That's not a man's job."

"Oh Tom, you know it's the custom! We stand side by side and you put your hand over mine as I cut the first piece."

"Oh, right."

Jeremiah gives me a sympathetic look as Sarah twirls around to talk to two of her girl friends.

"I sure wouldn't have known I was supposed to do a fool thing like that." His expression is so comical I burst out laughing, and Sarah and her friends glance at me, curious. The next minute I see the Dexter brothers arrive. They crowd around the food table loading up their plates and then join a few other young men. I feel Jeremiah tense up beside me. He too is watching as Hank pulls a flask from inside his jacket and drinks deep before offering the flask to the others. The only one who takes him up on it is his older brother. Hank takes another long pull before he puts the flask away. I can't help wondering if Mr. Long notices. He's with his neighbor Mr. Schmid, no doubt talking farm talk. Like many farmers, their conversation is full of long pauses, which means they have plenty of time to see what's going on around them. I wonder how early Hank started drinking. I'm sure it was before he got to the church. His brother is finishing Hank's barely touched plate of food.

Oh no, it's time to cut the cake. Mrs. Long is making an announcement. Sarah grasps my hand, walks me over to the cake table. How will she cut it? It's so high. Up close, I see the bottom layer is wider than the one above and the top one even smaller. So all she has to do is cut a piece out of the lowest layer. Nope, she chooses the top. I do my part, liking the feel of her smooth hand under mine. She slides the slice of cake onto a small plate and surprises me by lifting a forkful up to my mouth. Am I supposed to eat it? Only babies get fed this way!

"Tom, open your mouth." Sarah is laughing, so I guess everything's all right. It must be part of what she calls the custom. I take the bite, beginning to enjoy myself. She sets the plate down.

With no warning, Hank Dexter lurches up from his chair and staggers over to us. "Do I get to kiss the bride now? Isn't that the custom?" He seizes Sarah by the waist, pulls her close against his chest and kisses her smack on the mouth, breathing his stinking drunken breath into her. What happens next is blurred. I move to protect her. Maybe I yank him off her. A fury takes me over. I want to kill him. He's fouling the beautiful whiteness of the wedding. Sarah is innocent, pure, and he's spoiling her wedding day. It's my fault. If it weren't me she's marrying, these insults wouldn't happen. He wants to ruin the life I'm trying to build, and he could, that's what eats me up. He senses something's hidden, something's wrong, something that could bring me down, and goddammit he's right. He don't know yet what it is, just smells it, like a dog sniffing out a dead rat.

I beat on him like marse Tom beat me. If only I had a whip. But Jeremiah is stronger than me and my fury. From behind, he pins my arms to my back, says words I can't understand. Finally they get through. "You got to calm yourself, Tom. Let him slink away like the drunk skunk he is. His brothers are taking him out. Show you're the gentleman here," he adds in a low tone.

Sarah, her father standing by her, her face flushed, whispers to me, "He's right, Tom. Don't let it bother you. Hank Dexter's really drunk. He's always been a sore loser."

She thinks that's all this is about, a jealous former suitor? Well, I wouldn't want her to suspect anything more, would I? Her mother and Carrie join us and begin cutting and serving the cake. People break the silence, covering us with chatter about the wonderful cake.

Mr. Long frowns at me. "You have a temper, son. Like I tell my own boys, you've got to harness that energy, put it to good purpose." He speaks these words in a low voice that others won't overhear. Then in a normal voice, "Come sit down with Eric Schmid. He needs to talk to you about trading a horse. I'll take the chance to speak with Dan Fullerton. He's looking a bit peaked. This must be way more activity than he's used to."

"Yessir, you're right. Thank you. Jeremiah will take him home right quick." My whole body is trembling.

"I'll get him a piece of cake first," Jeremiah puts in, still standing near me. "He wouldn't want to miss out on the cake."

I straighten my suit jacket and cross the room with Mr. Long, grateful he's by my side. The Dexter brothers are gone and I'm grateful for that too. If only Hank would stay out of my life. Is that too much to hope for?

CHAPTER THIRTY

Riding home in the buggy, Sarah beside me, we don't talk at first. Now she's wearing a pretty pink dress with white pokey dots and she acts like she wants to rest. She closes her eyes. What is she gonna say about me losing my temper like I did? Does she think poorly of me? Did I scare her? Have I spoiled everything?

"Are you glad it's over?" she opens her eyes to ask. I'm surprised at the question. I give her a long look.

"I am. I have to admit it."

"It's all right, I know it was a strain. I'm glad it's over too. I'm used to a quiet life. Folks in my family don't really talk much, you've surely noticed."

She lays her hand on my forearm for a moment. "What I'm most glad about is we're finally alone."

I sigh with relief at all she's saying. And not saying. "Except for Daniel." I tell her. "He'll be asleep though, I'm pretty sure, or else he'll pretend to be. Our room's upstairs and he's down next to the kitchen in the back. We'll be way to the front of the house."

She'll be blushing now. Yes. She's pink up into her hair roots. I reach my arm over, lay my hand on her knee.

"Tom, you better keep both hands on the reins. Dolly and Louisa might take a notion to gallop." Mischief shines bright in her eyes.

I really do love this woman. The feeling washes over me like a patch of sunshine, like that moment I rolled out from under the willow tree to feel the sun, the freedom. And then that man came along with his rifle. That's the day I started down this path of being a white man, though I didn't know it then. Yes, I rolled away from Mama and kept on rolling, didn't I?

"Tom! You're doing it again."

"Doing what?" Her annoyance shakes me out of my thoughts.

"You do that to me, Tom. You suddenly go off somewhere. You seem so far away, like you're in another world that I'm not part of."

It's not you I'm doing it to, it's got nothing to do with you, I think. And it's not something I do on purpose or even know I'm doing.

"Say something, Tom. Come back!"

"I'm right here, Sarah. Doing my best."

Her face shows a mix of feelings. At last her features soften. "I'm sorry," she says quietly. "We all have a right to the privacy of our thoughts. It's just hard to be close one minute and the next I don't know where you've gone. Maybe I'll get used to it."

"I hope I won't be hard to get used to. I want your life to be wonderful, Sarah. You know that, don't you?"

She smiles into my eyes with the warmth I love in her. "Yes. I actually do know that, Tom. I knew it when you jumped on Hank Dexter like you were about to kill him.

May seem a funny example to pick, but . . ." She trails off into a rueful chuckle and I grab her hand and squeeze it tight. Thank God she's mentioned it, brought it out in the open in a way that makes how I acted seem okay. That's my girl.

We're home now. I go around the buggy and lift her down.

We tiptoe into the house, hearing not a sound, then go up the creaky stairs, bumping into each other in the dark, which sets us giggling.

Up in the bedroom, sudden rain slams the roof like thousands of bucketsful poured all at once. There was still a glimmer of light in the sky when we were outside but now darkness closes in.

"Do you need a light?" I ask.

"No. I washed up at home."

I move toward her, drawn by the huskiness in her voice. When I take her in my arms, her clean, flowery scent spreads around me with a new layer underneath, a musky odor that arouses all my senses. Kissing her, I reach around and begin to unbutton the back of her dress. She doesn't stop me, her dress slides to the floor. I lift her onto the bed, pull off her shoes and stockings. It thrills me when she arcs up to meet me as I pull down her bloomers. With quick movements, I strip off my shirt and trousers, shoes and sox. It's so humid, it feels wonderful to get rid of clothes, free our feet and bodies. I reach my hand down inside her bodice. Her heart beats wildly. I feel it under my palm.

"Oh Tom," she murmurs, her head tilting back. She's the first woman I've had. I'm very tense. She reaches up, strokes my face, then my shoulders and arms. It's the best feeling in the world. I enter her softly, where she is wet and ready.

But something snaps in me and I am back in the slave cabin, rain pounding the roof, marse Tom plunging himself into Mama, Mama letting him. I am a small boy in the dark, knowing Mama steels herself to take him into her, knowing she hates it, hates the man.

My body goes rigid. "I'm sorry, Sarah, I won't hurt you! I'm sorry."

I am inside her, still hard, afraid to move.

"Tom, please, it's all right. You're not hurting me."

"I'll stop."

"No, no, don't stop. It's all right."

My body starts shaking. "Sarah, are you sure? I'm not hurting you?"

"No, you're not hurting me."

"Hold me, Sarah. Hold onto me tight. Please. Tell me again I'm not hurting you. Can you tell me you want me to do it? Is that asking too much, dear Sarah? Can you hold me tight while you say that?"

Magically, she says the words I need, holding me tight.

"You're not hurting me. I want you to do it." She says it again. "I want you to do it, Tom. I want you to. You're the best man on earth, Tom."

Mama would never have said that to marse Tom. Not in millions of years. I begin to understand this is different, what Sarah and I are doing. This is what love is. I ease into lovemaking with joy, protected by darkness and Sarah's arms.

CHAPTER THIRTY-ONE

I open my eyes to sun streaming through the windows, casting a glow over the "Pinkie" picture Ned Riley left us, the walnut washstand, the flowered porcelain pitcher. How remarkable they can look familiar when there is the newness of my bride sleeping beside me. I've never seen her asleep. She looks more innocent than ever, sleeping so sweetly. I think about what we did in the night, my strong feelings for her, and try not to remember my fears and the awful memories that got in the way. What a relief and comfort it is to see her face smooth, unlined, untroubled. She flounces over suddenly, grabs my pillow, buries her face in it. Sure looks like she plans to go on sleeping.

I pull on the gray workpants and green and white checked shirt I bought last week, and head downstairs. Daniel will be up. I must have slept late since sunlight was coming in. Surely a man's entitled to after his wedding night. I start whistling "When the Saints Go Marching In."

Daniel opens the door from his bedroom into the kitchen, peers in.

"Lord, the groom's whistling. A good sign for sure."

Self-conscious, I say, "I'm just gonna make some breakfast for you and me and Sarah." I dash down the narrow stairs to the cold cellar to get the salted slab of bacon.

"Golly," I mutter. "I forgot to start the fire."

When I get back with the slab, Daniel is fussing with kindling.

"Here, I'll do that. You sit at the table and rest yourself."

He grins. "You can go on whistling. Don't bother me none. What is that tune anyhow?"

His eyes have the merriest twinkle I've seen in them.

"When the saints go marching in," I mumble, wondering why in hell I'm so embarrassed. Will I feel calmer when Sarah comes down? Or will it be worse? I notice Daniel is all spruced up. He's got a clean, pressed, light blue shirt on.

"I'll just slice off some bacon and fry it up. Don't know how many eggs she eats. Or how she likes them. I do know she's a good, strong farm girl. We got bread and fresh butter. Oh! I forgot to make coffee, what's wrong with me?" Here I am muttering to myself like a fool. Daniel looks amused. Out the corner of my eye, I see him hiding a smile.

Sarah comes in at the moment I get the coffee brewed and am pouring out a cup for Daniel. She looks all proper now, in a red and white print dress with her lace-up black shoes. She pauses in the doorway, and I feel suddenly shy. Might she be feeling the same way? I've never seen Sarah shy. Not really. But it must be hard to walk into a room different from the one where she's eaten breakfast all her life, and have to face me and Daniel. Especially after the night we just had. It was wild. God, am I the one blushing now? I get busy setting out plates.

"Good morning," she says. "How are you this morning?"

"Just fine, my dear. That was quite a spread your folks put on."

"Oh, thank you! A lot of people helped."I pull out a chair for her.

"Sit here, Sarah. I'm frying up bacon. How do you like your eggs?"

"Three over easy, please."

I relax, push the sizzling bacon to one side, crack open the eggs one by one into the cast iron skillet. We have time, Sarah and me, we have time.

CHAPTER THIRTY-TWO
Nellie

So Tom's getting himself married. To a white girl. From a good farm family. I checked with Miz Walker about all that, just led her around to talking about it.

That dear boy Jeremiah brought me a little note from Tom when he came riding up on his horse Paint to buy more salve and any potion I might have to fix up that poor man whose heart is slowing down on top of all else gone wrong. I cooked up something gonna help him real good. While it was cooking gave me a chance to get that quiet Jeremiah to talk.

I'm sitting in my room right this minute looking again at Tom's note, how he write so nice and pretty. I want to eat it up so it'll be part of me. Maybe I just ought to do that and not give anybody a chance to come across it and start figuring things out. I can tell Tom sat a long time staring at nothing trying to write that news to me and just coming up with one sentence: 'Mama, I gonna marry Sarah Long, a fine woman like you.' I cry over that. My boy's saying a lot in them few words.

I made sure to read it before I let Jeremiah ride off. I came back here to my bedroom to do that, told him to wait. I needed to know if Tom was asking for something else or what moved him to lay words on paper where they be a danger to us.

It means he's going on a new path, one he don't know where it goes because he's making it by himself.

How will the children turn out? No, I'm not gonna worry along those lines. That's the road to going plumb crazy.

I sat then and I sit now doing my own staring out into emptiness. Will I see him again? Could I bear it even?

When I went back, I told Jeremiah I hoped he'd come again real soon. I gave him some good little corn cakes I made for him to eat on his way home. "You come anytime. Y'all be welcome as the sunshine and the rain. Now don't you forget that."

He gonna be my tie to my son. I gonna get that boy to tell me things when they happen, like about the children that be borned and all.

I feel my face squeezing back tears trying to come out. They come out anyhow.

Chapter Thirty-Three

1841

Sweat runs down my back as I put away the plow I spent hours fixing. I grab a rag and wipe my face and neck.

Soon it'll be suppertime. Sarah will ring the dinner bell and the children and me will go in the house after washing up at the outside pump. They've been out here playing with the new batch of kittens. We said to wait till the kittens got bigger before they started fooling around with them. Now the kittens are big and the children can't get enough of them. Our little Sophia, who talks so clear at two, she says, "Three of the kittens are black and white and two are white and black." That tickled Sarah. I love it when something makes her smile and her face goes soft.

Leaving the barn, I see a cloud of dust headed our way. Men on horseback. Can't see yet who they are. A whole bunch of them, riding hard. I make them out as they get closer and rein in their horses. It's the saloon crowd. All three Dexters plus faces I do and don't recognize. Fifteen or twenty men, I'd say. My heart beats so loud I hear it in my ears. Hank brings his horse ahead of the others.

"Tom! Tom Jones! Join in with us! We're headed for Cincinnati. Niggers there rioting. We gonna beat em up."

I motion Mariah and her twin sisters to go in the house.

Hank's eyes are bloodshot, his slurred speech that of a man well on his way to being drunk.

"Don't you wanna get yourself a nigger?" He leers at me.

The children have gone inside, but I see Sarah watching through the screen door. She'll hear every word.

"Go on without me," I call out to the men. "I've got family here to take care of."

"So do we!" One of the men I don't recognize answers me, wild-eyed, shifting in his saddle. His horse paws the ground, picking up its rider's restlessness. "Men from Cincinnati rode over to give us the alert."

I keep staring at them, not knowing what to say.

"Aw come on, Hank." It's the wild-eyed one talking. "There's enough of us to help those Cincinnati fellas. Let's go!" He swivels his horse around, leads the pack off, the beat of horses' hooves pounding dry ground.

Hank stares hard at me. "Don't want to go, do you? What are you? Chicken?"

He backs his horse up slowly, eyeing me. "I'll mess up a nigger real bad just for you, how's that? And set houses on fire in your name, Tom Jones!" He jerks his mount around, races off after the others.

My hands are shaking. Did I think they were coming for me?

Sarah lets the screen door bang behind her as she steps outside. "Thank goodness you're not going with them, Tom. They look like the riffraff of four counties. The Dexter brothers are always ready for excitement, and don't care how they get it. But I never knew they could be this bad. Come in to supper. I made potato hash, scrambled eggs and string beans. I took Daniel his in his room. He didn't feel up to coming to the table."

She seems fairly calm. Has she seen this kind of thing before?

At the supper table, I find I can't swallow, so I just watch the children, taking comfort in them. Mariah at three is so pretty it's all anyone notices about her, that and how naturally sweet she is. Two-year-old Sophia talks up a streak as usual, babbling about the horses. Elizabeth, her twin, listens with eyes wide. Baby Henry slumps in the high chair that Sarah's parents passed on to us. He can't stay sitting up straight for long. The twins look very different from each other; Elizabeth is taller, with stronger, coarser features. Looks like Mama is who she looks like but I'm the only one knows that. All the children are what Sarah calls "little curly heads" and have brown or black hair and green or brown eyes. They all have a golden tint, not Sarah's pinkish tones, and tan quickly. I'm relieved no one has commented on Henry's skin being darker than the others even though he's a baby, hardly ever out in the sun yet. I guess all our children gonna turn out pretty much like these first four, and that's a relief.

Always sensitive to my moods, Mariah keeps her beautiful dark eyes on me, herself not taking a bite of food. Finally Sarah says, too sharply, "Don't worry, Mariah. Daddy's not hungry tonight. You go ahead and eat." Mariah's expression grows even more worried. "The men are gone. They won't be back."

"I'm glad you're not with them, Daddy." She must have been watching at the screen door, listening. She's wise for her years. Like Grandma Long says, they're all smart as a whip, every one of them. I'm so proud of them I could burst.

"I'll take you upstairs and read you a story," Sarah tells the girls. She sighs. "We'll have these leavings for breakfast."

I give baby Henry another spoonful of hash and then carry him up. He holds tight to my neck, lays his little head against my shoulder. I know from the smell of him he needs his pants changed. So I do that when we get upstairs where we keep washcloths and a couple pails of water.

Later, in bed, Sarah clings to me, pressing her body up against me. I know she wants to make love, though she'd never say it, but I can't. My body won't respond, with my imagination conjuring up pictures of those colored folks in Cincinnati down by the river where they live. I been there a couple times on business and seen those shacks. They'll burn like kindling. Folks will run out in their nightshirts to save themselves from burning up. They don't have much to start with and what they have will burn in minutes. Then they'll get drug around and beat up, all because they came north looking for work. That white trash up there in Cincinnati, I've seen them too. They think the coloreds take away their jobs. But most of them couldn't hold onto a job if they had one. They're shiftless no-good bums from what I could see. Drinking ale in the morning with their white bellies hanging out.

Sarah finally rolls away from me, falls asleep, but the pictures go on running through my mind, won't let me alone. I see fear fill the wide-open eyes of the colored folk. I hear their screams, smell the wood and clothes burning, see the children hanging onto their mamas, see daddies with little ones in their arms. Would those white men rip a child right out of its daddy's arms?

Sliding out of bed, I go to the window, peer into the darkness. Are we really safe here, Sarah and me, Daniel, who's so weak, Mariah, Sophia, Elizabeth and the baby? It's hard to believe we are. First light streaks the sky when I crawl back under the covers and hide in sleep.

A few days later, in town, I run into Hank on the street. Startled by the wound on his face, I stop dead still. A long deep gash cuts diagonally up his right cheek.

"What happened?" I blurt.

His expression turns surlier. "What happened? You wanna know what happened? A nigger gal cut me with a rusty knife is what happened."

"Has Doc Kilroy seen it?"

"Yes, Doc Kilroy has seen it. As if you care! You couldn't be bothered to go. We could've used you. Maybe there was more of us than them but I didn't expect no woman to pull a knife on me."

I stare, wondering what he did to her.

"Talk about getting between a hen and her chicks," he mutters.

"Was there a baby there?"

"Not after I threw the damn thing in the river. One of them could of gone in and pulled it out. Current wasn't all that strong. It was the woman I wanted. I didn't give a damn about her kid."

A trembling starts deep inside me. I feel pure hatred.

"You son of a bitch." I grab hold of him. "All you'll get is a scar and you killed somebody's child!"

He's afraid of me. I see it in his eyes.

"Calm down, fella. What do niggers know about family? They're animals. They copulate like animals."

I shake him when he says that, holding onto him by his shirt lapels, I shake him till his teeth rattle in his head. Next thing I'll do is knock his teeth right out.

"Break it up, boys!" Five or six men crowd around; it takes three to pull me off him. Straight away, Hank appeals for their support.

"What's wrong with this nigger lover? Standing up for them. You one of us or not?"

No, I want to scream. Of course I'm not one of you. Are you blind? Can't you see who I am? Am I invisible?

Instead of screaming, I come to my senses. Do I want to tear apart this life and family I've created? I hate it that rage can take me over like it did marse Tom the time he beat me so bad and couldn't stop. I vow never to let it happen again.

It galls me, but I reach out my hand and after a moment Hank Dexter grabs and shakes it. That's what men here do after a fight.

Why do I feel I've just made a bargain with the devil?

CHAPTER THIRTY-FOUR
Sarah

I wonder if it's wrong to have such thoughts about my own husband. It's not something I can talk to Mother about. Somehow I doubt she's ever had such feelings. I've tried to pray on it, but that's when my feelings seem most wrong. And is there really a God listening? How does He feel about women? Does He understand us? How could He? I know He's not an ordinary man but He's a he.

I get so muddled up trying to think these things through.

If only I had a woman friend I could talk to. The friends I have are from my schooldays. For years now we've seen each other in passing, at church, in town. When we women do get a chance to talk, and how rare that is, we're putting food on the table, clearing it off, tending to babies—we talk about what's going on right then and there. Helga and I get together for canning, and sometimes Bertha joins us, though she tends to spend a lot of time recovering after childbirth and resting before the babies come or else she loses them. She's lucky her husband's sister never married and lives with them. It's Lizzie who does all the work around their place. Lizzie looks thin and worn and old before her time. Kind of like my mother.

It's what we do that makes us have the babies I'd like to talk about with somebody. I've even thought of talking to Tom, but I'm afraid of shocking him. He thinks I'm such a lady.

I love it so. It frightens me afterward how much I love it. Somehow I have this idea I'm not supposed even to like it. It must be the way Ma talked about it, though it was little enough she said. What she did say was about this duty we have as wives, a duty God wants us to fulfill and bring forth children. She never said it would feel so good. She never said how I'd want to do it over and over again even when Tom and I are both all tired out from our work. What a comfort it is! Afterward I sleep like a baby. Our lovemaking makes life a joy.

When Tom touches my skin my body springs alive. But I'm afraid to let him see I feel that way. I try not to show how excited I get and that makes me even more excited, to be feeling so much pleasure in the rich deep darkness and trying to keep it from bursting out in squeals and shrieks. Would it just terrify him if I let my excitement out? He'd think, what kind of woman have I got here? This can't be my good Sarah.

But I know he likes it too! It's so clear to me when he wants to do it. I can tell from the special light in his eyes and the way he sidles up close and shoos the children off. Or even if he's got the children on his lap, it's the way he looks at me across the room. His look makes me tighten up down there where we fit together. And he sees that in me sometimes and smiles in a charming, mischievous way, but other times I try to hide from him that I'm wanting it as much as he does and even act like I don't, and then he gives up, disappointed. I get confused. I suppose I get him confused too.

Am I a bad woman?

Can people see that in me?

Is that why Hank Dexter looks at me like he does?

But it's only Tom I want. I can't imagine it could feel so good with anyone else. See, I'm bad for even imagining it being with someone else!

Tom is strong yet gentle as a spring lamb. He'd never hurt me. I know that. I trust him so much. I want to produce more sons for him.

Could God be punishing me by making baby Henry so sickly? Dr. Kilroy came and listened to his chest and said he can tell from his weak heartbeat there's something wrong. But all he told us is to feed him good, make sure he gets lots of milk. I wonder if Mother knows any tonics or remedies. I almost never see her. Life carries us along so fast.

MARY ANDERSON PARKS

CHAPTER THIRTY-FIVE

I do it with Sarah often as she'll let me. I find ways to make her want to. I take a dishtowel and dry while she washes, snapping the towel on her backend now and then, playful-like. The girls in the front room with their dolls and doll beds Sarah and I made, baby Henry crawling around, I put my hands on her shoulders and rub her neck to relax her. Then I blow down the back of her dress to get her roused up. Later in bed, making love, I can truly believe she loves me and my body.

I used to worry in the beginning she'd know somehow I wasn't a white man. Maybe there's something different about me I don't know. But then I'd think how innocent she is. I'm the only man she's ever seen naked. So how could she tell if I'm different from a white man? For god's sake, I don't even know myself! When I first got to Milford, I put off going to the barber because I feared he'd see my hair's different from white folks. He didn't say anything the first time. The second time he frowned. "Don't know why I have trouble cutting your hair so it lies the way it ought. It ain't a cowlick either. I know what to do with cowlicks. No, it's something else wrong." But in time he got used to my hair. Now he cuts it real good.

Sarah and me, we're close at night, snuggling together, but in the daytime she's different. She's busy keeping the kids in order, gardening, canning, cooking, sewing, cleaning. I admire how she gets the children to help with everything. Mariah's four now and the twins three. I'll walk into the kitchen and she's got them standing up on stools mixing dough for piecrust or biscuits, sitting at the table snapping string beans, shelling peas, or depending on the season they'll be out hoeing the garden with a little hoe she got them, even slopping the hogs, they can do that too.

Sarah and me milk the cows together. At first I had fun squirting her but she got mad, said it was wasteful and she'd have to sponge off her dress, so I stopped doing it. I try instead to use the time for talking. We don't get much time alone. Even when we're in bed, a child might come knocking at our door. I taught them to knock and wait for me to call out they can come in. That's one rule I insist on. Sarah didn't like it but I overrode her. So mostly they go to each other when they need something.

Sarah isn't much for talking. Never really has been. I remember that from our courting days. Maybe a person should take more notice of such things before they up and get married. I wouldn't want a big talker though. I see women like that. They jabber away to each other and maybe to their man but it's like they're talking at him, not to him. I want a woman who talks mainly just to me and then listens to me and has things to say back about what I said. Sarah says back things like, "Is that right?" or "What ideas you do have, Tom!" I'd like more than that. Of course there's a lot we don't have no choice but to talk about, what with the children to care for and the farm.

She likes the bed part and I'm damn glad. After she gives birth, she's always ready to start doing it again in a few weeks. Sarah's a healthy woman. She seems like such a fine lady to me. I do what I can to make her life easier. I get up first and start the wood fire, then slice bacon strips off the big salted slab we keep in the cold cellar. By the time she gets up at five, I have the coffee made. All she has to do is fry up bacon and eggs and make biscuits. That's more than plenty for a girl not yet twenty-four with four children. I'd do more to help her those chilly early mornings but I have chores out in the barn.

I look forward to when our three girls and our boy can take over more of the work. Our boy though, he don't seem to have much strength in him. It took him the longest time to sit up in his little chair, and even now he kind of slumps forward. The girls all sat up straight as you please when they were just six or seven months. Not Henry. He's a sweet little fellow. His sisters take special care of him, carrying him around everywhere so he don't tire himself out. That isn't normal. Doc Kilroy says maybe he'll grow out of catching every damn thing that comes along.

It's on our minds but Sarah and I don't talk much about it. Don't know what to say, I reckon. I see the worry on her face when she watches him play, the girls toting him around like he's their little doll.

Henry likes it when I sing. He lays his head back against me and gets a peaceful look on him. The best time of day is after supper when I gather them all up on my lap and sing to them, like I'm doing right now. I've picked up new songs at the church we go to. I like the energy of those gospel hymns white folks sing. They've got harmony. Once in a while though, I can't help myself from humming one of our own black folk songs.

"Where did you learn that one?" Sarah asks, pausing in her mending. "I've never heard it."

"Oh, I pick up tunes easy. Don't remember where." I go back to humming "Motherless Chile."

"Beautiful," she murmurs. "But fearful sad." She studies my face. I'm glad she can't read on it my memories of singing with the other slaves out in the fields to make it through the long days, the back-breaking work, with no way to escape the hot sun beating down, only music to take your mind and spirit to some other place.

Next morning out in the barn, I rest my hand on Mariah's black curls, still humming that song I've got stuck in my head. Mariah's learning to milk. It's a joy to have her sit next to me on her own milking stool with the heavy warm odor of the cows around us, the comforting swish of their tails. I laugh at the curiosity in Belle's eyes as she turns her head to see who's trying to milk her without knowing to do it firm enough. She's the only one I've let Mariah practice on so far. I can't help trying to imagine what cows be thinking. Some sort of thought's going on in there. Or have they been bred to be placid. Did they try to do that with us slaves? They had some slaves they called breeders. Big strong men and women. When those thoughts pop up, I find it so terrifying I shake my head over and over to get rid of them. Mariah shakes hers too, laughing. She loves to copy me. That's how she learns. But I am troubled. Maybe I've been doing that with a whole lot of my thoughts these past years: shaking them off. That's not good, is it? There's so much I keep trying to put behind me, hoping it'll stay there.

The children help me be happy and forget. They are always caught up in what's right in front of their eyes. I learn from them to do that. Sarah complains I'm like a little boy sometimes. First she had to look after her younger brothers and now me. Does she mean that?

I can't help wishing she'd be more playful herself. She seems almost ready to settle down into being a grownup woman and let go of her girlish ways. I guess she always knew what she'd grow up to be. Every day I wake up full of thanks that I'm free and Mama's free. I think back over the past year and pray I've been a good man like Mama would want. But when can I see her? I just can't figure out a safe way. I'd be risking too much.

I want Mariah to stay happy and fun-loving like she is. I want a man for her who's strong and good and kind. Sometimes I think I'm closer to her than I am to anybody. It feels like her dear little hands are wrapped around my heart. It scares me to think what a happy family we are yet we're built on a lie.

When our boy Henry takes sick and dies and we don't even know why, I remember how God tested Job and all his family along with him. Is that what God gonna do to me? Is that my punishment? Sarah takes it hard. She named him after her beloved Grandfather Long. She clings to me for comfort and for that I'm grateful. We cling to each other.

Henry was eighteen months old and had only just begun to learn to walk. It's in March, when I thought we were about to come safely out of winter.

Is more testing coming?

MARY ANDERSON PARKS

CHAPTER THIRTY-SIX
1849 Eight Years Later

Sultry air warns of a rainstorm. I smell it, not far off. Usually gets me giddy as a highstrung colt, but riding under this fearsome, low-hanging sky I feel an unknown force headed our way, a stronger bad feeling than I've had in years. It is late afternoon when I rein in at McKinley's feed store and hitch Midnight to the post. I stroke the white streak that runs the length of his black face. He lifts his head in pleasure. Then I turn to walk into the store. None of the old men are settin out on the porch today. Must of got scared off home by the weather.

First thing I see is Hank Dexter buying a sack of feed. Only other customer is a farmer I know to nod to, and I tip my hat to him and Hank and Mr. McKinley, who gets stouter with the passing years, stuck here in his store.

At corn planting this year, Hank and his brothers came and helped, saying they'd need help themselves later. It was the biggest crop we put in yet and we knew heavy rains would be here soon. Jeremiah and I returned the favor and they too got their crops in before the big rains hit. They've settled down some, the Dexter boys, leastways the oldest. He got married and his wife cooks for them all. The mother's in a wheelchair since she broke her hip. Their father died of something or other. I wish Hank would take a wife. Seems strange he hasn't. His other brother hasn't either, but he's painful shy and Hank's the opposite, fancies himself a ladies' man. I surely did not appreciate the looks he gave Sarah at dinner around our big table. Mariah helped Sarah with the cooking and serving and he'd even give Mariah those once-over looks. She's a beauty, Mariah is, at almost thirteen. Everybody says so. She's small for her age and slender. Her curly black hair and flashing dark eyes put me in mind of my sister Janey, though Mariah's a gentle, trusting girl. Of course she's never had anything to fear.

Quickly I grab what I need and bring it to the counter, anxious to leave.

Mr. McKinley says, "Just as you rode up, Hank here was remembering those race riots in Cincinnati in 1836. He said they started on a day like this one that sets folks' nerves on edge. Hank, sometimes your imagination runs off with you like a wild horse. Why would you even remember what the weather was like then? What set you thinkin about it in the first place? You keepin a record book or somethin?" He chortles at his joke.

"Yeah, I keep track of things," Hank drawls. "I like to know who's who and what's what. That's the year you came to these parts, Tom." Hank's eyes are on me with new sharpness, watchfulness. Or do I imagine it? I fall back on the way of speech of most farmers here, like they're in a contest to see how few words they can make do with.

"Was it?"

"Yeah, I suppose you heard about the riots in your travels, seeing as how you were coming up Cincinnati way and Milford being so close to Cincinnati. What'd you hear?"

"Nothin I recall."

"That's peculiar. Everybody was talking about it. Those folks in Cincinnati had to put the damn niggers in their place. It took a lot of roughing up. Seems like you'd have heard talk, once you got up here from Virginia. Or maybe you had other things on your mind?"

No, I didn't hear nothing no more of my own people, I want to say. Not after Mama and I went separate ways. Why is he asking me this, all these years later?

He takes out a plug of tobacco, packs it in his cheek. "I don't believe you ever told us just where you came from in Virginia and how you got up here." He leans against the counter, clearly waiting.

"Ain't much to tell."

"Aw come on, Tom. Everybody's got their story." He narrows his eyes. "Betcha I could dig it up if I tried."

"Mine ain't much. A poor farmer's boy. More mouths to feed than him and Mama could manage." I'm nervous and the word 'mama' slips out. They say 'ma' don't they? Or 'mother?' My palms start to sweat. I wipe them on my pants and see Hank notice me doing it.

"Don't like to talk about this, eh?" His grin is not friendly. It brings to mind a cat playing with a mouse it's caught. Torturing it. So it's glad I am when he picks up his saddlebags. But he doesn't leave.

"Sarah just gets prettier all the time, don't she?

My face muscles stiffen.

"You keep her busy having babies but it don't hurt her figure none."

Jaw clenched, I take a step toward him. This is no way to be speaking of my wife.

He takes his time fastening a saddlebag. "Yep, I miss that good cooking of hers we got to enjoy at corn planting. Maybe I'll drop by one of these days at suppertime. Just to be neighborly." His wink and grin are downright evil. "We can do some more talking then." He goes toward the door. "About where you come from."

"Oh!" He turns, and I know by the falseness in his tone and his expression like the cat after it eats the mouse, he's about to say what he's been fixin to say all along. "I'm going to Blan next week to check out an interesting rumor. Could be I'll have a story to tell when I get back." He leers at me and as he leaves shoots back the words: "I'll be sure to drop by."

The farmer, at the counter now, exchanges a puzzled glance with Mr. McKinley. They heard everything. What are they thinking?

I stand there feeling like a wrung-out rag as I clumsily pay out my money. I mumble, "I better get on home before the rain starts," and push the door, then remember I have to pull it. It has suddenly become very heavy.

Did they hear the shakiness in my voice?

Blanchester. Blan. He's going there. Where Mr. Arnett has his grocery. Where they know my name. Am I the biggest fool on earth? Why the hell didn't we keep on till we got to Canada?

I mount Midnight, who tosses his head, restless, but I don't have energy to move yet. I sit there, my mind racing. Not making sense. Going around and around asking how can this be happening? After all these years, why is it happening now?

"I don't know what to do," I hear myself say, and realize I need to ride off. I need to go home. To Sarah. Sarah is where home is.

"No," I mutter. "No!" What am I saying no to? What is even happening? My head feels like it's splitting in two. I can't let a son of a bitch like Hank Dexter split my world in half. My fists clench. I open them and feel Hank's neck under my hands and then clench harder. Finally I take hold of the reins. Midnight starts off at a trot.

What will Hank find out? Could marse Tom still catch me and take me back? And Mama? Tom, wait! Wait and see what Hank knows. What he finds out. He's a bluffer, you've seen him play poker. Try to stay calm.

But the urge is in me to kill him. Something in me aches to destroy him. Before he destroys me and my family. He don't even have his own wife and family, don't know what it means to a man. It isn't fair he could hurt me so much.

CHAPTER THIRTY-SEVEN
Sarah

Tonight is the worst I've ever seen him. He came back from the store, jumped off Midnight, rushed into the kitchen where Mariah and Elizabeth were helping me get supper, grabbed and squeezed me so tight he took the breath from me. When I let out a squeal, he backed off.

"Sorry, Sarah. Last thing I'd do is hurt you or the baby." I've got another child inside me is what he means. He looked about to cry. I had the strongest feeling he wanted to tell me something and I couldn't help hoping maybe this is it, the loosening in him that some part of me is always awaiting. He went over to Mariah where she stood staring, gave her a long hug, then held her off from him, looked in her face and pulled her close again. It's clear she's a great comfort to him. Seemed like he forgot about Elizabeth. And he sure didn't say whatever it was he was holding inside, though I was still wishing he'd trust us with it. How can I help him if he won't share his troubles?

He went to the dining room and slumped down in an armchair next to Daniel, who sat watching little Amanda roll a cloth ball to baby Tommy. I told Mariah to go out and take care of Midnight. The stallion was standing there in the barnyard where Tom left him and a big storm was coming up fast. The sky went dark gray, almost black in the direction of town. Must have hit the store soon after Tom left. I called Sophia to come help and soon we had supper on.

Tom came to the table sunk into that mood I'm used to where he closes everything out. He concentrated on cutting his pork chops and as he slowly chewed it was obvious his mind was a million miles from us.

Daniel saw how it was and started up a conversation, asking the girls what happened interesting at the schoolhouse today. "It didn't burn down or nothin did it?" he teased. They love him and the attention he gives them. He's an old man now but he's actually doing better. Here we thought we might lose him last winter and then he started to gain back strength. I told him how my German grandmother Holstein used to swing her arms back and forth at her sides hundreds of times, walking down the lane in good weather and standing on the porch in winter, breathing in and out deep as she could. He started doing it and after a few months doctor Kilroy noticed his heart and lungs had grown stronger. But I think what helps him most is the children. He loves them so.

When Henry died, I'd find Daniel sitting with a book in his lap, tears running down his face. The girls started spending more time with him. I suppose it helped them with their own pain over losing their brother. "Can you teach me to whittle like you do?" Elizabeth asked Daniel. Now the two of them sit out on the screened-in front porch and make the most cunning little animals. We have them setting all around the house.

What on earth happened at the feed store is what I'd like to know. He didn't even buy most of the things he went for. Mariah emptied his saddlebags and all she brought in was the scissors and bolt of navy blue wool I wanted for a coat. Tom finishes eating and shoves his chair back. "Sarah, I need to go up and lie down awhile."

All four girls look surprised and worried. Usually he gathers the children on his lap and sings to them after supper, and oh how they love that. Even baby Tom is staring at his daddy, frowning. Mariah picks him up and hugs him. She always sits next to the baby and cuts his food into tiny pieces.

"Daddy," she says. "I'll take the lamp and light your way up. Hold little Tom, will you? He's tired out and needs to get in his own little beddie-bye, don't you, Tommy boy? He likes it best when you're the one lays him in his cradle."

I sigh heavily. She knows her father so well, knows it will comfort him to hold the baby. When I get up, the other girls rise to help me clear the table. Daniel says goodnight and goes off to his room.

Maybe Tom will talk to me once we're in bed. Sometimes in the dark he tells me things. But he's asleep by the time I finish in the kitchen and go up. He quivers and cries out but doesn't wake when I crawl in. He must be having one of his nightmares. I lay my arm across his chest to calm him.

The storm hits our roof with a vengeance.

Chapter Thirty-Eight
Mariah

It is two o'clock when I wipe down the oilcloth on the kitchen table. Daniel lifts his plate and glass so I can do the whole surface. He's finishing a second giant piece of blackberry pie. We already ate most everything Mother left for us. I fill his tea glass, pour more into my own, then sit across from him. My feet touch the ground now. I'm glad I grew some this summer.

"When do you think they'll get back, Uncle Daniel?"

"Your mother said it will be past dark. You sorry you didn't go?"

"Not at all! I love being here with you. I've been to county fairs before. But how often do the two of us get to talk all we want?"

"We do find lots to talk about. I appreciate your not leaving me alone all day."

"I love your stories of the old days and how you met Daddy when he first showed up in town and he became like a son to you."

"He's been a wonderful son I can tell you, Mariah. Get our deck of cards, will you? We'll play some euchre. Just to keep in practice. Your mother won't mind, am I right? Your school don't start up till next week."

I wink at him as I go to get the cards from the sideboard drawer in the dining room.

Around half past three, I stand up and stretch. "I need to check on the horses. Did you hear one of them whinny a few minutes ago?"

"Nope, didn't hear a thing. Of course I'm deaf as a post."

"No you aren't, Uncle Daniel. You've heard everything I said all day. Even my jokes. You laughed at every one!"

"You're a girl worth listening to, Mariah, you truly are."

I smile, pleased. "Anything I can get for you? I'll be out there a spell giving them water and new hay. Do you want me to walk with you to the outhouse again?"

"Nope. I'll quit drinkin this tea so you and me don't have to make so many trips out there. Don't worry. I get around fine here in the house. Got my cane, you know."

"All right!"

I close the screen door behind me and step into the warm, lazy afternoon. As I cross the barnyard, a flash of movement at the corner of the barn catches my eye, but maybe I imagined it. A trick of light. Daddy says I see things other folks don't. Like I have special powers. Still, I did hear a horse whinny. The only horses in the barn right now are Cinnamon, Midnight and the two plow horses. I'll get my own horse when I'm sixteen, Daddy said. Four years to wait! But I can't complain. Mother lets me ride Cinnamon whenever I want. She seldom rides anymore. It's good for Mother to be getting out. Having some fun. No work for one day at least.

In the barn, I stroke Cinnamon, then Midnight. They miss the other horses, I suspect. They seem restless.

Midnight's pawing the hay, tossing her head. The family's been gone for hours already. All the way to Loveland. I bring water in a bucket from the pump and am on my way to the hayloft for a fresh batch of hay when I hear that same whinny and the clip clop of a horse's hooves coming around the back of the barn, then stopping.

A visitor? Will Uncle Daniel hear and come to the back door? Truth is he doesn't hear that well and likely he's dozed off by now. Eating all that pie.

I'm standing stock still, staring at the open barn door, when a man appears in it.

"Remember me? I'm Hank Dexter. You were the pretty thing serving us when we was all here at corn planting. Saw your family today riding to the fair, you not with them."

He moves toward me. Something doesn't feel right. His tone is mocking, menacing. He walks unsteadily.

"Can I help you?" I say, hoping to make things more normal. But he keeps coming at me. I take a step backward, then another. I back into stacked bales of hay. His eyes up close are scary, and he's got the smell of liquor strong on him.

"Yes, nigger gal. Take your dress off."

Nigger? Take my dress off? What does he mean? I hug my arms tight around me. He's way too close and there's no room for me to back up any more. My throat's gone dry.

"Come on, prettiest girl in the county." He's snarling now. "You're a nigger. You don't even know, do you? You're any man's for the taking."

He pushes me down hard onto the floor and yanks my bloomers down. He drops his own pants to his knees and thrusts part of himself into me. He's breathing hard and noisy and he's doing to me like animals do. I can't think. It hurts too much. I pray for the horrible jabbing to stop. Finally, the full weight of his body falls on me.

He doesn't see Uncle Daniel hobble in with his cane, carrying a rifle. Uncle Daniel lets the cane fall and points the rifle at Hank Dexter.

"Get up off her and move away from her." It is not a voice I've ever heard him use. It is deeper, stern with command. Hank Dexter does get off me. I pull my bloomers up as best I can. They are wet and sticky.

Uncle Daniel trains the rifle on him, fires, shoots him in the right hand.

"Whatcha doin for god's sake? Listen to me, Dan Fullerton. This gal's got colored in her. Tom Jones isn't a white man. Fellow name of Arnett in Blanchester hired him —"

Uncle Daniel shoots him in the leg, and Hank Dexter crumples to the barn floor, starts crying. "Don't you hear me? Tom Jones lied to you. To all of us. Arnett said a man last name of Jones came there twelve, thirteen years ago lookin for his property, two runaway slaves, one of them named Tom. Arnett sent this here Mr. Jones to Cincinnati where Tom said he was going—don't shoot again, Dan! Please! I'm a white man like you!"

"Don't, Uncle Daniel," I whisper. My voice has no strength but he hears me, looks down at me. "I'll be all right. You can stop now."

"You're no kind of man." Uncle Daniel spits the words at him. "Drag your sorry self out of this barn and onto your horse and don't ever come back. And keep your goddamn mouth shut about whatever those fools in Blanchester said." He gives him a hard poke in the chest with the gun barrel.

Hank Dexter starts to get up from the barn floor, grabs hold of a post to steady himself.

"Come on, Mariah. We need to get you inside." Uncle Daniel reaches for my hand, pulls me to my feet. I pick up his cane and we leave the barn leaning on each other for support. Hank Dexter's hateful words throb in my head. I find I can hardly walk for the ache where he hurt me. We go very slowly.

In the house, Uncle Daniel helps me lie on the couch, brings blankets to cover me. My legs won't stop shaking. I'm so cold I don't think all the blankets in the world could warm me. He raises my head, puts a pillow underneath, then pushes an armchair close to me as he can get.

"Why are you clutching at your chest, Uncle Daniel?"

"Got a pain there," he says. "It'll go away. Usually does. I never shot nobody before. I'd of gone on till I killed him if you hadn't made me stop."

"Don't talk anymore, Uncle Daniel. Try to rest and breathe."

"Pay no mind to what that drunken fool said. Likely all lies."

"Yes. Just rest. Close your eyes."

I wish to God they were lies. What will Daddy do?

"You're the one needs rest." His voice fades away.

I hear the slow clip clop as Hank Dexter's horse goes by.

I guess we sleep then. It is completely dark when the buggy rolls in on the gravel and both of us startle awake. Daddy will unhitch the horses and lead them into the barn. He'll have to light a lantern. That's when he'll see the blood.

Mother and the children come in chattering.

"Yoohoo, anybody up?" Mother sounds happy and light-hearted. How I wish we didn't have to tell her. If only we could just go on with our lives, pretend none of it happened.

"In here," Uncle Daniel answers, his voice feeble. He reaches for my hand and keeps hold of it.

Mother comes in with a lamp. Sophia carries one too. Elizabeth holds little Tommy. Amanda, tired, trails behind. The room is bright now. Their eyes focus on me. "Send them upstairs, Sarah," Uncle Daniel says. Mother's eyes widen in alarm.

Nothing is ever going to be the same, I see that with awful sureness.

She tells the girls to take baby Tommy and go up.

"But we—" Elizabeth begins.

Amanda says, "What's wrong with Mariah?"

"No questions now," Mother cuts them off. "Put Tommy in his bed and go straight to your own beds."

They are upstairs when Daddy rushes in yelling, "There's blood in the hay! Blood streaking all the way to the barnyard!"

He stops, stares. "Why is Mariah here like this?"

He hurries toward me but Uncle Daniel raises a hand to stop him. "Wait, Tom. I need a word with you both." I can tell he still has the pain in his chest by how he winces when he stands.

He takes a while telling them, that worries me. He's led them to the far side of the room. The only words I catch are my father's, "I'll kill him for this!" and Uncle Daniel's raised voice answering: "Even Hank Dexter's not so stupid as to tell folks what he did to get himself shot. Don't you be the one spreads it around, Tom." He leans on a chair to hold himself up, talking louder now. "I messed him up bad, Tom. Would of finished him off but Mariah stopped me. She's a saint, that's what she is, our Mariah."

He won't tell Mother what Hank Dexter said, will he? He mustn't! She'd never be able to hold her head high again. Mother is so proud of who she is. Good, here she comes, and Uncle Daniel's pulling Daddy into the kitchen. She won't hear if they talk there.

Mother kneels beside me, lays a trembling hand on my forehead. "Have you had any water, Mariah?" I've never seen her look like she does now, like she doesn't know what to do. It frightens me.

"No, but please don't leave me alone. It hurts up between my legs. More all the time."

She stands up. "Can you walk? Can you make it upstairs with me and use the chamber pot?"

"Please let me rest here. When Daddy comes back he can carry me up."

She clasps her hands together. "Oh Mariah, I'm so terribly sorry this happened. If only we hadn't gone off to the fair and left you here. My poor sweet innocent girl!" She kneels and lays her head on my chest. I stroke her hair to comfort her.

"But how could you ever have imagined a thing like this, Mother?" I shudder, cold again. "I'll be all right. Won't I?"

She raises her head. "Oh yes, Mariah. I think you'll be sore a few days but you'll heal. You'll be able to start school when it opens."

"School? Do I have to go to school?" How could I face anyone after what he did to me?

"Yes, Mariah, you do have to go. No one will know."

Mother begins to pace around the room, muttering angry words I can't make out. Finally Daddy comes to lift me in his arms and carry me upstairs. She follows. Daddy's face is wet with tears and they are still flowing. He is the only one of them who cried. Uncle Daniel must have told him what Hank Dexter said. I'm just glad he'll never hear the words Hank spoke when he was alone with me. It would kill him, or else he'd kill Hank.

I wrap my arms tighter around his neck. "I'll be okay, Daddy. In just a few days, Mother said."

What a comfort to breathe in Daddy's good honest smell. He always brings the outdoors in with him, the freshness.

After I use the chamber pot and Mother carefully washes my bottom, he stays with me, kneeling by my bed. He holds onto my hand to help me bear the pain. Every time I wake, my pillow is soaked through with his tears.

Finally I open my eyes to daylight and see from his tired face he has not slept. There are dark circles under his eyes. He clenches his fists on top of my bedcovers.

"Why is it you he had to hurt? Why you of all people? Is he the devil?"

I try to think how to calm him. "No, Daddy. He's a very unhappy man. I saw that in his eyes. Uncle Daniel made him pay for what he did. He might never walk normal. He's lucky to be alive and he knows it."

I lay my hands on his and whisper, "He won't talk, Daddy. Uncle Daniel warned him." I've never seen such grief as I see in Daddy's eyes.

"No, I'm pretty sure he won't. Try to rest your mind."

Is he talking to me or to himself?

I feel older than when I woke up this morning. I look down at my arm. All of us children tan every summer and the tan stays with us. With a jolt, I recall baby Henry almost never spent time outside like the rest of us, often sick with something that kept him in. Yet he was the darkest-skinned of us all.

What a secret for Daddy to bear.

'Nigger' is what Hank Dexter called me. Hate in his voice.

Daddy feels me shiver, and hugs the covers closer around me. Oh how I want to stop hurting.

Chapter Thirty-Nine
Nellie

It's a crisp beautiful morning and I already delivered my loads of laundry. Now I'm fixing to have me a day to myself. Ain't that something?

I'm settin out here on Miz Walker's porch drawing the leaves that turned gold and brown, orange, yellow, red. Russet red. That's just how the red ones' name ought to sound. Russet red. Squinting my eyes, looking across the road, I start another picture.

It's way down deep in November and the air is uncommon chilly. I'm wearing my old dark gray sweater I ran away in. It's worn thin from washing and holds together by mending. Under it I got on another sweater and then my new orange calico dress Miz Walker made me. She used the left over cloth and sewed me an orange scarf to tie around my hair. I look like I belong in the autumn picture with my beautiful orange color. I changed clothes because I'm not gonna work more today. I'm waiting for Jeremiah is what I'm doing. This dress is mostly for going with Miz Walker to church. She's about the nicest lady in the world so I go to church with her. Ezekiel don't. I believe he thinks he's some kind of Jew because of that Jew man Mr. Davison who taught him everything he knows about shoemaking. And how to buy his freedom. He loves that man.

I look close at the tree I'm drawing, then shut my eyes and see it in my mind. Gives me a good feeling drawing, thinking my thoughts.

I've been having lots of feelings, some of them not so good. Fact is, I had some nightmares. When nightmares come on me, it means something bad happened or it gonna. So which is it?

We hear things in colored town. Gossip flashes around like lightning. That Hank Dexter, he's bad news. Him that once tried to beat up our Jeremiah, them three Dexter brothers ganging up on Jeremiah and him sending them all running. I always have to chuckle.

Anyway, a couple months ago Hank Dexter got himself shot in the hand and up near the top of his leg close to his parts he supposed to keep private but don't from what I hear. He's mistreated that poor halfwit girl Sadie Mae all these years. Of course he's not the only one, but I bet he's the baddest. First a rumor went around he'd got shot in both feet, but some men seen him coming to take advantage of Sadie Mae and he was limping but still walking. A man with both feet shot up can't go back to walking after a month or two. So that quieted the fool who came up with that story.

I've been thinking and thinking on it but don't know enough yet to figure things out. Nobody does. Hank himself won't say anything. Probably first time in his life there's something he don't yak all over town.

And Jeremiah hasn't come around these past couple months. Now why's that? I know they're out of tea and ointment.

I remember how at Tom's wedding Hank Dexter got drunk like he always do and grabbed hold of the bride and kissed her. Tom went after him. Had to be pulled off. White folks talked about that a long time, and what they talk on most often comes to our ears. Picking up dirty laundry, taking it back clean, I hear things. Being a housemaid, Miz Walker hears heaps and of course she lets me in on it. We know Hank Dexter was first to court Sarah Long and then she chose Tom over Hank. Everybody here breathed easier for her when she didn't go and marry a man we know is a mean drunk. She's from a respected family and a fine girl, and my Tom's earned a reputation as smart and honest. Of course nobody knows his past. They sure don't know I'm his mama. Though who can be sure? Around here in colored town not much escapes notice.

"There be time way out yonder when we go." Why do I start singing that one line's been stuck in my head all morning? "There be time way out yonder when we go."

Jeremiah is coming soon. My bones tell me, ringing with gladness. He's my link. I know Tom wants to come and I know why he can't. It's how it has to be. It's the way the world is, even here in the North. If a body goes over to the white side, there's no coming back. Not unless the whites find out.

Mean old Hank pops up in my thoughts. It's my worries keep bringing him to mind.

Nobody's gonna think one way or another about Jeremiah coming to buy medicines from me. He don't look like me, for one. Jeremiah's a blond blue-eyed fellow. He's not the sort folks think matter much. He never made himself no money. I asked him once to draw me a picture of his family, all however many there be of them. I have to say they're a sorry-looking bunch. Them eyes! No spirit. Poor white trash, I suppose they'd be called. But not our Jeremiah. He stands out like a prince, leastways for me.

I'm hoping he'll bring what I asked for. Might be he didn't have time to do it yet. I'm hoping it'll be today he comes. It's been almost two months since he was here, maybe more. He didn't stay long. Seemed in a terrible hurry. We didn't have a good talk like usual. Another thing different, Tom wanted a gentle balm for healing could be used on a youngster. Now who's that for? And why? I've been thinking on it ever since. Keeps me wide-eyed in the night. It's at night things come to me if I open myself up. So far it's just the nightmares. Leaving me muddled up in my mind. Shaking and shivering in my nightdress, I come out here and stand looking toward where Tom's family lives.

My drawing lies in my lap. I've been forgetting to work on it with all this figuring I'm doing. Conjuring is more what it is. Well, look here! I conjured up our Jeremiah. Here he comes, riding up smart as you please.

But something's wrong. He's trying to smile and his mouth's not working right. There. Now he's got it in place.

"Howdedo, Miss Nellie."

"Howdedo, young man. You see that tree across the road?" I hold up my drawing for him. He slides down from his horse, comes over to look at it up close. Then he glances across the road at the tree I drew. Now a real smile lights his eyes, chasing out some of the worry.

"Those last two leaves ready to fall. That's a real special moment you captured, Miss Nellie."

"Yes, I just set out here and wait for these moments."

He chuckles, but something's powerful wrong and I aim to get it out of him. He's not leaving till I do. I can bide my time, do it my own slow way.

"So. You had you any free time for drawing?"

He won't meet my eyes. He's shy as a barn cat, I know that, but it isn't the reason he's not looking me in the eye. He has something to tell me he don't want to.

"I drew pictures of Mr. Jones and his family like you asked, Miss Nellie, but they aren't much good." He's hiding now in his mumbling.

"Let me have a look for myself." I push my feelings down, afraid he'll see how much it means to me.

He walks over and strokes Paint. He don't even have to tie her up. She feels that much at home here. He reaches in the saddle bag, pulls out sheets of paper. I try not to breathe so loud. My hand trembles, accepting his three drawings. It's taken me years to get up enough courage to ask for what he just handed me.

The pictures rest in my lap like something alive. I say a prayer before I look at them. Lord, please let me not show what I feel.

I say to Jeremiah, "Good. You done them in color like I wanted."

"Yes ma'am. It helped me too because I've been working on skin tones."

What is he telling me by that? I always wonder how much Jeremiah knows. He's a deep one, our Jeremiah, and I suspect he knows a whole lot.

"Well." I take a breath and let it out. "I'll look at this one first."

I stop breathing. It's Sarah. He printed her name on it.

"She's a real pretty woman. Looks nice, too."

"Yep," Jeremiah says softly. "She is."

I give him a sharp look. Is he in love with her? Or does she put him in mind of the kind of mama he wishes he had?

Can't tell. He's got those eyelids that droop down and cover up his expression. And them long eyelashes. Oh he do be a pretty boy. Guess I should start thinking of him as a man but I can't. He's my boy. He comes and sees me. Brings me pictures when I ask. Why didn't I ask sooner? When they were younger? I'm almost afraid to look at these.

"Sarah Long," I say, trying out the name. "She married Tom Jones." I know I'm muttering to myself. Can't help it. "Look at her dark hair. Natural curl, is that it?"

Jeremiah nods.

"Black hair."

He nods again.

"And her eyes. They're dark brown?"

"Yes ma'am."

I think a while on how smart Tom was to pick a dark-haired, dark-eyed girl with curl in her hair.

"There's sadness in her eyes. When did you draw this?"

Jeremiah scrunches up his mouth like he does when he don't want to answer.

I go on to the next picture and draw in a quick breath. "The four girls and the baby. And this one's Mariah. The oldest. Lord, what a beauty."

Jeremiah nods, sadly now it seems to me. "Look at those dark flashing eyes." She puts me in mind of my Janey but she's so pale, Mariah. She seems as gentle as a dove. There's that spark though in her eyes. Intelligence? Is that it? But what else? Something's happened to the child.

"When did you draw this, Jeremiah?"

He pretends to think. "About two months ago, I reckon."

About when I had my first nightmare.

I look at her three sisters next to her, names and ages written under them, Mariah on the left, then Elizabeth, she's the tallest. And she has my bones. I smile, because there I am in Elizabeth. Nobody can know what satisfaction that brings me. Her twin, Sophia, leans into her like they're good friends. Then the smallest girl, Amanda, her chubby arm around baby Tommy. I breathe in slow and let out a sigh. Then I turn to the last picture.

Yes, there's my Tom. But oh the torment in his eyes! I never saw anything like that in him. What is so wrong, so hard? He's still handsome, but there's misery in his eyes.

I look up at Jeremiah. He gazes back at me, sad as I've ever seen him.

"These are real recent, Miss Nellie." His voice is full of meaning. None of it good.

"Tell me, Jeremiah."

"I can't. Mr. Jones doesn't want anybody to know."

"What kind of fool do you take me for?"

He lowers his heavy eyelids. "My commission today, Miss Nellie—" He can't go on. He takes a deep breath. "It's to get something from you to make a young girl lose the baby growing in her, something gentle as can be that won't hurt her."

Finally I say, "There ain't nothin like that."

He looks up. "There's got to be, please Miss Nellie. She's the best little girl on earth."

I knew it was Mariah, didn't want to know it.

"You have to bring her to me tomorrow, Jeremiah. All right? I'll need her here three days. She so young."

I see him worrying how he's gonna do that.

"Wrap her up good and cover her face and hair. Ride her here horseback."

"You can't just send a potion or something?"

"No, Jeremiah. This is Mariah. We ain't taking no chances." I think about the chances we do be taking. "Not with her body. She's a precious beautiful girl."

He looks me full in the eye. "I know that, Miss Nellie. I'll bring her early tomorrow if they let me."

He leaves the drawings with me and climbs up on Paint.

I stand close to them. "I won't let anybody know who she is. Not Miz Walker, not nobody. You tell Mr. Jones that."

CHAPTER FORTY

Jeremiah knows to find me here. These past days since Sarah told me she was sure, I've come here a lot to sit and think. Today I sent Jeremiah on a mission.

Belle's used to me being here. The other animals too, except Midnight, who's jumpy as I am. Course it's my mood he's picking up on. We're too close, me and that stallion. He wheezes and I know he's tossing his head looking for me. Can he smell where I'm at? When I tried sitting in his stall, he got nervous as a cornered cat.

It's Belle's stall where I've ended up, piling hay to sit against. We're keeping the animals inside because of the cold spell. No point taking the cows out to pasture till the ground thaws. Maybe it won't. Winter's only a month away.

Cows are funny creatures. Seems like they contemplate, the way they chew their cud and gaze off in space. They look you in the eye too. If you want to see who looks away first, they'll play that game. They win most every time. Belle and me aren't in the mood for that. I chose her stall because she's the one I taught Mariah to milk on. Belle was here that cursed day we went to the fair. So was Midnight. I come here often as I can. Only Jeremiah knows this is the spot to find me.

The odors of manure and fresh hay, the soft neighing, lowing sounds the animals make, their steady breathing, all that comforts me. Even though this is where it happened—or is that the reason I come? Wanting to understand what she went through, how she feels? She herself don't ever come near the barn anymore.

At first I didn't see how I'd go on living. There's nothing I can do about any of it, that's what I hate! And I'm deathly afraid of folks finding out.

Watching Mariah helped. She goes to school every day like Sarah told her she has to, and we all seven ride in to church like before. Her sisters know something bad happened that day, but I'm sure Mariah never talked to them about it. I catch Elizabeth studying her, worrying. I see Mama so plain in Elizabeth's face and strong bones. It makes me powerful lonesome for Mama.

With Mariah going to school, doing her homework every night, I began to think we'd make it through. I started throwing myself even more into work, riding all over buying and selling, getting things done before winter closes in.

Then Sarah figured out Mariah's pregnant. That's a horror beyond anything, knowing who the father is, Mariah so young and small, the shame that could come to her and all of us.

I lie back in the hay, close my eyes but can't escape my thoughts. Jeremiah hasn't had time yet to go there and come back with whatever damn thing we'll have to give Mariah to kill the monster in her. I was afraid she'd want to go ahead and have it. She's so kind, don't even want to kill fleas. But she didn't say she won't do it. I expect she knows it'd kill me if she had that baby.

Maybe I doze off. Suddenly there's Jeremiah alongside Belle, watching me with fearful eyes.

"What?" My voice comes out hoarse. I notice his empty hands. I thought he'd be carrying whatever it is gonna save us all.

"Tom, I-I need to tell you straight off. Miss Nellie says I got to bring Mariah to her. She'll have to k-keep her a few days. Tom. There ain't nothing a girl can just drink and be done with it."

I stare hard at him, trying to take in what this means.

"She told me to wrap her up so nobody will know who she is. And she said she won't tell anybody. Ever. She guessed who it is, Tom. I didn't say. But I know she won't tell."

I bury my head in my hands. "No. She won't tell."

How do I explain this to Sarah, to Mariah? The less I say the better. I'll just tell them what to do and they'll do it. What choice have we got? I look up at him.

"Did Miss Nellie say when?"

"T-tomorrow."

"Tomorrow," I repeat, shaking my head. I stay quiet, admiring Mama's spunk, her quickness to act. Well, that's my mama. She sure don't let grass grow under her feet. And I begin to feel better. Mariah will be safe in Mama's hands. I've heard awful stories of girls dying but I feel sure Mariah will come through all right. Mama won't let her die. She just won't.

Mariah can use my leather travel bag. She'll want her doll she sleeps with. She and the doll have matching pink flannel nightgowns Sarah made, with white ribbons. I better go talk to Sarah. Get it over with.

When I walk into the kitchen they're all there, helping Sarah make supper.

"Elizabeth, you and Sophia please take Amanda and Tommy upstairs to play."

"We're not playing, Daddy," she beams at me. "We're working."

"Mother and I need to talk to Mariah." Elizabeth's face right away turns serious. She swoops up Tommy, and Sophia leads Amanda away by the hand. I wait till I hear them go up the stairs.

"Mariah, there's no simple way to do this. I'm sorry. I thought there was. Miss Nellie says she'll need you to stay with her there at her house a few days."

Sarah drops the bowl of biscuit dough. It clatters onto the table. "Are you out of your mind, Tom? Mariah go to colored town?" Her eyes are wide with fright.

Mariah speaks up quickly. "It's all right, Mother. Jeremiah's told me about Miss Nellie. He goes to her every couple months to get Uncle Daniel's tea and salve. He says she's nice and kind and clean as can be."

"Mariah, go to your room please." Sarah keeps her eyes on me.

Mariah gives me a last look as she leaves and a small smile to reassure me. What a wonder of a girl.

"Pack enough for three days," I call out to her.

"Three days! You really are crazy." Sarah stares at me, disbelieving.

"Sarah, what choice do we have? This woman is a healer. She knows what she's doing."

"She's colored! Mariah can't stay in her house! What's wrong with you, Tom? They're different from us. You know that."

Her eyes plead with me. I feel my face flush.

"Sarah, she's going to Miss Nellie's." I force the words out, afraid of her resistance. "Nothing you say will change that. Jeremiah's taking her tomorrow morning before daybreak."

"You've made up your mind, have you? Why don't you use the good sense you were born with? What will people think if anyone sees her?"

"They won't. She'll go before dawn. Sarah, Miss Nellie's promised. She'll never tell anyone. She'll keep our secret!"

Sarah's hard gaze penetrates into me. "How did you even come to know of this woman? How can you put our daughter's life in the hands of a colored?"

I turn away from her. I didn't know her face could change like this. Hard as earth scorched by the sun. Where is my soft sweet Sarah? Am I really seeing what I'm seeing?

"I have to get out of here. I have to."

I wipe cold sweat off my forehead. "I'll sleep in the barn." Dazed, unsteady, I stumble out of the kitchen.

She don't know she's talking about my mama. My head hurts so bad I wish I could tear it off. I want Sarah to help me and she won't. I guess it's not her fault if she thinks like they all do. But it scares me. Her feelings about coloreds never came up before, with us living out here on the farm, happy keeping to ourselves, busy with our work.

I never slept away from her in the barn. We won't have the comfort of each other. It's strange here at night. Belle shifts her weight, restless. I tell myself it's only for one night, I'll want to sleep in our bed with Sarah tomorrow night when Mariah's away, and she'll forgive me for sending Mariah to Mama, she has to! If only I could tell her everything, make her understand!

I burrow deeper into the hay, trying to make my mind blank. Well before daybreak the sound of Jeremiah riding into the barnyard wakes me. I get up, boots still on, stride over to the house and up the stairs. Mariah is sitting on her bed, fully dressed, looking very tiny with her back straight as can be. She has her things packed in my travel bag next to her on the floor. We've given Mariah her own room since this happened. Sarah must still be sleeping. There's no sign of her.

"Jeremiah's outside on Paint, waiting for you. He'll ride you in front of him on the saddle. Just lean back into him and you'll look like one rider. Is that your warmest cloak, Mariah, with the big hood to pull over your face?"

"Yes, Daddy." She reaches out and touches my hand. For a moment we look into each other's eyes, hers so full of trust. She seems very brave to me. I want to carry her downstairs but I let her walk in front of me.

She'll be with Mama soon! My heart beats strong and I have to breathe deep to let the rush of feelings pass through me. She'll be with Mama. And I'll be here where I can't do anything but wait. I watch as they go off, Mariah riding sidesaddle in front of Jeremiah, melting back into him so they look like one rider.

I'll have to face Sarah, try to break through the wall building up thicker between us, give her what comfort I can.

Here she comes, in her nightdress with a big brown sweater of mine over it. She's shivering. I put my arm around her but at this moment I'm far away, riding toward Mama.

MARY ANDERSON PARKS

CHAPTER FORTY-ONE
Nellie

I wake up a good spell before dawn, run barefoot to the kitchen, get the fire going, start making coffee. I'm surprised I slept a blink of a yellow cat's eye. I'm about as excited as I've ever been.

I'm sure he'll bring her early when most folks aren't up. That's if they're all cooperating over at Tom's, nobody standing in the way. I bring out Sarah's picture. Can I really expect to understand a white woman raised up like her? Something in her face troubles me. The innocence? Does it mean she hasn't seen much suffering? But their son dying, that had to be a trial to her. She's had more children since and probably she'll keep having them. She's strong and healthy. Now this trouble's come on them, but she looks in Jeremiah's picture like she'll know what to do, in a coping kind of way. She'll keep going on.

It's us she don't understand. She's got no notion how it feels to be one of us. Probably never met a colored person the way these Ohia farmers live. Now isn't that just the strangest thing, with her married to my Tom? Oh I do wonder what she had to say when she found out they're bringing her daughter here to me. And how Tom felt if she didn't take it well.

Look at that expression on her. She don't know what it is to fear a beating, or worse. Course now the worst happened, to her daughter.

The more I think on it, I'm almost sure who done it. Why else did that devil get shot where he did and he's not talking about it. But there's more. I feel that in the way my blood runs cold when I try to imagine how it happened. And who it was shot him.

Will Mariah tell me? Will she even talk to me?

Miz Walker bustles in and I push the picture back in my big pocket, pour her a cup of coffee. Her eyes are full to busting with questions. All I told her is Jeremiah's bringing a little white girl for me to take care of a few days, while I help her lose the baby growing in her and there ain't gonna be no talk because we ain't gonna let anybody find out she's here. Except Ezekiel of course. "Of course," she nodded at me. Acting like she knows about such things though it's the first time any of us ever heard of a white child staying overnight in a colored house. Her eyes been wide as pie pans ever since I told her what's gonna happen. I didn't ask, I told her. My heart couldn't stand it if she said she wasn't up to taking a risk like that.

"I can't tell you the girl's name," I added, watching close how she'd take that. "We'll jes call her the little girl." Oh but did she throw me a sharp look. I could see her mind dashing through alleys and byways trying to chase down what's going on. Kind of like I've been doing, I suppose.

"I'll help you, Miz Jones," was what she finally said. "That little girl will find herself welcome here." Then she added, "Whoever she be." And I swear she winked at me. I pretended I didn't see. It's hard keeping all Tom's secrets.

"When she comin?" Miz Walker says while she's hard-frying eggs.

"I expect Jeremiah gonna be here with her before daylight."

She gives me a knowing look. "That'd be smart. Here's a fried egg sandwich for you. You need to eat something. This be a real big day for you."

Now what does she mean by that? What does she know?

She eats her own sandwich quick. "I better be off to work. Yesterday I was late cause I twisted my ankle." She takes her time collecting stuff to go in her purse, then puts on her old coat and scarf, mittens with holes she hasn't found time yet to mend. She keeps glancing out the window. I know she's hoping they'll ride up before she leaves. But that don't happen and I'm glad to be left here alone to go back to my rumination. I like that word. Always puts me in mind of a cow. How patient cows are. Tom has cows, horses, chickens, hogs . . . I sure do like thinking about those animals he got for himself and how he goes around selling and trading, making enough to bring up a family, growing his own crops. Then this—

I hear Paint snorting from the cold and rush out wearing just my old sweater over my everyday dress.

The girl is bundled up in front of him and when Jeremiah lifts her down off Paint, I can't see her face until we get inside the warm kitchen and she pulls back her hood.

I will never forget the moment I look into her face and see the strength of her spirit shining in her dark eyes and the trusting smile she gives me. It's like she reached out her little hand and wrapped it around my heart. Those eyes of hers express so much. She's not thinking about herself. That's the marvel of it. She's thinking about me, looking in my face to see who and what I am. What she finds brings gratitude to her eyes. Yes! She's grateful I gonna take care of her. Oh we'll be fine together, me and Mariah.

I can't help it my face scrunches up and tears come. I hug her close. And she hugs me back! Oh I sorry Lord but this do be the happiest day of my life, even knowing the sorrow that brings her here. I know what to do about that.

Jeremiah takes his leave of us, reluctantly. He loves Mariah. There's a special friendship between them.

I take her cloak, then give her a cup of the special tea I brewed up strong last night and set myself down across the table from her.

"Now Mariah, I gonna tell you what to expect in these days you'll be with me. Today I have to go off to collect laundry and bring it home to wash."

I watch her eyes widen.

"Yes, that's what I do is wash rich white folks' dirty laundry. It brings in enough for me to live on. Your mama probably does her own washing, am I right?"

She smiles the prettiest smile anybody ever seen. "Yes, Miss Nellie. My sisters and I help."

Lord, I don't think she has any notion how startling beautiful she is. I try not to get distracted.

"Well, that's a fine thing to do your own washing. I sure as snow in winter wouldn't let some stranger mess in my personal things.

"Now here's what we'll do. I'll scurry fast as I can and Mr. Davison, my good friend Ezekiel, he'll work outside in the yard so we can be sure you're safe in here. This is Miz Walker's house I live in and she's at work. Mr. Davison won't come in and scare you or nothin. You'll jes see him out through that window. He'll stay out there. He's a real gentle man, but big. Don't be put off by how tall he is."

I pull out the table's only drawer. "Here be paper and pencils for you to draw with. Jeremiah told me you like to draw."

"Miss Nellie, please, I hope Mr. Davison will feel all right about coming in if he needs to. He's your friend and I understand he's coming over to keep me safe. That is surely nice of him, and I won't be afraid. I brought two of my schoolbooks so I can keep up with my work. I'll be busy while you're gone. Don't worry about me."

Oh, she talk so good, that Mariah. Like a real lady. "Yes," I say. I don't know how to express how much I appreciate her words about Mr. Davison.

"Yes, you gonna be fine. It goes without sayin don't let nobody in. except Miz Walker was she to come home early. She knows you're here. And Ezekiel, I mean Mr. Davison, if he really needs to come in. But don't let nobody else in. Especially white folks. There do be some come to colored town and they most times up to no good. Like that Hank Dexter fellow."

Now that be cunning of me. I throw the name at her real sudden, all the time watching her, and the little honey shrinks back. I see it.

"Why would he come here?" Her voice is tiny and scared.

"Not here. He's never been here. I ain't gonna say no more about why he comes to colored town. He jes allout no good—" I check myself. She's white as a sheet blowing on the line.

I go lay my hands on her shoulders. "I ought not be upsetting you. You jes keep drinking the tea, that'll comfort you. The chamber pot's over there in my room next to the bed. You can do your reading and writing at the table here. Here's a bowl of apples and in this tin some corn cakes you can have when you get hungry. When I get back, I'll feed you good as if you was a turkey we fixin to eat." I want to bring back her smile.

"Tomorrow's the day I'll be keeping you in my bed with the linen all washed clean and a rubber sheet under, because I have to give you some evil-tasting stuff. Three tablespoonsful. That's what makes the thing come out of you that oughtn't be there."

I see her lips quiver.

"Yes, Mariah, it'll hurt. And it'll take time. But I'll put compresses on your tummy to keep you warm and I'll be right with you all the time. Mr. Davison gonna do my deliveries. He'd wash the clothes too, if he knew the first thing about it."

Mariah smiles at that. Through the window, I see Ezekiel swing into the yard twirling a rake, showing off his strength. That's my sign to go.

Making my rounds, I'm up in my head not knowing if my feet on the ground or in the air. It a wonder I don't fall in a hole. I'm thinking how precious these hours are. The lord seen fit to separate me from all my grandchillun but gave me these few days with Mariah. I'm quivering with the bigness of it. How can I hold a gift that big? I want to fall on my knees thanking the lord or whatever power it is that can just as likely rip us apart and play sport with us, like happened to poor Job. Oh yeah, I heard his story. Mistress Elaine used to read the Bible to her own girl and I listened right along. I'm like Mrs. Job, though I don't remember any mention of the poor lady, or what she might have been thinking. I'd draw her in if I was drawing a picture of the Job family. At marse Tom's, I heard a slave tell the Job story and we all wanted to hear it again the next night and the one after. We all knew what we love most can be taken away and there's nothing us can do. Don't seem fair white folks get to claim that story for their own like they do everything else.

So I'm doing all this thinking and before long I'm back home. A man who knows when he's needed and when he's not, Ezekiel murmurs she's safe and goes off about his business. I find her working away at the table, right smack where I left her. I'm glad to see she ate two of the apples.

"Hello little darlin. How you been while I was gone?"

"I've been fine, Miss Nellie. I did a lot of my lessons already. I can't wait to use the drawing pencils."

"You jes draw with them pencils all you want. And you can take them home with you."

I get busy setting out a healing meal to keep up her strength. Broth from beef bones I boiled up all day yesterday with good chunks of meat on them, throwing carrots and onions in at the end. Onions cure most anything.

"And here's my special bread, Mariah. It's got three different grains in it, walnuts too. All buttered up, it be the best thing in the world."

MARY ANDERSON PARKS

CHAPTER FORTY-TWO

Nellie

"Miz Walker! How did your day go?"

"I'm a bit early. I worked fast. Wanted to get home and see how y'all doin."

"Oh we doin fine. This the little girl I told you about. She'll still be here tomorrow, then a day after that, restin up, healin."

"You come to the right place, little gal. Miss Nellie knows all there is to know about healing. Folks around here all come to her. How'd you happen to hear of her?"

Before Mariah can say anything, I rush in with words. "Miz Walker, this gal needs to finish eating, then I'll put her in my bed. She got a big day comin tomorrow. She needs her rest."

So that's what we do. We get ready for bed early. I make up a place for me on the floor with extra bedding and a pillow.

"Miss Nellie, you mustn't give up your own bed! There's room here for both of us."

My heart squeezes up when she says that. I'm powerful tempted. Sleeping the night with my own granddaughter, that'd be something to remember all my life. But she's a white girl. It wouldn't be right. What if Jeremiah came to know? Or anybody? It'd be jes like Mariah, the little trusting thing, to go and tell Tom or her mother or sisters. She wouldn't think nothin of it! She's a walking miracle, that's what.

"No. We'll both sleep better if we have our own place to spread out."

I tuck her in and go settle into my covers.

I commence to singing real low. "Dee-e-p River . . ."

After a few lines, she murmurs, "Daddy . . ." and then her breathing tells me she's sleeping.

Next morning, I'm across from Mariah at the table, drinking coffee. She ate her eggs and bread and now she's reading in her book.

"Today's the day. We gonna go real easy, Mariah, like fine ladies taking our time eating and resting. Miz Walker, she'll be gone to church most of the day. I got your medicine cookin away. I was up before sunrise mixing it. You jes go on with your reading and pay it no nevah mind till it be ready."

I get my own drawing pencils out. Next thing I know I'm drifting into my thoughts like I do.

Tom, why did you go off the other way from me? Will I be asking that my whole life long? Because I do, you know. Well no, you don't know anything about what I'm thinking. You've got no idea I ask myself that all the time. And the answer I come up with is you don't think coloreds are good as whites. Well I think a whole different way. All my life I knew I'm not just good as whites but I'm better. I'm better because I don't treat nobody bad as they do. Our people, we're mostly kind. That's because we know how it feels to be treated like a mangy dog, but the fact staring me in the face, like a snake I met on a tree limb as a girl climbing high, the fact is we're better than whites. Deep in me I always knew it. But you Tom, letting me walk off from you that first day we came to Milford, then going off to the white part of town and staying there, you showed me you thought they was better than us. That's not a happy memory.

I look at this girl of yours, Mariah, and I think, would she have all that book learning if you hadn't gone on the path you did? I know the answer. Course not. But if you'd married colored, stayed with your people, couldn't your daughter still have a noble character? And dammit you could have learned her to read like I learned you. Even if the laws of Ohia won't let us in their schools!

Mariah raises her head. I got so worked up I broke my pencil in two!

"Sorry. My thoughts carried me away."

That little marvel of a girl, she reaches over the table and touches my face oh so gentle. "The bones of your face are beautiful, Miss Nellie. Your face reminds me of my sister Elizabeth. It took me a while to realize that's why you look familiar to me, and I feel at home here."

I swallow, not trusting myself to speak.

"Miss Nellie, were you born here in Milford? Is your family here?"

She's scaring me now. I meant to be the one doing the finding out, but she's getting way out in front of me. I try to think what she might ask next. Be careful, Nellie. I get up and busy myself ladling soup.

Setting the bowl close to her, I say, "I grew up on plantations down south."

She fixes her gaze on me as if she's waiting to hear more.

I take a deep breath. These are probably the only days I'll ever have to talk to her.

"I was born a slave," I tell her. "You learned about slavery yet in your schoolbooks?"

"Yes." A fearful look comes into her eyes. Is this more than she's ready to take on? No, my Mariah, she draws in a breath I can hear, like she's gathering courage to ask me something.

"What was that like for you, Miss Nellie? Can you tell me please? Our teacher told us people might go to war over slavery and she thinks that would be tragic."

What should I say? I hear talk about how there may be war. Especially at church. That's when we do our talking.

"Mariah, I hardly know which end to take hold of on that. If there was a war, and it ended slavery, do you think that might be worth fighting over?"

"Well, no, Miss Nellie, I don't suppose I do. A lot of people would die who don't have anything to do with slavery. I mean, it's not our fault those people in the south need workers to help them on their big plantations. I guess cotton's a crop you need lots of farmhands all year round."

I stare at her. What kind of woman is this teacher of hers? I add kindling to the fire, start heating water for more coffee, slice and butter my special bread and lay it on a plate on the table. When the coffee's ready I pour Mariah half a cup, adding lots of cream the way she likes it. Then I set myself back down across from her.

I look her in the eye. "Mariah, slaves be slaves; they're not farmhands. They be owned, like a man owns his furniture. They're property. They can be sold by the master to anybody he takes a notion.

"I always knew who my daddy was and loved him something fierce, like you love your daddy. He was a tall, strong, deep black man. He'd set me on his big hand and carry me around, both of us proud as roosters. That didn't happen often. Mama and him was gone every day to the fields. I saw Mama's stomach growing and knew she had another baby in there about ready to come out. But before the time came, massa took it in his head to sell Daddy. Massa, that's what we called the master on that plantation. Mama heard massa tell the missus he had such a good offer for Daddy he couldn't turn it down. She said those were his exact words. I was peeking out from under the porch the day Mama went down on her knees to beg him not to sell Daddy. She was a light-skinned pretty woman, delicate and slender. Massa yanked her to her feet, 'Get up. Get back to work.' 'Can they do that?' I asked my mama later, disbelievin. 'Jes up an sell us?' 'Course they can,' my mama said. Daddy was taken away the next day by his new master. At the last minute I jumped up on him and he hugged me, sobs shaking his body. A house slave took me from him when the new master yelled at him to get on the wagon."

"Oh Miss Nellie, how awful!" The poor girl is quivering. "Tell me what happened after that."

"Mariah, what am I thinking? You calm down now and after a while I'll give you the medicine. We can talk about this tomorrow when your treatment's all over and you'll feel better."

"Yes, tell me tomorrow. Please. I want to hear what happened to you and your mother."

The doorknob turns noisily and Miz Walker bursts into the kitchen. "It be cold as a sow's tit out there."

"Miz Walker!"

"Oh, our gal here's a farm gal, right?"

Mariah smiles. "My mother says that sometimes. Though she wasn't allowed to growing up. My grandfather is a very strict man. They had to read the Bible a whole lot. My daddy is much more fun. He sits us on his lap and sings to us."

"What do he sing?" I can't help asking.

"He can sing anything! He likes all the liveliest hymns from church, and we join in on the harmony. Some songs we don't know and maybe he doesn't know the words so he mostly hums. I love it when he does that."

And I love it when she bursts out with something like this about her daddy. I can see him doing it.

"So he likes to sing." Thinking about Tom, forgetting everything else, I start humming "Motherless Chile." I stop when I see Mariah staring at me like she's watching a ghost.

"That's my favorite," she says slowly. "How do you come to know it?"

I need to move her mind away quick from this track. I've been putting off giving the medicine, knowing it'll be the end of our talking time.

"It's time for the medicine, honey. We'll get you in bed. Miz Walker, don't you need to be changing out of them nice church clothes? That's a lovely hat you're wearing, with those pretty pink feathers."

All I gonna say about the rest of that day and night is I did end up in the bed with her, holding the poor child in my arms. I ached along with her, maybe more than she did. She cramped up bad and that's what hurt her most. She didn't vomit, my tea helped her. Then the thing came out of her, all of it. I was hoping for that. I cleaned her up gentle as I could. What a blessing when the Lord let her sleep. I knelt on the floor and prayed. A lot of my praying was for Tom. There's more to his trouble, and Mariah knows what it is. I seen it in her eyes when she asked how I come to know the same song her daddy does. Things be coming together in her mind, Tom, I can't help that. You're on your own path now. I can't come along it with you.

When Mariah wakes from her long sleep. I see her open her eyes and watch me cleaning up the room. I set by her on the bed. Her sad eyes tell me she wants to say something hard for her.

Her voice comes out real small. "Am I bad, Miss Nellie? Is that why this happened to me? Because sometimes I don't do what Mother wants right away or I tell my sisters to leave me alone when I want to read my book?"

So those are the poor child's sins. And she thinks that's why she got raped?

I take hold of her little shoulders and look straight in her eyes. "No! What happened to you ain't no way because you're bad. No girl or woman should have to suffer a man forcing himself on her. The sin is in the man. The sin ain't in you, Mariah. Believe me, I know what I'm saying to be God's truth."

"Thank you, Miss Nellie. There's nobody I can talk to about this. They'd all gone to the fair. Uncle Daniel and I were alone. He was in the house and when I went out to the barn. . ." She closes her eyes and falls back to sleep, comforted.

I told my white ladies I'd be missing a day. They don't like that, but I said to just save up their laundry for me. So now I can doze off when she does.

MARY ANDERSON PARKS

CHAPTER FORTY-THREE
Nellie

Time is going too fast. Mariah's been sleeping and sleeping. I know it's the best thing for her but tonight Jeremiah will be coming to get her already. He'll wait for dark and then he'll come. I've been watching her sleep. She got through it all just fine. Her color's good and when she finally opens her eyes I see how bright and alert they are.

"Miss Nellie, please tell me about what happened to you and your mother after they took your father away." It makes my heart glad she hasn't forgotten.

"It's a sad story, Mariah. Are you feeling up to it?"

"I want to hear it all. Please, Miss Nellie, I feel just fine."

I draw a breath, let it out slow. "My mama was out in the field the day her baby came. She fell over on the cotton and the overseer smacked her with his whip to make her stand. He whipped her over and over, because she wouldn't get up. She couldn't. I heard about it later when the slaves trooped back in starlight. She and my sister died out there. Two of the men carried them back. I'd jes turned six."

Mariah sits up in the bed, reaches out her hand and lays it on mine, her eyes wide. "But you were all alone. Who took care of you?"

"I worked for the young missus for two years in the big house. When I was eight, I had to go work in the fields. Least that place gave us big hard shoes to wear for field work."

"You mean later you went to another place?"

"I was sold when I was thirteen. I can't talk no more about this, Mariah. Makes me feel like it's all happening again."

She gets up, pulls on her dressing gown and follows me into the kitchen, where I get out the bread and pour coffee and milk into a cup for her and black coffee for me.

I bite off a small piece of bread. "It don't taste good like it's supposed to."

"Yes it does," she says. "It's wonderful bread. It is making me strong, that and your stew and the tea. When I get back to school— I will, won't I?"

I rest my hard hand on her soft one. "Yes. Soon. Mebbe even tomorrow." I set out a bowl of applesauce and a hunk of cheese.

"Miss Nellie, I have to get back to tell my teacher and schoolmates. They have no idea what slavery is. They like to talk about how happy the slaves are; they say you can tell because they sing while they work." She looks at me, a question on her face.

"They sing, Mariah, so they won't drop dead in the field. They sing to remember they human beings, men, women and chillun that belong to God as much as white folks. Our songs carry messages. Could be our grief pouring out, or anger. Or hope. A body needs hope.

"Don't stop asking questions, Mariah, and thinking for yourself, not jes believing what folks say who may know nothin about it."

"Yes! I want to tell my teacher I talked to someone who was a slave and—"

"Mariah, that's not such a good thing to do, though I know you be meaning it in the best way."

"But why not? They should know."

"For one thing, you mustn't tell a single soul you been to colored town and stayed here with me."

She raises a frowning, puzzled face.

"Promise me, Mariah. You must never tell. Do you understand why?"

"I do," she says at last. "But it's sad how things are. The way some people think scares me."

"Yes, my darlin. Try to put all this out of your head."

That last day with Mariah, I push myself to stay busy. Too busy to think on things is what I'm aiming at. She helps me bake a pie using cherries Miz Walker put up in summertime, and we pack up herbs so she can make tea at home to speed up her healing. The pie's to offer Jeremiah. Give him coffee and cherry pie and he'll set for a spell. I'll get a little more time with my girl.

"I like this tea, Miss Nellie. I'll think of you every time I take a sip, and I'll remember the things we talked about. These days have been important to me." I can't stop myself hugging her, my arms all floury up to the elbows. She seems to know well as I do this likely the only time we'll see each other.

"You smell so good, Miss Nellie. Like pie dough." We have a laugh about that.

Then a question pops out of me like a fish slipping out of your hand when you grab it and it's not even yours yet. "Have you ever spoken with a colored person before me?" Now why'd I ask that?

"No, I haven't." I see her turn my question over in her head. "Well not a person you'd know was—" She stops, blushes up into the roots of her hair. She stares at me, her mouth open. In shock at what just came out? What in hell is she saying? A chill runs up my arms, down my back. Did somebody tell her about Tom? That's what comes to my mind. I've got that feeling I get when my mind opens for spirits and such to come in.

Jeremiah rides up just then. We hear old Paint snorting in the yard. It's almost a relief. Something unsettled hangs between Mariah and me and we don't know what to do about it. I reckon stuffing ourselves with cherry pie gonna help as much as anything.

Jeremiah smiles broad, seeing her look so healthy.

"You better go out and say howdy to Paint, Mariah. Take a lantern, it's dark. That old horse won't calm down till she sees you. I never saw a horse as smart in my life."

When she's gone he says, "She's going to be all right?"

"She's fine." I take in a breath. "Jeremiah, I have to know. Was anybody near when this happened to her? Could anybody have heard words said to her by him who done it?"

He looks at me through his eyelashes, frowning. His words come slow. "I don't know. Mr. Fullerton came out when it was too late. With his shotgun."

He just told me what I suspected be true. But what did that devil man say to Mariah before he got shot? If it what I fear, how did he find out? Guess I don't need to know that. I don't think she's gonna tell her mama. Or nary a soul. She loves her daddy too much. I bet she's gonna keep his secret. But Hank Dexter will talk. Probably already has.

CHAPTER FORTY-FOUR

I'm out on the road a full hour before I see them. Jeremiah's riding slow, trying to go easy on old Paint and not jostle Mariah, tucked in front of him in her cloak, leaning back into him. Midnight and me, we've been riding the length of the property, up and down checking fences. It's almost a full moon and when the clouds part I see clear as day. Why I'm really out here is to talk to Mariah before Sarah does. I guess I'm afraid what Mariah might say.

I've been back in my own bed with Sarah, but I worried about Mariah so much I hardly slept. I want to see for myself she's healthy and strong.

There's more to it though. She's been with Mama all this time and my mind's been right there with the two of them, trying to imagine what that's like. It'd be real different for each of them. Did they talk at all? Mariah's always got something to say, she's a talker, but how she'd take to Mama is what I don't know. Mama would be feeling pure love, and she'd be holding it in, knowing she couldn't express it the way she'd like. One thing's sure. She'd take the best care of our girl anybody in the world could. She'd treat her like the angel sent from heaven that she is.

She's waving now. Oh Mariah! Don't break our hearts. Not any more than this already has.

I dismount and wait for them.

As Jeremiah reins in Paint, Mariah leaps off into my outstretched arms.

"Oh Daddy! I'm so glad to see you!"

I bury my face in her hair. "You can't know how glad I am to have you back. We'll get you home now and wrap you up on the couch."

"But I'm fine, Daddy, I really am. Miss Nellie took as good care of me as if I were her own granddaughter." She looks at me carefully, Mariah does, saying that, and a shiver runs through me.

I'm quiet, riding her into our barnyard on Midnight. Jeremiah follows close behind.

"Shall I head home now?"

I ease Midnight around so I can look at him.

"Yes, there's no more to be done today. You've brought her back safe and kept her covered up in her hood. Thanks for your help." I come close to choking on how poor words are to say what's in my heart.

His blue eyes, looking from me to Mariah and back, are full of love for her. Maybe even for me? I see a new appreciation for him in Mariah's eyes when she looks at him. He reaches into the saddlebag, then leans forward and hands me a packet wrapped in brown paper.

"Miss Nellie sent this with her. It's tea to help with her healing." Next he gives me my traveling bag, then Mariah's schoolbag. "Here's the work she did while she was there." He glances at her shyly. "Don't she look fine, our Mariah?"

I smile, and the urge I have is to embrace him. But we're both on horseback and he turns and rides off.

Why do I feel so close to this man? Is it because he's unhappy in his home family and I feel the suffering running deep in him that somehow makes him kind? Hank Dexter's the opposite. It's like when lightning hits and for an instant you see something clear and sharp. Hank Dexter's suffering, whatever cause it might have, makes him mean.

Sarah comes out to meet us. Good. She's been strange these last few days. Her reaction to Mariah going to colored town has come between us like nothing ever has before. I've been praying over it. I don't know who exactly I pray to but I've become a praying man.

Mariah is sidesaddle in front of me. She slides off into Sarah's arms. Sarah takes her by the shoulders and holds her away from her. "You look fine and healthy, Mariah. I'm thankful you're a good strong girl. You'll be just fine. You can go to school tomorrow with your sisters."

"Are they in bed already, Mother?"

"Yes, though I think Elizabeth's probably staying awake to see you. She's left their door wide open."

I settle Mariah on the couch and pull up a straight-back chair to sit next to her. I want to be as close to her as I can. It's a relief when Sarah leaves for the kitchen and says, "I have to make your lunches for tomorrow."

I want Mariah to tell me about Mama. She's been near Mama all this time, what have they been saying to each other? If only there weren't all this stuff we've got to hide! Sometimes I think it'll drive me crazy. I just want to feel close to Mama through Mariah. I need that so bad. I need somebody to feel close to and it's Mama. I'll never be close to Sarah. I know that now. She's a white woman. What made me think she could be a real wife to me? She belongs to that whole different life she grew up in. She don't know what slavery is. Never seen it even. She don't know how splendid it is to me that I own this place, that I can take off from work and sit here next to my daughter and talk to her and no old marsa's gonna take the lash to us.

"Daddy!" Mariah reaches out and shakes my arm. She's smiling. "What on earth are you thinking about? You should see your face!"

I gaze at her a moment. "I'm thinking how wonderful it is to be here with you." I hesitate. "Was it hard, what you had to go through?"

"No, Daddy." Her little hand squeezes my arm. "Miss Nellie was so gentle and loving with me." She looks off beyond me as if she's seeing pictures in her mind. "She seemed so pleased to see me studying, doing my schoolwork. We had good conversations, Miss Nellie and I."

I scoot forward on my chair. "You did? What about?"

Sarah looks in the door at us. I notice Mariah waits till she's gone and only then says, "I told her how we've talked in school about the war that might be coming, and about slavery." She lowers her head, not looking at me. "Miss Nellie was a slave. She told me some of her experiences." I stop breathing. Mariah is silent. I don't know what my voice would sound like if I tried to speak right now. Mariah takes hold of my hand. "It is so awful to realize slavery is still going on and it might take a war to end it. Daddy, please don't go to war!"

My God. I had not thought of such a thing. The poor child, worrying about that.

She stares at me strangely now. "It must be the awfulest thing in the world to be a slave." She is waiting for me to say something.

I swallow, try to look into her eyes, swallow again. "I can't tell you, Mariah, how glad I am you and Miss Nellie got to have those talks." I get up and leave because I am close to tears. I'm not sure Mariah hears my words as I leave the room, tripping on the rug, "I wish I could have been there with you."

MARY ANDERSON PARKS

CHAPTER FORTY-FIVE
Sarah

Something's wrong. I feel cut off from what's happening. It hurt me deeply when Tom sent Mariah to that colored woman in Milford. How could he? Folks don't do such things. How does he know about the woman in the first place? Jeremiah buys tea from her for Daniel, and salve. But why would Tom trust our daughter to her? Who is she? Awful thoughts have come to my mind these past days. How old is she? I tried to find out from Mariah. She just says she's a grandma. She calls her a "lady," or "Miss Nellie." What has Tom done to our Mariah, leaving her in the care of coloreds? I feel more distance from him than ever. We haven't made love and that's what brings us close, reassures me. But we haven't for too long. I count the days on my fingers. He wouldn't ever go to another woman, my Tom. Would he? He's the best husband there could be. Except for this.

Mariah too seems distant. I missed having her here to help me and talk to, yet when she came home I held back from telling her how I missed her. Even though I was so glad to see her. Now it's her father she wants to be near. And he, my goodness, he hangs on her every word.

I think I'm jealous. Of Mariah, and the colored woman, whoever she is. My feelings are all mixed up. There's no one to talk to. Certainly not my mother. I know she can tell something's bothering me. She's been watching me in church. Asked why Mariah wasn't with us. "She's not feeling well," I said. "Still?" Mother asked. She must think I'm the one acting distant, the way I've avoided talking to her.

Daniel's been affected too. He hardly came out of his room those three days Mariah was gone. I hope he doesn't feel responsible for what happened to her, but I think he does. He feels he should somehow have kept it from happening.

I wonder what folks are saying about Hank Dexter getting shot in the leg and the hand. To think I considered marrying that man! I worry folks might connect it with us. They seem to be treating us differently, kind of skirting around us. Makes me not even want to go to church if it means more people I end up feeling separate from. Course it's Tom matters most. He's the one I want to be close to.

He sees me sitting out here on the back steps in my apron. He's already waved a couple times but he doesn't come over and join me like I wish he would. He's always kept a distance between us. It's almost like he's playing a part in a play. I enjoyed reading Shakespeare in school. We read *As You Like It* and talked about all the world being a stage and all the men and women merely players I wonder what part does Tom think he's playing? Somehow that makes me smile.

He comes out of the barn, a hoe balanced on one hand, and looks over at me. "Hey young girl. Good to see you smiling!"

Does he finally want to make love again? I see he does from the gleam in his eyes. It's been eleven long days.

I pat the spot next to me on the step. After a moment, he leans the hoe against the barn, walks slowly over to me. I feel my belly tighten as I watch, drawn to him by the strength and grace in how he moves.

I glint my eyes up at him. "Tommy's sleeping. It's his naptime. The girls won't be home from school for an hour or more." I stand up.

He slides his arm around my shoulders and squeezes me against him. I wrap my arm around his waist and we go upstairs, headed for our bed. Makes me remember our first night together. As always, I push away the memory of his fear of hurting me, though it feels important, it feels connected to the distance that lies lurking, ready to plant itself between us. For the next hour we erase the distance in the way that works best for us. I always thank God after we make love. What an amazing gift it is.

Tom is urgent in his lovemaking, forceful. At one moment he raises his head to look at me and I see fear and sorrow in his eyes. A kind of torment.

MARY ANDERSON PARKS

Chapter Forty-Six
Sarah

Sitting at the table peeling potatoes, I gaze out at the hollyhocks, not my favorite flower but hardy. You can count on hollyhocks to keep coming up on their own.

Snow will be late this year. Sometimes we get it in October, but not this year. I like it when we're snowed in, deep down in winter. We make love more. Daydreaming about when Tom made love to me two days ago, I feel the soft pressure of his hands on my face as he leaned back to look at me with that odd torment in his eyes. Yet his hands cradling my face were full of gentleness, made me feel special, like I'm a princess. A thrill of pleasure runs through me. I miss him even when he's gone just for the day like he is now. I don't understand all of what he does. I know he trades, buys and sells livestock, does an occasional real estate deal. Daniel has left everything under Tom's management, but Tom always reports each transaction to him to help him feel part of things. He used to with me, but now I have all the children to take care of. Daniel sleeps most of the time these days, but when Tom goes over accounts with him he perks up a good deal.

I'm surprised to hear a horse's neigh. I was so lost in my thoughts I didn't hear the rider come up. I run to the kitchen door, open it to see my oldest brother dismounting.

"Matthew! It's glad I am to see you!"

"Sorry it's been so long. Father's had me working on repairs and I have to make use of the daylight hours best I can, but even with Luke helping—well, you know how it is."

"I made two apple pies today. They're cool enough to eat. Let me cut you a big piece." I pour a cup of coffee to go with the pie. "Oh Matthew, it's just so good to see you. And have you all to myself for once!"

"Not for long. Mother sent me here on an errand. Gosh you're looking good, Sarah. Married life agrees with you." Then he blushes. My family's not much on compliments. Or on talking about things as personal as married life, come to think of it.

"You look fine and healthy too, Matthew. What errand?"

"Oh not exactly an errand. We saw Tom ride past earlier. Is he off somewhere for the day?"

"Yes. Yes he is." I frown, puzzled, and ask, "What does Tom being away for the day have to do with Mother's errand?"

"Oh it's just that Mother had the idea she'd like to come visit you. She asked me to ride over and see if you'd have time for that. Fact is, Sarah, something's worrying her, but course she won't talk about it."

"No. She wouldn't. I know how she is."

What could it be? Does she know about Mariah? Despite all our efforts to keep everything secret? Oh please don't let it be that.

"Well, I'll probably never find out," Matthew says cheerfully, leaning his big frame against the chair back. "My guess is she has something she's going to tell you and nobody else. Oh, there's one more thing. She said for me to find out when the girls get home from school."

Oh no. Then it must be about Mariah. "They get home around half past four, Matthew. She better come right now because Tommy's taking his nap and it sounds like she wants to talk to me alone. Tell her Daniel sleeps all afternoon. I mentioned that to her on Sunday when she asked about him."

"Okay then. I'll ride back and tell her. The pie was delicious. Good as Ma's. The Lord sure blessed us with a fine apple crop this year."

Watching him ride off, I think about the short distance between our two farms, yet how seldom any of us see one another. Only at church. How like Father he is. Though I don't imagine Matthew ever questions any part of his religion, and I happen to know Father does. Tom told me about a talk they had when we were courting, and Father expressed he had doubts on some things in the Bible. It made me happy Tom told me. Brought us closer, having a secret to share. It hasn't happened often. Hardly at all.

Mother keeping things to herself is different from what Tom does. I can't put my finger on it, but it's different. It's like . . . oh my, how wintry-looking our maple trees are, the rich vibrancy of russet, gold and orange gone. They held their leaves longer this year. To soothe us? It's like . . . like Tom has one foot in some other world.

Chapter Forty-Seven
Sarah

Mother arrives in the one horse buggy. She looks very small in it by herself. Her hair, almost all gray now, is in a tight bun at the back of her head. And yes, she looks worried.

"Sarah, come help carry in these jars I brought you. Vegetables and fruits both. I did a lot of canning this summer with cousin Minnie helping and we've got more than plenty."

"Let me take your coat and hat and gloves. I have a nice fire going in the fireplace."

"Well, carry these jars in first. I put them in boxes to carry easier. You'll make good use of the boxes."

"We'll make good use of the food, too, Mother. Everybody has a good appetite in our family."

"Yes, I know. Now you have as many as I did. If we count Henry, poor boy. Amanda's almost six, right? And little Tommy?"

"Tommy's twenty-two months."

"You're sure he'll nap longer?" The frown lines deepen between her eyebrows.

"Yes. Just sit down and rest, Mother. He's due to sleep at least another half hour. And he always plays in his crib when he first wakes up."

"Sarah, finish the job and put all the jars down in the cellar. You started down with one box and then stopped. I don't like to see a job left undone."

"All right." I barely suppress an exasperated sigh. "Let me pour you a cup of coffee first. I've got it steaming hot the way you like it."

I pour her coffee, then carry one box down to the cellar, come back and get the other one.

"Don't hurry on those narrow steps, Sarah. You're not pregnant again, are you?" She gives me a sharp, critical glance.

"Why, what if I am? We might well have several more! Tom loves children." And, I smile to myself, we don't really know how not to have them. "You know what a help children are on a farm." I hurry down the short flight of stairs, defying Mother's cautions, deposit the box and run back up. Keeping on the run helps me hold off thoughts of what Mother may know about Mariah.

As I close the cellar door behind me, Mother says in a low voice, "I don't think you should have more children."

My face must show that her statement stuns me.

"Oh Sarah, I'm so nervous I hardly know what I'm saying."

"Let me cut you a slice of apple pie. Maybe you're hungry. That could be why your nerves are acting up. You probably haven't taken time to eat properly. You're too thin, Mother."

"Sit down. I've come to tell you terrible news. You must never speak of it to anyone. Never." Her thin forearms lie tensely on the table. "I wouldn't be able to eat a bite of pie. I'd be sick to my stomach." Her mouth locks itself into a grim line.

I finally sit, disappointed to have no excuse for another piece of pie. I'd been looking forward to it.

"Sarah, pay attention! I'm not going to say any of this twice. And before we know it, the girls will be home."

"Mother, what on earth are you going to tell me? If this is about Mariah—"

"It's about all of you. And I don't know if I should even be telling you because it's a rumor and not for sure true. But when I think about your children, all with that curly hair and tanning as brown as berries in summer, never getting sunburnt . . ." Her voice trails off and she sighs deeply. "It is my duty to warn you not to have more children."

"You're not making sense, Mother. We have fine healthy children. Except for Henry. He wasn't strong enough to make it through that hard winter when he got the sickness in his lungs. It was his heart too, that was weak."

"Sarah, listen to me! There's a rumor going around, it was cousin Minnie told me, she'd been talking to a cousin of the Dexters, a rumor that—" She stops, draws in her breath. "That your Tom has colored blood. That he traveled up here from Virginia with a colored woman."

My body goes cold. Cold in my bones. The room shifts and moves around me, unfamiliar. The edges of the teakettle blur, the checks on the blue and white tablecloth run together. I want Mother out of my house. Right this minute! I can't stand her sitting here saying these words. Dizziness sweeps over me. I close my eyes and grip the sides of the wooden seat I'm sitting on so I won't fall off.

Mother rises from her chair. I half see her do that but it's unreal, it's happening somewhere else.

"You've gone all white, Sarah. You're white as a sheet." I hear the words from far away and I hear their irony because my mind is working. It is working furiously fast. Things are coming together, falling in place. I glimpse answers to questions that have been in my mind since we married. Tom always wears an undershirt when we make love. Even in the hottest weather. This one time he forgot. I was thrilled, feeling his bare back under my moving hands and then I cried out, "What are these ridges across your back?" I remember he said, "It's from an illness only poor children get, you wouldn't know about it." But he couldn't go on making love. We didn't talk about it then or after. I decided it bothered him to remember his family being so poor and the suffering they must have gone through. He never talks about them and I've gotten used to that. But now, in my mind, I see him getting lashed across his back with a whip.

Mother slaps the sides of my face, hard.

"Stop it," I say. "Just stop it!"

"I thought you were going to faint. It's only a rumor, you know. It might not be true. You know how people gossip."

"The way you talked about our children, how tan they get and their hair—" My voice breaks.

"Sarah, I came here to tell you so you wouldn't hear it from somebody else first. What Minnie heard was about a slave owner from Virginia, name of Jones, coming through Blanchester many years ago looking for a light-skinned runaway called Tom, traveling with a woman slave this man Jones said was Tom's mother."

Every word hits me like she's still slapping my face. "Stop, Mother. I mean it. I'll pass out if you keep on. I can't take this."

She lifts her chin, her stubborn chin. "Well let me tell you, Sarah. It will kill your father if he hears of this—I pray the Lord he won't—and if you leave Tom and come running home to us, that will for sure kill him. There's never been anything like this in the Long family."

I stand up trembling, unsteady on my feet. "Go away, Mother. Don't worry about me running home to you. I love Tom. I don't know if you can even imagine the way I love him. I don't think you've ever loved anybody like I love Tom."

I see in her face how frightened she is by my rage. Desperate to get her out of my house, I yell. "Go!"

"Well, I never!" She starts gathering up her things.

As I leave the kitchen, I hear the back door close. I make my way to the couch our Mariah lay on during those awful hours. My legs don't work right and I stumble. When the girls get home, I'll send Mariah upstairs to take care of Tommy. Sophia and Elizabeth will start supper, Amanda can help.

My body is so cold. I pull the blanket over me that I keep folded on the back of the couch. That's the last thing I remember until I wake to hear voices coming from the kitchen.

"Mother's sick, so we made supper. We couldn't wake her."

"Your mother's never sick."

"But Daddy—"

"All right, Elizabeth. We should let her sleep. But we'll fix her a big plate of food. She'll be hungry when she wakes up." I close my eyes.

"I want my mommy!"

"Shush, Tommy. You'll wake her."

"Elizabeth, ask Uncle Daniel if he wants supper out here with us or in his room."

"There's pie, Daddy," Sophia says. "I bet she's tired from making the pies. She made apple. She knows apple is your favorite."

"And she pared lots and lots of potatoes," Amanda puts in.

"Uncle Daniel is sleeping really soundly."

"Well, let him sleep then. Oh I forgot. Whose glove is this? I found it outside."

"Not mine, Daddy."

"Not mine."

"That's Grandma Long's glove." Mariah's voice. "She's the only one has those little pads sewn into the finger tips."

"Yes," Amanda pipes up. "She wears those gloves to church."

"Well, why was her glove out in our barnyard? Was she here today?"

"We don't know, Daddy."

"She wasn't when we got home."

"What's wrong, Daddy?" That is Mariah's soft voice.

"It's not like her to lose track of anything," Tom says. "She hardly ever visits your mother, and she always wants to see you children when she's here. She must have come earlier, when your mother was up and about and you were still in school."

"Yes," Elizabeth says. "Somebody had eaten part of one of the pies."

"Maybe she left in a hurry was why she dropped a glove." Tom goes on in that same voice, as if talking to himself. "I better go check on your mother."

I turn my head toward the back of the couch, pretending to be asleep. Tom's footsteps come in, stop, then move closer. He lays his hand on my shoulder. After a few moments, he takes his hand away and I hear his steps go back to the kitchen.

"All right, girls. After you clean up, start your homework. I've got chores to do."

The kitchen door bangs.

I open my eyes, feeling very wide awake. Will he notice a difference when I have to get up from here and talk to him?

A sudden thought stops my breath. If I don't tell him what Mother said, what I am now sure of, will I create new distance between us? I feel terribly cold and pull the blanket tighter.

The house is quiet when I wake again. Tom is sitting next to me like he did with Mariah when she lay here. I reach out and he takes my hand in both of his.

"Are you all right, Sarah?"

He sounds worried.

"Yes, I'm all right. Just tired. This baby is maybe the most active one yet. Kicks me with its little feet like it wants to come out."

"Was your mother here today?"

"Yes. She brought us two boxes of canned fruit and vegetables she put up this summer."

"She came over just for that? Any news or gossip?"

"Snow is right around the corner. I guess she wants to get out while she still can."

"I found her glove outside. We'll give it to her on Sunday. I'm worried about Daniel. He hasn't had any supper. Slept right through. First time. Come in the kitchen, Sarah, and have something to eat. I'll get the fire going stronger and heat up your food. Then I'll check on him again."

Chapter Forty-Eight

Sarah holds me in the night. Snuggles up close. She seems full of tenderness toward me. Maybe it's the baby affecting her that way. She's like that. I think it's about two or three months till it comes. Or could be the sudden change in the weather. It's turning cold. The smell of snow is in the air, the crisp feeling of it. I'd say two days at most and we'll be up to our ears. Little Amanda will be, at least. I smile, thinking that.

I hope Daniel's warm enough down there. That's my last clear thought as I drift off. And a sense that Sarah is awake. Maybe she's not ready yet to sleep for the night after her long nap. Did she say her mother had news to tell? Can't remember, don't want to think about it.

I wake early, hurry down and kindle the fire up good, then go in Daniel's room, calling out his name. He lies in bed with the covers up to his chin, eyes wide open.

"Cold, ain't it. Spect snow's comin."

"Yes. You must be hungry, Daniel. Don't know what you had for lunch but you plumb missed supper altogether last night."

"Well Tom, I'm done eating. I'm fixin to be gone before we all get snowed in. Don't want to make things harder for you. That undertaker broke his sleigh makin the turns too fast. How would you ever get me out of here? No, I'm gonna go today."

"What the hell, Dan?"

"Just accept it, Tom. That's best. I would like to see everybody though, before they go off to school."

He closes his eyes, appears to be sleeping, but then speaks. "Tell Mariah to bring her Bible. I want to hear the twenty-third psalm."

"All right, Daniel. I'll get Sarah too. It's still a bit early."

His eyes flicker open, a slight glaze over them. "Yes, Sarah's mother was here yesterday. That Sarah's a damn fine woman. She'll have something to tell you one of these days." A hoarse sound comes from deep down in his throat. "You better get all of them up. I don't have long."

I take the stairs two, three at a time. "Everybody up! Uncle Daniel's dyin. Mariah, bring your Bible." I can't believe how quickly they come, Mariah with her Bible, Elizabeth carrying Tommy, Amanda holding onto Sophia's nightgown. Sarah's first though. She goes right to Daniel, kneels by his bed, lays her cheek on his. We all crowd around.

"The twenty-third psalm, Mariah. That's what he wants to hear."

"The Lord is my shepherd; I shall not want." Mariah begins before she finds her place. She likely knows the whole damn thing by heart. When she finishes, she bends closer to him. "Anything else, Uncle Daniel?"

"Psalm one hundred, Mariah, about mercy."

"That's a short one. You've asked for it so many times, I can say it from memory." When she comes to 'his mercy is everlasting,' she bows her head.

"I love you all, more than I can tell you. You're my family," Daniel says, his voice cracking. "Tom, hold your head high, you hear me? You're a successful man and a good, honest man. Everybody in this community dang well better respect you. You've done a lot for them."

I can't hold the tears in any longer when he says all that, weak as he is.

His head falls back on the pillow.

"I wish Jeremiah was here too. Tell him . . ." His voice stops and our Daniel slips away, his hand lifeless in my own. I'll never know what he wanted me to tell Jeremiah. People carry some secrets with them into death.

Chapter Forty-Nine

Sunk in the worn comfortable chair by the front window, I marvel at our little world blanketed deeper and deeper in snow and silence. Whiteness everywhere. Snowed in, I feel safer. Means we're in the north. Means nobody can reach us easy.

It started falling late evening of the day Daniel died and kept on steady through the night until by morning the girls couldn't get out to go to school. The undertaker carried him away in the afternoon, in a wagon. Daniel wanted to spare us trouble and he did. I choke up when I think of that.

I'd wanted to tell him about the real estate deal I closed the day before. It made us a heap of money and the folks on both sides were happy. I always looked forward to reporting to him, as if a thing hadn't really happened until I told him the details of how it went. Daniel had given me good advice how to handle the matter and he would have liked hearing how well it worked out.

But those days of talking things over with him, knowing he's standing by me, are gone. Except not really because I hear his voice most every day, suggesting, warning, praising me when I do good. Not just work, family things too. He's right here with me like a guardian angel. Like Mama.

It's been well over a month now. We're a good ways along through January. The only service we had was in church the Sunday after his 'passing' as the preacher called it. There weren't many in the congregation because of snow but Sarah insisted on going. Jeremiah crowded in our buggy with us and he and I got out and cleared space around the wheels every time we got stuck. Longs made it in too but they still have Matthew and Luke home to help. Carrie's off and married and so is Mark, their middle son.

I heard Sarah tell her mother another baby's coming and she'll likely need help with the birthing. Lately they've been acting awful stiff toward each other, and I've been wondering about that.

"I'd be fine with just Doc Kilroy," Sarah declared, staring at her mother stern-like, "but he'll never make it to our place if winter keeps on hard as it started."

"You're not far along. I didn't even know when I was over to your—"

Sarah gave her mother another one of those cold looks. "No, you had other things on your mind. You know how I am, I don't show much the first six or seven months, then I pop way out in front. And this baby wants to come early; I can tell by the kicking and turning."

As I run that conversation through my mind, it worries me. I'm tired from all we been through. I close my eyes and feel I could drift right off to sleep. Winter's good for that. A man needs to rest from his labors. Says so in the Bible. But they don't tell slaves that part. No wonder folks don't want us to learn to read.

I lean my head back, loll it around. Must be I doze off because I jerk awake with the question in my mind that's been lying there since Daniel planted it. What did he mean, Sarah would have something to tell me one day? And saying that right after telling me Sarah's mother had been here to see her.

So he was awake. Sarah would have thought he was asleep because he'd taken to napping right through the afternoons. He heard whatever it was Sarah's mother came to tell her. That was the day I got home and found Sarah sleeping on the couch, the children saying she was sick. Since then she's been nicer to me even than in our courting days. Could be she's sorry for me because of Daniel dying. Here she is now, coming to find me.

"There you are! I've looked all over. Even out to the barn. You've been so good about clearing a path. I can walk over lively as a spring chicken."

I cleared a horse path to the road too, but it's not much use with the road like it is. I worry about when the baby comes. How will anybody get in to help us?

"Do you have a minute to sit with me, Sarah?"

"Of course I do!" She smiles, real pleased, I can tell.

"You always smell so good. You been baking?"

"Yes, that dutch oven in the fireplace works much better since you cleaned it out."

She pushes an armchair closer to mine, settles herself in it carefully. She's getting big.

"Sarah."

"What, Tom?"

"I miss Daniel awful bad."

"I know you do. I miss him too. He's been here in this house all our married life. He loved the children like they were his own. And you, Tom. He loved you powerful hard."

"I don't feel as safe with him gone." I speak low, but she hears. I see a new kind of listening come into her eyes. "He's been sort of like my protector from the first day I got to Milford."

"Were you alone when you met him?" Now she's the one whose voice drops low.

"Why do you ask that, Sarah?"

She looks me in the eye, doesn't say anything. I feel a wave of fear and try to ride it, conquer it.

"Sarah, Daniel talked to me before I went upstairs and called all of you that morning."

"Yes?" She says it encouragingly and I go on.

"He was awake, Sarah, the day before that when your mother visited you. He heard something important."

She stares at her hands folded over the big bump that is our baby. A hush builds between us.

"What did she tell you?" I ask at last.

Sarah returns my gaze, her eyes full of the love and sympathy I've been feeling coming from her these past weeks. Sympathy, yes! That's what it is. Why? What does she know?

She swallows. "Just rumors, Tom. She'd heard some rumors."

My hand goes to my forehead, shading my face. I'm afraid to look at her. "About me?"

"Yes, Tom." She lays her hand on my arm. "We don't have to talk about this if it's too painful. As Mother said, they're only rumors."

I don't want to cry. I've cried too many tears. For Mariah. For Daniel. For all of us. I can't go on talking with her. I don't have right words to say. But she scoots her chair even closer, leans over to grasp my arm with both her hands.

"Tom, I can live with this. So can you. They just gossip, you know. Nothing may come of it."

She shakes my arm urgently. "Tom!"

I lift my head and despite mighty efforts my face is streaked with tears. Hers is too.

"Sarah, sit on my lap. I can hold you both. You're not heavy even with the baby."

I hold her a long, long time. I hear one of the children come in, stop, and tiptoe out.

MARY ANDERSON PARKS

CHAPTER FIFTY
Sarah

I dive in and start ironing everything in my ironing basket. I still don't like niggers, don't want to be around them. The iron says it for me, presses the thought hard and hot into the shirt.

But Tom's my love. He's the father of my children. And now he's my friend. I won't tell him, of course, how I feel about niggers, though I did once, before I knew. Looking back, I see it hurt him. I pause, suspending the iron in the air, remembering when it was. It was when he had Jeremiah take Mariah to that woman. I upend the iron, the shirt only half done. Mother said the rumor was that a colored woman walked up from Virginia with him. Who was she, how old? Where is she now, right there in Milford? Is she the woman he trusted to help Mariah? Did Ma say she was his mother?

I'd best not think on all that. I don't want to know. I want it to be all over.

I pick up the iron, plunge it into the shirtsleeve. The action calms my mind.

After the ironing, I'll bake a custard pie. They all like custard pie, especially little Tommy, and we've got lots of eggs on hand.

I feel so restless. I can't wait to see the baby. I want to hold him in my arms. I'm almost sure he's a boy because I'm carrying him high like with Henry and Tommy. I rub my hands on the sides of my belly. He seems big enough to pop out right now.

Tom comes up from behind and his arms go around me. "What are you up to now, young girl?"

I turn in his arms to face him. "Watch out or I'll poke you with my baby!"

"He's a tough one, ain't he? Yessir! I've felt those kicks of his. He's out to get me, that one."

He gives me the look I know well.

"The girls are busy at the kitchen table doing schoolwork. I told them they can play charades when they finish. They love that."

"Is Tommy napping?"

"I hope so. Do you want to go up with me and check?" I give him a look of my own.

Tommy's still sleeping soundly and within minutes Tom and I are in our bed making love, with adjustments for the bump. Afterward, I roll over onto my back, stretching out full length.

"You were relaxed, Tom. I loved that."

He looks deep into my eyes. "I love you, Sarah."

Has he ever said those words to me before?

"I wish I didn't have to go off and leave you tomorrow. I was waiting for a thaw and tomorrow the roads will be passable. It's melting fast."

I keep silent.

"It's a livestock transaction. I have to stay away one night. Will you mind too much? You won't be frightened, will you?" He's never asked me that until now.

"Not if Jeremiah keeps coming over to help every day like he's been doing."

"Have you noticed how when you're pregnant he helps me watch over you?"

"Yes, I have." My face grows hot. I wish it were night with soft lamplight. Tom wouldn't be able to see me as well. There is so much unspoken between us. I see in his eyes and the tender way he made love to me that a great burden has been lifted from him, knowing that I know and still love him. In an odd way the burden has shifted to me to carry, and the fear of exposure is something we will now face together for the rest of our lives. The great thing is, I feel truly close to Tom for the first time.

"I hear little Tommy. I'll get him out of his crib." At the door of our room I turn, fear gathering substance, gripping me. "I wish you didn't have to go out in the world. It felt safe being snowed in." I run to the window to look out. "It's thawing for sure. Did you see that wagon go by earlier? It was bumping right along."

"I did. But remember what Daniel told me. I have to hold my head up, Sarah. I have to keep my confidence."

"Yes, you're right." I walk over, take his hand and hold him with my gaze. "We haven't done anything wrong, Tom. We just love each other. And we're raising our family in a good way."

CHAPTER FIFTY-ONE
Sarah

He's gone already when I get up the next morning. I walk into the kitchen carrying Tommy and settle him in his high chair, the smell of good strong coffee reminding me I am loved. As always, Tom has sliced bacon and left the fire well kindled. I'll have cows to milk though, and later chickens to feed. Eggs to gather.

"We can go back to school today, don't you think?" Mariah asks, peering out the window. Elizabeth rushes in, flings open the back door. "Yes, the Jones girls will be comin round the mountain, trudging through the snow. Nothing keeps those girls from learning! Lucky we've got good high boots. Look at that snow melt!"

"Let me see the snow melt! Can I play in it?"

I give Amanda a quick hug. "No, dear. When you get home, maybe."

"I wish Tommy could go to school. He and I could play at recess."

"Well he can't, he's still a baby. Sophia, feed him some applesauce, please. He's been waiting patiently for the four of you to come downstairs."

Elizabeth starts giving him a tickle. His grins get wider and wider until he laughs uncontrollably. "Tickle, tickle," she says. "Tickle tickle little Tommy."

"Now stop laughing everybody. How can Sophia feed him if he's giggling?" I ask.

"I can't," Sophia says. "It's like spooning food into a spitting baboon."

Elizabeth responds to my half-hearted command to stop laughing with a frown of mock sternness that sends them off again.

Wanting to set an example, I try again to be serious. "Your lunch boxes are packed from last night and lined up by the door with your boots."

"Wonderful!" Elizabeth crows. "We'll jump right in them as we go out." She winks at me, and I smile back. I never can resist her when she's cutting up. Where does she get that energy and irrepressible spirit?

They eat their fried eggs, bacon, and leftover cornbread from last night. Tom did the milking, I realize when I see the bucket of warm milk at the far end of the counter. So the children have milk with breakfast. As they leave, all four of them take time to give Tommy a kiss in his high chair. He looks after them wistfully when the door closes.

I sit down with a cup of coffee and eat what cornbread is left. I'll fry up the rest of the bacon later. Tommy watches me. He looks more and more like his father. A handsome little fellow.

"Sissies go school," he says soberly.

"Yes, your sisters go to school."

How much it helps to have the children. They keep me rooted right here in this place, this moment. And now comes Jeremiah's rap at the door.

"Come in, Jeremiah."

He takes off his hat and stands awkwardly just inside the door.

"Oh please Jeremiah, pour yourself a cup of coffee and sit with me and Tommy."

He does pour himself coffee but stays standing. He aims a grin at Tommy, who grins back and bounces up and down in his chair.

"Well no, I need to get to work. Tom doesn't want you out in that slippery slush."

"It's good for me to get out! I need exercise. Have you had eggs and bacon this morning?" He mumbles something I can't make out. He's always like that around me, gets real shy, especially when Tom's not here.

"Sit down!" I tell him. I fry three more eggs and the remaining strips of bacon, slide them onto a plate and set it in front of him. Then I sit down myself.

"Oh Jeremiah, we rely on you so much. What will we do when you take a wife? I see young girls at church giving you the eye."

Well that was the wrong thing to say! He goes red as a beet, gets up to pour himself more coffee. Perched again on the edge of his chair, he eats hungrily, turning now and then to make funny faces for little Tommy, who adores him. Tommy giggles, beside himself with joy. Though Jeremiah can't often be coaxed into the house, today he lingers. After he's done eating, he gives me a worried glance.

"Sarah, I saw Tom before he left, helped him finish up in the milk house, so that's all done."

"Why thank you, Jeremiah."

I watch as he gathers up his plate and cup, fork and knife, carries them to the sink, comes back to the table and sits down awkwardly.

"Did you have more to tell me?"

"He said I wasn't to leave you alone while he's gone. Not for a minute. I guess because of the baby due to come soon." He lowers his voice. "And what happened to Mariah. He isn't the same since."

"Yes, I know."

"I'll sleep out in the barn. It's warm there with the cows and horses." He mumbles his next words.

"What, Jeremiah?"

"Just said my stuff for making drawings is out there. Don't know why I went and told you that." He shakes his head and gets up. "I better go out to the chicken house, give them their feed. That scratching shed Tom and me built works real good. When they can't go outside in winter, they go in there and scratch in the straw, pecking and strutting like they do."

I know he's talking to cover up his embarrassment about telling me he does drawings. I never knew that about him. If I can, I'll make him come in the house with his drawing things but I doubt I'll succeed. At least we'll make him join us for meals. It's not just Tommy; all the children adore him.

"Tommy and I will come with you," I announce. "He loves to see the chickens. And that one hen that's in there setting? He especially likes to visit her."

I pull on my boots and a coat. Then I button Tommy into his warm winter coat and cover his head with a knitted hat with flaps that come down over his ears.

Jeremiah carries Tommy up on his shoulder, goes to the barn and slings a sack of feed over his other shoulder. We make our way along toward the chicken house, me following close behind.

"Thank you for keeping a path shoveled for me to get out here."

"Tom said to."

"Well anyway, thanks."

His long eyelashes are dusted with flakes of the light snow beginning to fall. "No way to keep her inside is what he told me, so you and me will make it safe as we can." I smile, wondering do they both think I should save them worry and stay in the house? Well, I don't intend to. The more I keep on the move, the easier my babies come. The baby gives a sudden kick and I catch hold of Jeremiah to keep my balance. He stops, looks at me in surprise.

"It's nothing. I'm fine now. Charlie gave me a really sudden kick." It embarrasses me to talk to him about the baby but after all, he may be the one who ends up delivering it. I grin at the thought. "He's more active than the other babies were. Charles is what we've decided to name him. If he's a boy, and I'm sure he is."

At the end of the path, we come to the tight-built chicken house Tom and Jeremiah designed and put up, with its lean-to scratching shed attached. We hear loud clucking from inside as we approach. Jeremiah holds the sack open. Tommy reaches in, grabs a handful of feed and throws it over the shed's wall made of wooden slats. The rooster and a clutter of hens rush from their roosts into the scratching shed. We join Tommy in throwing handfuls of shelled corn. They don't have to go out in the snow at all. They do have their little swinging door so they can run in and out at will, but if the snow is deep or soft, we close up the little door, like it is now. They might run out one by one, disappear straight down into the snow, and not be found till spring thaw. They aren't the smartest creatures.

"Tommy, that's enough feed for them. We'll go in the big door and visit the setting hen. Keep her company."

"Compy," he repeats.

As we three appear inside the dimness of the chicken house, the rooster rustles in from the scratching shed spreading his wings wide, two hens clucking close behind him.

Jeremiah laughs. "You have to get in on everything, Mr. Rooster, don't you? Wait till you see what that hen's hatching, you'll be more puffed up than ever."

"Remember, Tommy, how we put eggs under her when she was in a setting mood? First we candled them to make sure they were fertile." I turn to Jeremiah. "I always explain things to Tommy. Some day he'll make sense of it, if he hears it enough times and sees it happen."

It strikes me that I am like the setting hen. Maybe that's why I bring Tommy out to visit her so often. Even though I keep active, I'm brooding away inside, waiting, like she is.

"I'll be back, broody hen," I murmur. I wish Tom were coming home tonight. Is he safe, wherever he is?

Giving Tommy a quick squeeze, I tell him, "Just you wait, Tommy. You and Mr. Rooster will be so excited when the chicks hatch, all tiny and yellow, making little peep sounds." Tommy claps his hands. He really does understand.

Jeremiah listens and watches. I do wonder sometimes what's in that boy's mind. Can't help thinking of him as a boy.

Impulsively, I seize his arm. "Bring your drawing things in the house when you have supper with us tonight, all right? You can sleep in Uncle Daniel's room. He has a small desk in there." I bite my lower lip, not wanting to admit fear, but the words burst out. "I don't want to be alone in the house with the children."

He gives me a long look that seems to see right into me and understand. "All right, if you'd feel better," he says simply.

What has he heard? What does he know? There was much feeling in his eyes. He hides behind those long lashes but I caught a glimpse.

We're all hiding, especially baby Charlie inside me. I want to see him.

CHAPTER FIFTY-TWO

I start for home before midday. The Ludlows are nice folks and happy about the price I got the buyer to give for their cattle, and they want me to stay for dinner. I told them I have to get home cause my wife's baby is due any time now and by the looks of the sky more snow is coming our way. Mrs. Ludlow packs me up some fried chicken and cornbread and I start eating it soon as I'm out of sight. Before I know it I'm singing "I Stood on the River of Jordan." There's nobody to hear me and I sing out deep and strong. Can't help feeling good. I got a fair cut on the deal and both sides are happy. They'll tell their neighbors. It's likely to lead to more business. I'm known for good solid paper work. Learned that from Daniel. I wish he was alive to share in this. The buyer goes to our church. Word will spread there. Did he look at me funny yesterday when I was negotiating? Maybe I imagined it. Folks who hear those rumors, I hope they'll think about how it happened a long time ago and the story might have got mixed up. By now I'm part of the community. They rely on me. They trust me when it comes to buying and selling land or livestock. They know I'm smart and honest.

Tom, don't get yourself all set up. Honest, are you? How do you figure that? Remember, pride goeth before a fall, like Daniel and me read in the Bible.

I'm not as worried though as I could be, as I have been all my years here in Ohio. That's because Sarah's standing by me. She knows and yet she loves me still. I start up singing again, this time it's "Didn't My Lord Deliver Daniel?" I come to a curve in the road and when I round the corner I see another buggy coming.

"That you, Tom Jones? Singing like that?"

I know this young man, helped him buy his farm. "I'll see you in church Sunday," I call out, smiling. "If we don't get snowed in again."

"Watch out for ice," he warns me. "You'll hit some black ice up ahead."

"Thanks, neighbor. I'll watch out."

It's doing me good to make this trip, get out in the world and practice what me and Sarah talked about. The ones who hear the rumors may not take it that serious if we act like everything's all right.

We'll keep going to church regular. I quit stopping by the saloon quite a while back. Afraid I'd run into Hank Dexter and kill him. Better not to drink anyway. I need to keep my head clear.

Snow's falling now. Steadily. At least, if it gets deep enough, it'll help cover slippery ice. Seems like dark is coming awful fast. The horse slows her pace.

"We got to keep going, Lady. They're all waiting for us at home. Still about ten miles to go." She turns her head to the side, trying to see me, then starts off at a trot.

"Not that fast, Lady," I rein her in. "Don't want us slipping on a patch of ice. We can't see a thing, can we? But we know the road's there. Just keep on, don't stop. The way this snow is falling, the road's gonna get wiped out but you'll get us there, strong mare that you are."

I talk to her like that all the way. Almost miss the turn to our place when we get to it but Lady knows, comes to a stop. Durn that Jeremiah. He's tried to shovel a path out to where the road has disappeared under a half foot of snow.

There he is still shoveling, floundering around in fast deepening snow.

"You can stop shoveling now, you damn fool!" He sees me laughing with relief at being back home and joins in. He's as relieved to have me back as I am to be here.

"I'll get out and we'll walk Lady in, leave the buggy here till a thaw comes."

"Yep," he says. "It's not a far distance but I couldn't make the path wide enough."

"You gave it a good try!" I poke him in the arm. "Were you afraid you'd have to deliver the baby?"

His face, already red from the cold, turns redder.

"Just glad you're back safe," he mumbles.

MARY ANDERSON PARKS

CHAPTER FIFTY-THREE

Three days of unrelenting snowfall. Turns out I can't make Jeremiah go home when I give it a half-hearted try.

"They must be worried about you at home, Jeremiah. They must need your help. I sure don't know what we'd a done without it."

"You folks need me more," he says shortly. "You're the only man on the place. They've got plenty of help at home. Won't hurt my brothers to slog around in the snow, do some work." He turns away, mumbling, "Need my pay more'n they need me. Nobody else bringing in money."

"I heard that," I say. "Look. I've been meaning to raise your pay anyway, and if you're going to stay here nights to help us out when the baby—"

He interrupts. "I didn't mean for you to hear."

Gosh darn, he looks like he might cry. I squeeze my eyes shut, praying for him not to. I couldn't take that.

"I don't want more money. Forget it. Just forget it and let me stay on in Mr. Fullerton's room if I'd be a help." He lowers his head. "It's awful at home and there ain't a damn thing I can do about any of it."

"If you're gonna be working more hours for us, you'll get paid more, dammit." I glare at him. "Do I have to fight you over this, out here in the snow?" Somehow my temper rising up makes me feel better. I lean in and shove him in the chest with the palm of my hand, which of course doesn't budge him. I should of known.

Is he hiding a grin? Goddammit, I'd swear he is.

I feel my lower lip jut out like marse Tom's. "You're right. I'm afraid I'd lose. I'm in fact damn sure I'd lose. Grin at me all you like. You're the last man in this county I'd want to fight." I shake my head. "A man who wrestled cows!"

We stare at each other a long moment and bust out laughing at the same time Elizabeth's lusty yell reaches us. "The baby's coming!"

I hear Mama's voice in my head as I rush inside, Jeremiah close behind: "You two act like little puppies playin!" How I wish she could be the one coming to help Sarah do the birthing.

"Mother's up in your bed, Mariah's with her," Sophia tells me, vigorously pumping water at the sink. Elizabeth, with Tommy on one hip, hops sideways from one foot to the other, Amanda latched onto her skirt.

I head for the stairs, take them three at a time, the motion in my muscles recalling other times I've raced up these stairs. The house seems dark after the brightness of snow. In our room, the curtains are drawn.

I become aware of Sarah sitting on the side of the bed, Mariah helping her out of her housedress, lifting it over her head, then slipping a white nightgown over Sarah and fitting her arms into the loose sleeves, and I am conscious this is the seventh time we've done all this. We're going to have another baby with us soon. My heart pounds from excitement or the stairs or both.

Mariah moves aside and I take Sarah's damp hand. She lets out a sudden cry, then hurries to find words to comfort me.

"It's all right. Don't worry. Get my mother here. Soon as you can. Have Jeremiah go." She's short of breath and her words burst out in quick gasps. "Pains coming fast."

She tries to smile. "Mariah will stay with me."

"She said it'll take too long to get the doctor," Mariah whispers.

"He wouldn't be able to get in anyway, the way the roads are."

I vault down the stairs, my feet hardly touching ground. Jeremiah's in the kitchen lifting a huge kettle of water onto the stove. Sophia carries in an armful of firewood. Amanda and Tommy are jumping around in a corner.

"Stay away from the stove, children," Elizabeth cautions.

I make myself wait till he sets the kettle safely on the stove. "Take the buggy and fetch Grandma Long double quick. I think the baby's coming any minute!"

He frowns. "The buggy's out there where we left it. Frozen in. I'll ride over on Paint. I can carry Mrs. Long behind me or she can ride her own horse."

"Hurry then."

He's out the door.

I go back upstairs, slowly. Sarah and I don't know if the rumors have reached her father. When Mrs. Long gets here, she'll shut me out of the room like she always does. I'll feel useless as tits on a boar.

I go in our room and tell Sarah Jeremiah's already left to get Mother Long.

Sarah is doubled over in pain, still sitting on the edge of the bed. Usually she likes to walk around, but maybe we're past that point. Mariah holds a damp washcloth to her mother's forehead.

"Need anything, Mariah?"

"Yes, a fresh pan of cold water. Take that small pan there on the table, Daddy."

I smile my thanks that she found some use for me. In the kitchen, Tommy holds up both arms.

"Uppy uppy Daddy!" That is a plea I never can resist. I lift him high in the air, then hug him tight. Poor little fellow, he won't be the baby much longer. Still holding him, I pump water into the pan with my other hand. I carry him and the pan of water slowly up the stairs.

Mrs. Long arrives breathless, quicker than I thought possible, brushes past me without a glance, enters our bedroom and shuts the door firmly behind her. In a few minutes Mariah comes out.

"She told me to get a chair and sit outside the door. She'll let me know when she needs things. She wants Elizabeth or Sophia to wait out here too."

"Which one, do you think?"

"Well, Elizabeth is best with the little ones, so I'd say Sophia."

"All right. I'll have her come up. Here's that pan of water."

"I'll take it in soon as she'll let me." She sighs and shrugs her shoulders. I shake my head.

Back in the kitchen, I set Tommy on the floor with Amanda and give them a box of store crackers to munch. Jeremiah pokes his head in at the back door.

"I watered Mrs. Long's horse and put her in the stall next to Lady, with a blanket over her. Pitched hay for her and Paint and the rest of them."

"Come in, Jeremiah. You did a good job, getting her here so fast. Seems like you flew. No baby yet. Better close that door, cold air coming in."

It is a comfort to have him with me and I go on saying things that don't really need saying. "I'll gather the eggs. Or you can, Jeremiah. Maybe you already did? Or I'll be in the milk house separating the cream. Churn some butter maybe, while I'm at it. Good thing the spring's close to the house and we could build the milk house over it, ain't it? Nice to have it right between here and the barn. Sarah likes that."

He nods agreement, and so do the girls, but I feel strange, unreal. It helps to talk about solid things.

Jeremiah gives me a long close look. "You all right, are you, Tom?"

I nod, no energy to talk more.

"Mrs. Long is a hard woman," he mutters on his way out. I'm pretty sure that's what he said.

I dread facing her. Maybe she won't look at me and I won't have to. I hear a muted scream from above. "Sophia, you're to go sit with Mariah outside the door for when Grandma Long needs you."

"All right, Daddy." But she doesn't go. Is she afraid? Hearing her mama scream like that? For some reason I am.

"Your mother said everything's going as it should." I hope she said that but don't remember if she did.

Another scream, louder. Does Sophia see me wince? Elizabeth kneels by Amanda and Tommy, speaks softly to them.

"That's normal, you know. Women do that in childbirth."

"Yes, Daddy." Sophia leaves to go upstairs.

"And you, Elizabeth, are to take care of the younger ones." I sigh. Why do I feel so weak all a sudden?

Elizabeth smiles. Mama's smile. "They're fine, playing here. Here's a cup of hot coffee for you, Daddy. I'm having some myself. It'll buck us up." She sets the cup near me on the table, the cream pitcher too. She pulls out a chair for me and I sit down gratefully.

"Henry ought to be here. How old would he be?" I take a sip of the hot coffee.

"He was a year younger than Sophia and me, so about ten," Elizabeth answers. "He'd be a big help to you by now. We all miss him. Always will. Yes, he ought to be here with us."

"Families oughtn't be separated," I say. "That's the worst can happen to people."

She gives me a curious, worried look and I realize I shouldn't be saying these things aloud to her.

"Is there more coffee?"

She fills up my cup, leaving room for cream. I've sure learned to like our fine fresh cream.

"Good of you to make a pot of coffee, Elizabeth. It's what I needed."

She goes to sit on the floor with Amanda and Tommy and their rag dolls.

"We're playing baby," Amanda says. "Tommy, we'll have a live baby soon. It's coming out of Mommy."

He stares at her, eyes big with amazement.

I push my chair back. "Well, I better get on out there to the milk house. Just a few steps away if you need me."

A half hour later, when I can't find anything more to pretend to be doing in the milk house where everything is in tiptop shape as it always is, Elizabeth comes flying in.

"Daddy, come! I think Grandma Long is about to bring the baby out for us to meet."

I dash up the stairs ahead of her and we wait, breathless, Sophia, Amanda and me, Elizabeth holding Tommy. Mariah is in the bedroom with Sarah.

At last Mrs. Long steps out, grim and tight-lipped. She looks at Elizabeth. "I said I'd bring him out but I can't. It's a blue baby. Didn't get enough oxygen.

They usually die quickly," she adds. All the children burst out crying, even Tommy. She goes back in and shuts the door.

Everything's terribly wrong. I want my own mama, want her so bad I fear I'll scream out for her. Why don't they let the father in? Sarah needs me, I know she does. My eyes aren't working right. They've clouded over. I feel a gentle pressure on my arm. It is Mariah.

"Daddy, there's nothing wrong with the baby. Don't worry. He's fine."

The sobbing around me stops. They've all heard her. Mariah goes on, "You must come in. Mother needs you." She takes my hand, pulls me with her.

Sarah's face, white on the pillow, is a mask of worry and fear. Mrs. Long paces the room holding out at a distance a small wrapped bundle that must be the baby. Mariah pulls me nearer to the bed.

"Mother's weak, Daddy. You have to bend close to hear her."

Sarah's eyes burn with passion. She whispers hoarsely, "Make her leave, Tom. Make her go home. I don't trust her with Charlie."

I feel numb. But I'm the only one with authority to tell this small, strong-willed mother of Sarah's to go home. I stride over and take the little bundle from her forcibly, because she doesn't give it up easily. I look down into Charlie's tiny face that resembles all the babies I've ever seen born until our own, and through my tears I say, "Mrs. Long, you must go home now. We'll be all right on our own."

She seems confused, then straightens her back, gathering herself together from habit.

"Jeremiah's in the barn. Ask Elizabeth to take you to him and he'll make sure you get home safe. The snow's started up again."

She leaves the room babbling like someone not in her right mind. "I'll tell everyone it's a blue baby, can't live, not enough oxygen. No doctor. Lay him in a corner for the undertaker."

I give her a slight push out the door. "Elizabeth, take her to Jeremiah in the barn. She's not well. He'll know the best way to get her home."

The children crowd around me to take a peek at the baby I carry in my arms.

Amanda squeals with delight. "Look! He already has a little suntan and he hasn't even been out in the sun yet! How can that be?"

"He's special," Sophia answers. "Look how darling he is." She accepts Tommy from Elizabeth, hugs him tight, holds him up to see the baby.

I go back to Sarah who already, with her mother gone, looks better and holds out her arms for me to put the baby in them. I search her face and see the overwhelming love in her eyes when she looks at Charlie and then at me.

"She wouldn't let me hold him," Sarah whispers. "Said no use trying to feed him." Her eyes are big with questions. She's depending on me and I wonder, am I strong enough for what's coming?

Mariah throws her arms around my middle, looks up at me. "I love my new brother, Daddy. I'll help Mother take care of him and I'll help you take care of Mother. We don't need Grandma Long."

Sarah puts Charles to her breast so he can learn to suck.

"This is your seventh time," I smile. "You know what you're doing."

I get a smile back. How beautiful she is. And Charles. Will it be enough to have seven people loving him? Jeremiah too will surely love him. Won't he?

I'm grateful it is winter and snow falling again. Charlie will be too young to take to church in weather like this, maybe for months to come. Will Mother Long spread her wild story? What will people make of it? After the rumors they've heard.

MARY ANDERSON PARKS

CHAPTER FIFTY-FOUR

Sarah's been after me. Spring thaw finally came and now we can get the buggy out on the road, though we haven't gone anywhere yet as a family. The girls tromped through the snow to school all winter. Today it's downright balmy. Charlie is two and a half months old. He's the healthiest baby we've ever seen. He coos at little Tommy, makes him feel special in a whole new way. Tommy saw his first smile, came running to tell us. "Charlie laughing!" he yelled, jumping up and down. Those two are going to be close. I see it happening. But why do we have to spoil all the joy we're having by going to church with him?

Here she comes now. I lean on my shovel between two rows.

"Tom, you've been out here all morning. I want to talk to you." She speaks briskly, firmly. "Charlie needs to be baptized."

"Why so soon?"

"It's not soon. The other children were all baptized by now."

"Were they?"

"Yes Tom, they were. And he's so hardy, he's ready for anything."

"Don't know if I'm ready," I mumble.

"That's why I want to get it over with." She stares me down.

"That makes sense, I guess. I suppose we have to take him out sooner or later."

"Tom, please don't say it like that. We need to do it with pride, for the sake of all of us. Remember Uncle Daniel's advice? And he knew everything. It didn't stop him from loving us."

I sigh. "When, Sarah? This very next coming Sunday?"

"We need to give the preacher time. We'll all go this Sunday and ask him to do the baptism the Sunday following." She lowers her head. "My father hasn't seen him. We need to prepare him too."

I lift her chin, gently. Her clear eyes are troubled. "We just have to, Tom."

Sunday comes and we're clean and dressed in our best. We all took our weekly bath last night in the kitchen. Filled the tub twice with hot water. Sarah and the baby and the girls took their turns first. Then we changed the water for me and Tommy. Someday Charlie will join us and the numbers won't be as uneven. Sarah says we're going to have more children. That woman beats everything.

Our ride in is quieter than usual. Even Elizabeth seems sunk in silence. Only Tommy keeps up his usual chatter, making faces to see Charlie laugh again and again. "Charlie look funny in dress," he comments.

"It's the same dress you all wore when you were babies," Sarah says.

"But Charlie and me not girls."

I drive into the churchyard and the groups of people stop talking and turn to look at us as we unload ourselves. Had they been talking about us? Sarah goes right up to her old school friends who used to get together with her at canning time before she had our own girls to help.

"Isn't he a sweetheart?" Sarah smiles, lifting the blanket away from Charlie's face. "Sweetieheart!" Tommy echoes. "He can laugh!" Her friends smile politely, but I saw them flinch when they got their first look at him.

I go stand by Sarah's side. "He'll be a big help on the farm," I say. "Look how strong he is. Just like you, Tommy."

It is at that moment the Longs arrive. I take hold of Sarah's arm and feel the tension in it. She lowers her face to Charlie's and speaks soothingly to him. Her girl friends have moved away and are whispering together.

I have the sudden odd notion we are all part of one of Shakespeare's plays, though I don't remember one that has a baby in it.

Mr. Long marches straight over to us, worry plain on his face. "He's healthy is he, Sarah? Your mother was so upset about his condition, she wasn't making sense when she first got home."

"Yes Papa, he's very healthy indeed," Sarah says.

He looks now at Charlie, looks for a long time.

"So," he says at last. He turns to his wife, who has come up behind him. "He's recovered from whatever you said was wrong with him." Mrs. Long squirms under his searching gaze. "Don't you want to see for yourself?"

She takes a quick glance at Charlie and steps away, saying, "We'd best go in and sit down, Mr. Long."

As the Longs file past us, they peek in at Charlie, bundled up in his blanket in Sarah's arms. Charlie stares back with intelligent brown eyes. Matthew nods at me, uncertainly.

After church, going out the door, Sarah and I pause to ask Preacher Burns about doing the baptism next Sunday. He keeps his gaze fixed on Charlie, doesn't seem able to speak.

Suddenly Mr. Long is with us. "Holding the baptism of my new grandson next Sunday, Reverend?"

"Uh, well yes Mr. Long. I g-guess," Reverend Burns stammers.

"I'll stand up with them," Mr. Long says. "I need to go in now and talk to Alma about the hymn we'll sing."

"Uh, yes sir. All right then."

On our ride home I look over at Sarah. I can see it is by an effort of will that she fights back tears. She holds her head high.

I sit up straighter.

The next day, the girls go to school and arrive home chattering. Sarah and I hear them from the kitchen and go outside to meet them. We've been having pie and coffee, talking about anything but how anxious we are.

"How was school?" I ask right away.

Mariah has mischief in her eyes and the twins giggle. "Grandma Long has started a new rumor," Mariah says, trying to keep a straight face. "One of the girls told everybody Mrs. Long said to her mother when blue babies don't die their skin turns light brown but otherwise they're healthy."

I stare at her doubtfully. "Did they believe that?"

Amanda pipes up. "Of course, Daddy. Grandma Long always knows what she's talking about. She says so herself!"

Jeremiah has walked over from the barn to join us. I see the look he and Mariah exchange. There's a friendship between those two. A real closeness, and he's not an easy one to get close to. Elizabeth puts her arm around Sophia. Why do I always feel Elizabeth understands everything without being told; is it just because she looks so much like Mama with her strong bone structure and the firm way her mouth closes over her teeth? Sophia is confused. It's plain from her face. I suppose we'll have to have a family talk someday. Maybe Sarah could handle that?

"Come inside for milk and berry pie. You too, Jeremiah." Sarah takes Amanda by the hand. "Tommy's about to wake up. And Charlie." The worry lines I've seen in her face all day are gone.

On Sunday next, Mr. Long stands by our side for the baptism, and afterward we find out what hymn he chose for Charlie. Alma Stiles strikes up the rousing chords of "All Creatures of Our God and King." It's one the congregation always stands for, and during the final verses Mr. Long goes around and shakes the hand of every single person there, including his own family members and mine.

"Charlie good baby, Grampa," Tommy says to him when it's his turn for a handshake. "No cry when preacher throw water at him." His loud, clear voice carries and I hear a chuckle from Mr. Schmid. The music ends with a strong final chord. Mr. Long smiles and announces, "Mrs. Long made her oatmeal cookies to celebrate. They're on the table at the back, with apple cider."

CHAPTER FIFTY-FIVE

The next few days pass peacefully. I go into Milford where they have a big feed store, and take Jeremiah with me. I tell him I need him to help load the heavy seed bags on the wagon, but I suspect he knows it's because I feel safer when he's with me. I'm so alone when I go by myself. It's comforting to have him there to talk to, help me decide things. We're putting in more crops this spring: alfalfa, oats, clover, barley and rye along with soybeans and corn. We have more steers than last year. They'll need feed. Those crops sell well too. Some farmers don't have enough land to grow them.

Yep. Jeremiah knows I'm plenty strong to lift a bag of seeds. I smile to myself, thinking that. Folks in town seem to be treating me about like always. Guess they've got planting worries on their minds same as we do. Most farmers aren't given to chit-chat. They come to town, get their business done, pass the time of day and get home and back to work. I notice there's some staying clear of us altogether though, no wave or nod of greeting.

That night I have trouble going to sleep. I lie there in the dark, next to Sarah, and think about the six children sleeping in their beds, and my heart aches with wanting to keep them safe.

Friday night comes around, the Friday after the baptism. I've been in bed an hour, maybe two, maybe more, and I can't go to sleep. Friday nights some boys and men go into Milford and drink. Not Jeremiah. Not Matthew or Luke Long neither. They're all sleeping by now. Why am I so durn restless? I roll out of bed real quiet, not to wake Sarah, go to the windows of our bedroom and open the one that opens easy. I wish we had a window on the barn side or the other side, where the Longs live. I can't check on much from here. All I can see is part of our lane and across the road our empty fields. We've got the steers in the barn with the horses and milk cows, case a late freeze hits. And hay baled up in there roof-high. Jeremiah and me had a time of it fitting in all the bags of seed.

I push the window open higher and lean out, breathing in cold air. Jeremiah is sleeping down at his own house these days. If they had lamps lit, I could see their place if we had a window on the barn side. Don't want to roam down the creaky hallway to look out the window over the staircase. Might wake the children and worry them. You fool, Tom, there'd be nothing to see. No lights in the middle of the night.

I get back in bed. Must be I finally fall asleep, because I'm awakened by voices. Rough, drunken voices. I go rigid, listening. Can't seem to move a muscle. Worried about waking Sarah. I don't want her to have to face anything bad.

Finally I ease out of bed, pull on pants, then socks and shoes, and go to the window. Four men are outside on horseback, holding the reins of two riderless horses. Soon two other men come from over where the barn is. One of them has a bad limp. They both get on their horses, yelling like crazy. I hear the words, "Burn the nigger's barn down!" The one with a limp waves a lighted torch wildly in the air.

"What's happening?" Sarah sits upright in the bed.

"The barn, Sarah! I think they've set fire to the barn! Get a sweater on, get the girls up."

The men ride off fast. I grab a shirt, race down the staircase, through the house, out the kitchen door. Flames are rising in the barn, beginning to lighten the night sky. I hear sounds of panic from the horses and the cattle. I've got to get them out. I throw open the big barn door and rush in. The heat is scorching and smoke sets me off in a coughing fit, makes it hard to see. The flames haven't reached the animals yet. The fire's feeding on bales of hay. Midnight lets me take him out. I go back and get Lady. Daniel's mares won't come. Flames make a wall of fire now and Dolly and Louisa are spooked. I try to pull them but can't. So I go for the cows. Belle lets me lead her away and a few cows and steers follow. I herd another group out, but now I smell burning flesh.

Sarah runs in.

"Get out of here!" I yell.

She tosses me a bandanna soaked in water. "Tie this around your head, over your nose and mouth."

I do but I run to her and practically shove her out the side door. "Get buckets. Wet the ground between here and the house."

"We already did. The girls are at the outside pump. You have to come out, Tom!"

"I can't. Your horse is still here."

"Come out, Tom. Please. Come out." Her voice reaches me from a distance. And then Jeremiah is there.

"I saw the flames from our place. My brother's outside. He'll help at the pump." He plunges in among the cows, starts talking to them.

Sarah runs back in with another wet bandanna. Jeremiah ties it on quickly.

"My brothers are here," she says. "And Father. He says you two have to get out before the roof caves in. You're only got a few minutes." She coughs, choking on smoke. "They're herding the ones you got out into the fenced field on the other side of the barn. Father says if we don't, the cows may run back into the fire." She goes back out.

Smoke, dense and thick, wraps around me. I can see only a foot or two ahead. Jeremiah comes into view, his bandanna gone, his face blackened. He looks up at the ceiling high above. It is beginning to cave toward the middle, rafters cracking and breaking.

"Out, Tom! Now!" He's got Sarah's horse by the mane. On the hook next to him, I spot my old brown leather jacket.

"I'll be right behind you." I motion him to go ahead of me. Then I grab the jacket and feel my way to the corner where Daniel's beautiful old mares, my friends of so many years, huddle close to each other and stare at me wild-eyed with terror.

"Come with me, Dolly. Trust me. I'll lead you out. Tell Louisa to follow." She whimpers twice, nudges Louisa. I throw my jacket over her head, guide her along and keep talking. She's coming but I don't know if Louisa's following. I pull Dolly through the side door and know they've both come with me when a cheer goes up from the bucket brigade stretching out from the pump, and I hear the separate voices of my girls.

"He's got them!"

"Daddy saved Uncle Daniel's old mares!"

"Look, Dolly and Louisa!"

"They're alive!"

"Oh thank God, Tom."

Mariah's clear voice: "Mother, look over there, Jeremiah saved your horse!"

Moving slowly, exhausted, I go around to the front and see most of the cattle and the horses penned up with Matthew and Luke watching over them. Jeremiah comes bearing two full buckets of water. He hands them one at a time over the fence to Luke, who's in the enclosure with the animals. There is nothing for us to do now but watch the barn burn to the ground. Jeremiah's eyes are brimming with tears.

Mr. Long puts his arm around my shoulders. "We'll all help you put up a new barn, Tom. We can get twenty or more men. The work will go fast. I hope you have cash to buy the lumber."

I nod, unable to speak. Gratefulness crowds out bitterness. But I feel sick to my stomach staring at the charred remains in front of me.

Mr. Long tightens his grip around my shoulders, heaves a deep sigh. "We have to keep on, Tom, no matter what. The boys and I will be back tomorrow to help you clean up this mess." Then, as he drops his arm to his side, "I heard them ride by our place. I was up reading the Book of Ecclesiastes. Couldn't sleep. I recognized one of the voices and figured trouble was brewing." He pauses a long time, looking at me like he used to when we'd talk about the Bible. "You're a good man, Tom Jones. I'm thankful it was you Sarah chose."

Mary Anderson Parks

CHAPTER FIFTY-SIX
Sarah

I sleep the sleep of exhaustion. When my eyes open, Tom is gone from the bed and I see out the window a sky hazy with smoke. My eyes smart from smoke; smoke clogs my nostrils. I need to get up, wash my face, begin this day.

But not yet. I close my eyes and fall back into the pillows, sensing all the while that it is late. For once in my life I have slept late. It takes an effort to think. Images of the fire move through my mind.

The window has been left open and voices drift in. Jeremiah calling out to someone, "I could take little Charlie and give him some milk straight from the cow." Then Elizabeth, sounding almost cheerful, "No, let's wait for Ma. She'll be up soon needing to nurse him." She's right. Milk drips from my breasts into my nightdress. Where on earth is Jeremiah doing the milking? There's no barn. Nothing left. But somehow he's out there milking. Out in the open. I suppose he's taken the milk cows out of the enclosure with no danger now of them running back into the fire as cows have been known to do. I find the thought 'no danger now' relaxing. I stretch out my arms and legs and let my thoughts drift.

I have to be his support. He's going to need me more than ever. We'll be our own mighty fortress. I feel it in my body, slim again, still loving him, still able to please him, make him relax, if only for a while. He thrills me as much as always. I reach my arms out wider and my chest lifts up. We'll make our own happiness, here with the family.

All right Sarah. Up now. You can face the day. You have work to do. Both the boys must have woken at their usual time. They slept through everything last night. What a blessing. I noticed Charlie's empty cradle first thing on opening my eyes. Now I hurry, wanting to get downstairs and see what's going on, wanting to be part of it. I pull my green and white striped housedress over my head, splash water on my face. In the cracked mirror, I see the smudges. It takes soap and a washrag to scrub it clean. I wash my neck and under my arms, then brush my hair, fasten it back with a green ribbon and run down the stairs into the kitchen to find Tom sitting at the table drinking coffee. He's holding Tommy, feeding him bacon. They both look up at me with love in their eyes.

"Gosh, Sarah. You're a pretty sight."

"Pretty sight," Tommy echoes.

Smiling, I reach into my apron drawer and choose a dark green one with white stripes.

Tom always gets up before me to start the fire, make coffee, bring up the slab of bacon, but this time he not only cut off the slices, he fried them too.

"Sit down, Sarah." He pours me a cup of coffee. "I'll cook your eggs. How many?"

"Four, thank you. It's going to be a big day."

Elizabeth appears at the door and hands off Charlie for me to nurse.

Tom sets Tommy on a chair with a cushion under him, tells him to make a sandwich out of his bread and bacon. Tommy absorbs himself in buttering his bread.

"We don't know how many will come to help but my father will drive around and spread the word. He said he will. And nobody says no to my father."

Tom looks at me anxiously. "He'll actually take his buggy and drive around to the farms? He'd do that for us?"

"And New Columbia too, the town people there. I saw him do it once years ago for a farmer whose halfwit son accidentally burned their house down. The poor boy, he was over twenty but mentally like a child. He lost all power of speech when he saw the house burn. Never spoke another word."

Tom brings me a plate of eggs and bacon strips, buttered bread with blackberry jam, pours me more coffee. I can see in his eyes the emotion behind his offering. He takes Tommy back on his lap, wiping off Tommy's small sticky hands with his big handkerchief. Charlie is greedily nursing.

Tommy finishes his bacon sandwich. "See barn?" he asks.

"Again?" Tom sighs, carries him over to the door, opens it wide for Tommy to look out. The acrid odor of smoke enters the house, overpowering the aroma of bacon I'd been enjoying.

"Where horses go? Where Belle and her cow friends?"

"Remember? I carried you over to see them. Twice."

Tommy frowns, looks at Tom hopefully. "Go again?"

"No, let's stay here with Mommy." Tom shuts the door, hugging him close, and sits down across from me. Tommy turns his piteous face to me.

"Calf and mommy not with other cows. I looked. They not there."

Tom presses his lips together. "No, they're not."

"Why, Daddy?"

"Remember?"

Tommy nods. "Barn burn last night. They breathe too much smoke." Tears run down his smooth cheeks.

Oh no, not the yearling calf! Tom's eyes meet mine and I ache that he had to deal with telling Tommy all alone. I should have been up to help.

I force a smile. "Tommy, when all the girls are up, we have lots of baking to do. Pies! Bread and rolls! We'll cook good things to eat all day long, and you'll be such a help to me. You always are." His eyes brighten. "Neighbors will come to help Daddy and Jeremiah. They'll want good food after their work. First they clean up the mess, then tomorrow they start building a fine new barn. Daddy will buy the boards. The cows and horses will have a nice new home."

He looks very pleased. "Nice new barn home. They like."

"Yes Tommy, they will."

"Cows, horses watch barn get builded. They see from their field."

"Yes, we'll all like watching that, won't we? You can stand on a chair and watch from the window."

"Barn burn. Make new barn."

In the months and years that follow, I often think of those words as the pattern of our life.

CHAPTER FIFTY-SEVEN

Seven Years Later

I watch Jeremiah stride into the barn, his muscles quivering.

"Nellie's sick!"

"How do you know that?"

"I check on her, Tom."

I get up from the milk stool where I was mending a saddle. Does he just try on purpose to put me in the wrong? No, of course not! It's my guilt I'm feeling that in all these years I've never found a way to see her.

"She has double pneumonia."

Silence stretches between us loud as if we were hollering. I squeeze one balled fist with the other.

"Is it bad?"

"It's real bad, Tom."

When did he start calling me Tom? It wasn't when I first told him to. It took a long time. I turn away from his pleading eyes.

"She's asking for you, Tom." He scuffs the toe of his boot on the hay-strewn floor. "She was delirious or else she wouldn't."

How long has he known? How long have we both kept on pretending? He reaches out and lays his hand on my shoulder, leaves it there. He's never done that before.

"You don't have much time, Tom."

I pull my heavy work coat from the hook and shrug into it. The pungent smell of dried sweat and smoke surrounds me with years of memories of working side by side with Jeremiah and the night we led the animals out of the burning barn.

"I'll ride you in." It is an offer and a question.

"Thanks."

I can barely hear him when he says, "I love her too, you know." Does he really think I don't know that? Something in me softens, yields to him. We ride into town on the old horse I gave him years ago. It seems to me everybody in Milford sees us when we make the turn into colored town. Maybe they're used to seeing him go there, but not me they aren't. It is strange how instantly I feel colored, like it shows, when we enter those sorry roads. My vision takes in everything we pass, my arms hold onto Jeremiah. I don't even know where she lives. The residents of colored town watch me, curious, and at the same time it's like they know all about me. Little does it matter I've never come here. Those deep dark eyes watching me have always known I'd be coming. Coming home to my mama. Maybe they love her too, count on her to be strong, to be there with her medicines, her knowledge, her caring. Sudden tightness in my chest threatens to choke off my breath. I long to reach her in time. I want her to know me, know I'm here. Why can't I see?

It's my damn tears. Thank God I've got Jeremiah to hang onto, didn't try to ride in on my own.

"Here we are." He says it with the sigh I often hear in his voice, a sigh that means he'll deal with whatever life throws at him.

The house is small, squat, paint mostly peeled off. Jeremiah gives me a hand to dismount. How did I get so lucky to have this man for my friend? I sure as hellfire don't deserve him.

A woman peers out the back door when we walk across the path of stones. She steps outside.

"Miz Walker, this is Tom Jones, my boss." He is brief as can be with the introduction, but her face shows a whole history of dawning understanding.

"This be the Tom she askin for?"

Jeremiah nods.

She steps backward, away from me, in a kind of awe. Or is it horror? She turns and leads me into the house. "Come in here to her bedroom." Her voice has dropped an octave. The sloping linoleum creaks at every step of my boots. I've gotten heavier over the years. She motions me to go in the bedroom by myself.

I stop just inside the door. The smallness of the body in the bed sends a shock through me. Mama's tall, Mama's strong. This can't be Mama!

But her eyes focus on me, claiming me. I move quickly to her side, clasp her thin bony hands in mine. We don't have words. Neither of us. There aren't any words for what I've done. But the love is there in Mama's eyes. Unchanged. A miracle.

I fall to my knees, holding onto her hands.

Then pitiful words do come. "I thought we had more time. Time worked for me all these years, Mama, gave me a chance to prove my worth and for white people to accept me. I don't know. I guess I thought somehow there'd be a time you and me could get back together."

Her eyes close.

"Or maybe I wasn't thinking at all," I admit. Her hands move in mine. Does she understand how confused I am? But she can't talk. I've come too late for that.

Her breath escapes in slow gasps, like she had a fixed number and now she's coming to the end. I breathe along with her and I feel I'm breathing in her love. I hope to God she feels mine.

That's what's left to us.

Then the life goes out of her. And I'm alone with the empty body that was Mama. It is clear to me as anything's ever been that she's gone. Her mind and spirit left for some other place. This dying is too sudden. I didn't get to make things right. Time ran out on us. The years she spent with me are over, and we never got to have the years I stole from us. What they would have been I'll never know. And Mama won't neither.

Miz Walker and Jeremiah come slowly into the room.

"She was waitin for you was what she was doin," Miz Walker says.

I give Miz Walker all the money I have with me and tell her Jeremiah will bring more for the burial. The burial I won't be at. And that is all I can do, so I walk out of that room Mama has gone from.

A man slumped at the kitchen table with his head in his hands glances up through bloodshot eyes. Grief hugs round him like a shawl.

Miz Walker tells him as I go out, "It's all right, Ezekiel. Her boy came to her in time."

No, it's not all right, I want to turn to them and say. I didn't come in time. That would have been a day in 1836, twenty-two years ago.

Jeremiah rides me back to where I live.

I know we'll never speak on it again.

I'll live with it beating against the wall of my heart however many days are given me to go on without her, however many breaths I still have to breathe.

There's no way out from the path I chose.

I'm wrong though about Jeremiah not speaking on it. He does when we get off Old Paint back at the home place, me standing there not knowing what to do next.

"She knew, Tom, about all your children, little Charlie and the rumors, how you forged a place for you and the family, ten of you now, and are a respected man here. The first time Mariah made me ride her over to visit Nellie was a few months after Charlie was born. We both always drew pictures for her of the children, so she'd know them at their different ages, and of Sarah and you. Mariah and me, we both like to draw." He looks me straight in the eye. "Mariah's a fine young woman."

I've never known him to speak so long and clear, except in church one Easter when the preacher had him read scripture, and I found out he can talk real good. I step forward and embrace him for a long time, each of us leaning into the other.

CHAPTER FIFTY-EIGHT
Mariah

I lie with my face pressed into smooth marshy grass. No one in my family knows I come here. Have they forgotten this scum-covered pond with its smell of algae, overgrown with tall grasses? A big turtle lives down in its depths. It surfaced a while ago. Sometimes I can sense its silent turtle smell, its loneliness, its secret hidden life. I've been crying over Nellie and tears run down into my mouth, tasting salty. Jeremiah will tell me later if he got Daddy there in time to see her and for her to see him. Daddy will blame himself all his life if he didn't. I sit up, wiping my face with my hands and pray he did.

Jeremiah took me to Nellie two days ago. Said she told him there were things she wanted me to know. Before she died. When I got there, she whispered to me as I knelt by her bed, asked if I remembered the nights she took care of me and the night when I said she should sleep in her own bed with me and not on the floor. She told me that had been her dearest wish but she didn't dare because I was white. And then she did anyway when I was so bad off. She couldn't bear for me to go through that pain alone.

So then I stood up and climbed in the bed with her. Sick and sweaty though she was, I held onto her tight. "You're my grandmother, aren't you?"

"Yes, Mariah. And I don't want to die leaving only rumors behind, and secrets. I want you to be the one knows the truth. It up to you how much you share with your sisters or brothers. But somebody ought to know." I nod my head, tucked under her chin. "It too hard for your Daddy to carry his secrets alone. I know how that be. I'm all worn out from it."

I take her hand and squeeze it. "I think Mother knows and she helps him best she can."

"But she don't know me. Hasn't even seen a picture of me like I have of her." She talked to me then about my aunt Janey, still in slavery, and how after Janey was sold she never saw her or her three grandchildren again and how she and Daddy ran from the plantation when he was twenty-one, all the way here to Ohio, told me how mean his father, marse Tom, could be. Explained about Daddy passing as white, at first not even knowing it, and how that made her feel. I'll never forget any of it. I know I won't. It's my grandmother's last gift to me.

When I rolled a bit away from her, she looked into my eyes with deep sadness. "I woulda liked to know your mother and maybe even lived with all of you and been a help."

I lie on my back in the pond grass and gaze upward. Cloud shapes shift and a hawk swoops over. Could it be an eagle? I think it's Nellie's spirit that left her body and now watches over us. A great peacefulness fills me.

I have to get back to the house. They've gotten used to my absences but I don't want to be out after dark and worry

Mother and the rest of them. Just a few more moments to myself!

It was Jeremiah who showed me this pond, told me about the old turtle, said he's been trying to catch him for years and make turtle soup. It's hard sometimes to know when he's joking. He knows my secrets, all of them. And loves me. Hasn't said so, maybe never will. That's okay with me. What counts is he does, and he's the best man I know. Not that much older either. Sometimes I feel like I'm the older one. We have so much fun laughing, drawing, telling each other our thoughts, dreams.

I get up and brush leaves and insects off my dress and coat, anxious to see Daddy.

Nellie got very weak talking so long. Her last words were, "There is so much more to tell you. Not enough time. Bless you for your visits and bless that dear Jeremiah who brings you. You must marry him. Soon, Mariah. War's a comin.

You'll have to ask him yourself, you know." She winked, closed her eyes and rested.

Author's Note

1836 is the year my maternal great-great grandfather arrived in southern Ohio. The 1903 Atlas of Warren County reads at page 91: "Thomas Jones was born in Campbell County, Virginia, September 4, 1815 and died October 9, 1900, aged 85 years. When he was twenty-one years old he came to Ohio, a poor boy, with nothing but his hands and an honest purpose."

My mother began telling me the rumors when I was eight, rumors she mostly denied. She did admit it was true her great-grandfather Thomas Jones walked up to Ohio from Virginia with a colored woman and "she didn't understand what that was all about." As a young schoolteacher in rural southern Ohio she received anonymous notes she called hate letters: "We know you have colored blood." My sister, ten years older than I, later told me how distraught Mother was when she received the notes.

Several years ago, with both parents dead, I took a DNA test. I show two percent Subsaharan African and five percent East Asian blood. A slave ancestor from the West or East Indies? Am I the last of my family in whom the heritage with which I inwardly identified all my life is measurable?

Haunted by the fact I can find no history of Thomas Jones' ancestors, by the rumors, by stories from my Jones cousins, but mostly by the pain I saw behind my mother's eyes, I imagined a story that became this book.

Flight to Ohio

FROM SLAVERY TO PASSING TO FREEDOM

MARY ANDERSON PARKS

CPSIA information can be obtained at www.ICGtesting.com
Printed in the USA
BVOW08*2132200816

459226BV00001B/1/P